GRACE OF DRAGONS

MAGGIE HOOPIS

ISBN 979-8-9923469-0-9 (hardback)
ISBN 979-8-9923469-1-6 (paperback)
ISBN 979-8-9923469-2-3 (ebook)
Library of Congress Cataloging- in-Publication data is available upon request
Book Cover and Map by Anastasia Campo
Edited by Brittany Gossin
Proofread by Laura Ernst
First edition: 2025

Content Warnings

Grace of Dragons is a western romantasy. That being said, the stakes are high. As typical with the genres, you will read some dicey moments. Your mental health is important to me, though, so please note the following are topics in the book:

Alcohol
Death – humans, animals, on and off page
Gambling
Grief
Guns & shooting – it's set in the Wild West
Infertility
Masturbation – all consensual
Misogyny & sexism
Prostitution – all consensual
Sex – all consensual
Swearing
Weddings

For Daphne, who wanted me to write a story about the planets. Your unique words and your imaginative thoughts mold our world. The universe is yours, woman.

Part One

PROLOGUE

They came through the darkness. The cold. The void. The forgottenness.

They came for her.

Gnarled tree branches that spread like fingers arose from the ground. Desperation clawed at her insides much more than the branch protrusions at her ankles. And so, skirts hoisted, feet bare, lungs heaving, she fled. Lest they take her back. She had never run before, but today, her heart beckoned her feet forward as fast as they would go.

She could hear the echoes of Dimin's neurotic screaming carried through his cracked, yellowing teeth, from the balcony of the stone-white mansion on the hill in the distance.

"Get her back! Get her BACK!"

As the light from the swarming minions behind her brightened with closing proximity, her shadow on the ground stretched and darkened. She needed to move faster, but she was slowing, her feet dragging. She had trouble keeping track of what was shadow and what was reality. She misjudged a step and her foot caught on a branch hidden by the shadows on the ground.

Gravity pulled her down into a tangle of loose hair, fallen leaves, and ripped fabric. Oh, but she needed to hurry! *Get up!*

Gasping and lifting her head, she could see a clearing only fifty feet ahead. Hope reignited her flight. She would persevere.

"If I can't have her, no one will!" Dimin's voice reverberated through the nightmarish woods from the balcony where she had left him. His power had grown more than she had expected.

The spirits flew more rapidly, closing in on her. Some of the hand-sized flying blue spectres flew alongside her. She swatted the tiny nightmares away as she tore through the forest underfoot, hobbling from her earlier tumble.

Forty feet.

The tangled branches seemed to disappear.

Thirty feet.

The darkness gradually dissipated.

Twenty feet.

The spirits seemed to stop where the line of trees ended. Maybe she had a chance.

Ten feet.

WHOOSH!!

A large force pushed her forward, slamming her into the ground, where her lower back received the brunt of the impact. Air shot out of her windpipe as her chest heaved.

The energy in her body evaporated from her skin. With her face to the ground, she could feel the earth warming. But no, it was not warming–she was growing colder. A massive icy gasp punctuated this realization, seemingly slitting her lungs. She set her sights towards the light in the opening ahead. Grabbing the dirt and pulling her arms toward her, she dragged herself across the land. With every move, her body chilled. Her fingertips grew bloody from the dry dirt pushing its way beneath her fingernail beds.

Nonetheless, she would persevere.

Spirit bats flocked toward her, propelling her spirit forward. As she crossed into the opening, they hit an invisible line that made them drop to the ground. In the perceived safety of the clearing, she curled up into the fetal position, trying to warm herself. The violent chattering of her teeth and shivering of her body overtook her plight. The silence in the clearing provided her with a moment's peace before thoughts of her next moves entered her mind. How could she decide what to do next? Her head and her body warred in their desires as her consciousness began to fade.

Just then, a rough huffing noise reverberated through the clearing. Well, this was it. She had had a good run. She rested her head on the ground, submitting to the inevitable. May Mother Maker find enough pity upon her soul for a place on the fourth staircase.

A warmth embraced her as two tight leather blankets squeezed her chest and legs. Breezes shifted over and under her as her skirts blew all around. Looking into the clouds, she let herself go to the dark.

ONE

The green-black dragon had flown as far as his wings could manage while holding the extra weight of the woman in his front two leathery legs. The ground betrayed no signs of frost from the air, which upon touchdown, his two back foot pads verified. The tumbleweeds blew out of the street, kicking up dust as the dragon landed with a thud. He had needed to tuck his wings in tight to make his entrance in the middle of the street, an action which seriously detracted from his ability to gracefully glide to the ground. Despite being in the middle of nowhere with wide open spaces, these townspeople, for some odd reason, had decided to build their wooden structures, right atop each other, leaving barely enough room for dragon wings.

No, she was not the girl that he had been tasked with rescuing, but that woman was long gone. He had tracked that black haired queen to where he had heard whisperings in the meadows of her being: all the way east to that cold, disheveled town. She had never gone running to him anyways. He did not miss her, but the young miss did, and he never could bear to watch a heart break without hope. He had hoped to bring the woman home to her daughter. But he had not seen anyone leaving that area for months.

So when this tawny haired woman dug her way towards his resting location, he never thought twice about scooping her up to bring her out of harm's way. Espe might be lost, but this woman was found.

He tenderly looked down at his claws upon this humble creature with a resilient spirit. She was a fighter and without any sense of direction. He was a wayfinder. He would help her find one. Even if it led back home.

For now, he needed to ensure her life. The cold was turning her skin blue. While his father had always taught him to hold back fire, he added extra warmth to his breath in order to maintain her shallow breathing pattern. She needed a healer and fast.

From twenty feet up, his height on his hind legs, his eyes scanned the faces in the street, too busy to mind another dragon's arrival. He searched for someone, anyone, who might have a heart to help.

His eyes immediately softened as they landed on a brown-skinned woman, her black silver-streaked hair neatly pinned beneath a hat. She stood gazing at him, shifting on her feet. As her chestnut eyes met his amber ones, the dragon nodded slowly. Her footing became sure and she rushed forward to him. Her gentle touch on his claw gave him the encouragement to loosen his grip to reveal the middle-aged woman with blue-tinted skin. A gasp escaped from her mouth and she quickly touched the neck of his charge, testing for a pulse.

"I can help, but I can't carry her," she offered into the dragon's desperate eyes. At this point, a crowd was gathering on the sides of the street, wanting to know, but not wanting to look too interested in the whore's business.

Of course she knew better than to even ask for help. Sadie had learned long ago that men help themselves and women help each other, even if through the back doors. Looking at the street and the building, she placed her hand on the arm of the brave dragon.

"Wait for my call, I will be two minutes." She hoisted her skirts, high to her knees, partly for running, and partly for the free advertisement to the crowd.

"Gee, Madame Sadie, what do you think a little thing like you is going to do to help?" a male voice called from the side of the street.

The woman did not even have time to waste to remind him that she was taller than the average woman and she could still drag him out of her house by his ear as she had done the past Thursday. "Out of my way, Lars, unless you're going to help," she ordered, shouldering past him and nearly knocking his mite-filled, bearded face to the ground.

"Whaddyou care anyway?" he said under his breath.

She whirled around, eyes wide. "Lars, I run an establishment that serves others. Though the primary clientele is male, the women are always my number one concern. This person, regardless of her gender, needs help, and no one else seems poised to help her. So once again, I will come to the aid of the befallen, to the expectation that I will quite possibly be ignored by the very person that I strive to help. Human decency costs nothing."

The dragon snorted in assent, using his wing to flick the man out of Sadie's way.

As he waited, he watched the freezing woman in his claws. He put his snout near her, gently exhaling warm air upon her. When she did not move, he shifted her body to his right paw, lightly pressing his left front talon onto her. Her minor shoulder movement was the only response. The dragon nestled his cold quarry next to his heart, as a mother would with a baby. He feared he could not keep her alive much longer.

Bolting inside the house, Sadie tripped twice running up the front stairs, which were elevated to keep out the dirt and shit of the main unpaved street. Madame Sadie boasted a classy establishment. She had arrived at the town at its inception with the train of first settlers. Her ambitious nature and adventurous spirit quickly solidified her claim on the town for sexual company and entertainment. She commanded the industry with zest and shrewdness which meant the townspeople would never openly admit to one another their respect for her.

Just off the landing, a less seasoned girl lounged on her bed reading with an open door. "Get some blankets and hot water, Eve!" Sadie called to her. After a third time of tripping, she cast her boots to the side, holding onto the banister. Needing to improve her range of motion, she started stripping down out of her town outfit. Running to the upstairs front room, she pulled off her stays and her top skirt leaving her in next to nothing. Sadie did not have much experience with dragons, but she hoped the dragon had understood that she had a plan to help.

"Eve!" she called from the upstairs room. "Bring them in here!"

Three girls in various positions with their paramour clients occupied the large room. She had forgotten it was Lounging Hour. During this hour, the girls who wanted to work would be in the upstairs great room. They wore not their finery, but their undergarments. Lounging Hour allowed the girls to sit around and chat while still pulling in some money. Over time, Lounging Hour had developed a reputation as a good time for a half-priced quickie on a sofa. Voyeurs could lounge about as well for a price.

Having established the policy to never turn away someone who needed help, Sadie was setting an example for the women she had taken in as her own. As Madame of the fine establishment, her demeanor set the tone for her employees, as well as the clients that they serviced.

When the women piped up, the men who had come in for their midday pick-me-ups followed their lead, interested in the occurrence.

"Can we count on you to help?" Sadie's tone suggested that they would no longer be welcome at the brothel if they refused.

The men nodded in assent, shaking their heads clear of the half naked women, and their body parts, in front of them and trying to reconcile themselves to the situation at hand. A flurry of commotion and people clothed themselves to the minimum.

Sadie threw open the two french doors and ran onto the balcony. The dragon sat mid street where she had left him, breathing deeply onto his companion, whom he cradled in his claws.

"Slewja!" a voice came from near the dragon's head breaking the quiet whisperings of the town that had gathered around. He had no concept of what "Slewja" meant, but the word traveled down his spine like a gentle caress. Searching for the call's origin, he turned his head right then left. To his left, at the end of the row of buildings stood a cute little blue two story house with a white balcony on the second floor. From there, the "Madame Sadie" woman stood in her undergarments, waving both arms over her head. Opening up his wings on either side down the length of the street, he elevated off the ground enough to be able to release the cold woman from his claws onto a lounge chair on the balcony. Immediately, several people pushed the piece of furniture to the inside where he had a harder time seeing her. He craned his neck and flew in different ways to try to catch a glimpse of the action.

"I'll take care of her, I promise, you big-hearted hero," Sadie said, leaning over the bannister to rub his surprisingly smooth scales. He needed for the girl to know that she had nothing to fear anymore. He needed for her to be resilient. In a world that would crush her like an ice cube, she needed to be a diamond.

"You know, that's why I called you, Slewja. Where I am from, it means big-hearted hero. You rescued this woman, didn't you?" She calmly distracted the dragon's thoughts from his anxieties. He looked at her face. What else could she deduce? "Yes, we all need rescuing once in a while, whether by another or ourselves. You've done all you could. She needs to search inside and save herself, now. Why don't you go get some rest or some food? Take care of yourself. I'll let you know when she's turned for the better."

With a final pat, she walked back inside the french doors, shutting them behind her. He looked about for a better spot to sit. Spying the roof, he used his feet to jump off the bannister and land on top of the house. He pawed around a bit, trying to get comfortable on the angled carpentry.

Below him, shutters on a window flew open with a bang. "SLEWJA!" a voice yelled out. He craned his neck over the side to look at the speaker. Madame Sadie had a stern look on her face. "Slewja, you're knocking everything off the walls, including pieces of the ceiling. Go rest in the dragon clearing." She pointed at the end of the main street that opened to a wide barren area. Other dragons lazed about there, as was common in most locales. "I promise you, I will send word immediately."

Nodding his head, he stretched his wings and took off. He settled down between midnight-blue and chestnut-speckled dragons. With his head pointed so he could watch the brothel, he rested his head on his tail, waiting for any sign that a message was coming. His eyes blurred as his breathing relaxed. He let the creatures of the frontier town have their backs. No, this place was not his home, but it appeared safe enough for the time being. Eventually, he would make his way back to the safety of home, with the woman, if she so desired. But for that moment, he settled in to dream of the meadows, his family, and a brand new person that he had a funny feeling would become a friend.

TWO

Slewja awoke with a start to his spines baking in the sun, his eyes flying to the open french doors to the brothel. The other dragons still slept, shifting minorly to accommodate one another's tails that would swish across the ground like rattlesnakes. He wedged himself out from between the two female dragons that had decided to drape themselves across him. Heaving a deep breath of the already heavy morning air, he leapt into the sky.

Landing on the roof with a loud thud, he craned his head downwards, searching the room in desperation. No one seemed to be around. What had happened to the woman? A mound of blankets covered the chaise. Where was she? Moving his head as far into the room as he could, he sniffed the air. Dead roses faintly tingled his nasal cavities. The same scent that had followed her to him. Why was no one taking care of her?

"I thought I heard you in here." Eve entered the room in her robe, carrying her book and a mug. Casting an empathetic smile his way, she tucked her legs under her as she positioned herself near the patient. "She's fine. She's under there, see?"

He stilled himself enough that he could see the slight rise and fall of the blankets on the chaise.

"It's my turn to be with her. We took turns all night. I wish you could talk so I could hear your story. I bet it would trump this book's plot. Though again, I'm sure it's very similar to our stories here. Did it have to do with a man?"

Slewja nodded slowly in response, eyes looking down.

"Is he still coming for her?"

He looked up and around the streets, now on high alert.

"You go make sure she's got a few days. Otherwise, come back here so we can figure it out. Just flap your wing, or jut your nose in and snort or something. I'll tell the others and if we don't hear from you, we'll just let you know when she wakes up." With a nod of her head motioning him to head off, she turned back to her book in a chair across from the injured woman.

So, Slewja searched. He flew high, he flew low. He flew an hour out in every direction. But he could not find any scent or sign of the terror that had chased her away. Every night he would go out searching for any sign of the creature that wanted to bring her back. And every night he could find nothing that would indicate that she was in incredible danger.

But he did not let his guard down.

A week later, after alternating between waiting and searching, Slewja had just settled down in the clearing for a mid-afternoon slumber, after having been out all night. Eve arrived at the resting space with the good news as she ran through the clearing in her robe. "Slewja! Sadie says to tell you that your girl's awake!"

He perked up, eyes alert and jumped on to all fours. Flying low to the ground, he picked up Eve. Holding her in his claws, he hightailed it back to the brothel, her giggles filling the air the whole thirty-second ride. He soared high, exuberant with excitement that his rescue had not perished. He had saved her! Swooping back down, he felt the belly of the girl he held moving and heard her squeals of delight. A huge smile decorated her visage despite her nails digging into his scales.

Slewja hovered outside the balcony, flapping his wings in a steady rhythm in order to maintain a constant height, flying around to the different windows. When he saw the woman sitting up under piles of blankets, elation spread across his face into an open-mouthed smile. Sadie cleared the room of the people that had swarmed in to greet "the dragon girl."

The woman's eyes fluttered open, her fingers instinctively curling into the thick, layered blankets that cocooned her. Her breath caught as she registered the warmth enveloping her body—she was alive. A low, guttural sound rumbled from behind her, primal and unsettling, sending a shiver down her spine. Her eyes grew wider as she scanned from side to side, taking in the finely furnished large room. The animalistic grunting emanated from behind her.

Were people doing what she thought they were doing? While she was in the room? She did not mind sex. Mother Maker knew that she had had her fun times, but she had never done it in the open. She peeped over the high back of the sofa lounge where three couples, all in various states of undress, had appendages inserted into different human orifices. The woman was about to crouch back down and hide under the blankets to give them their privacy when the blonde, curly haired one made eye contact with her over her paramour's shoulder.

"She's awake!" The exclamation echoed throughout the room as people excitedly gathered around her couch.

"Sadie, she's awake!" the blonde called down the stairs as she threw her skirts back down to her ankles.

With that, the tall woman with wise eyes entered, parting the circle of people that had gathered around the settee.

"Britt, go get Healer Frumo. He's asleep in Eve's room," Madame Sadie commanded.

For being such a high priced establishment, Madame Sadie could afford to handle all of her customers. She maintained a healer on staff that would look over her girls to ensure they remained healthy. The venereal disease had taken down too many people too quickly and Sadie refused to risk their lives.

Healer Frumo walked in, buckling his trousers as he entered

the room. Attending to the new girl, he sat down, expecting her to immediately spread her legs as the workers typically did. When she merely moved her knees to her chest below the blankets, he gently placed his hand on where the shape of her foot showed through the blankets.

"May I take a look at you?" He peered over his glasses. Sadie looked at the girl, who seemed scared and unsure in her hunched position.

"He's okay." Sadie put her hand on the woman's shoulder. "I can vouch for him."

Britt chimed in. "Oh he's the sweetest man! Even when he comes in for a roll in the sheets, he is most gentlemanly and kind about it."

Healer Frumo cleared his throat without looking behind him at the source of his discomfort. "Um, thank you for that recommendation, Britt." His attention remained on the patient in front of him. "I'm going to do a *medgical* examination, a bit of the normal medical, a bit of the magical healing that I was trained in."

The bundled woman nodded at him, agreeing to the exam. Pulling several instruments out of his kit, he listened to her heart, and hit her knees. With his hands, he gripped her arms and legs before he declared them break free. Then, he pulled the speculum out of his bag, apologizing in advance. Madame Sadie assisted the woman in sitting back. He prodded inside of her with a tool that was shaped like a small orb on the end of a stick.

"Hm," he mumbled. "But it shouldn't be..." He poked more, ignoring the grimaces on the woman's face. He guided the stick in further. "Good thing this isn't your first time, or you'd be tighter than my aunt with her money."

"It still fucking hurts!" The woman exclaimed.

"Well, hold tight because I haven't even gotten to the rough part yet." Pushing down on her abdomen with his left hand, he spun the stick with his right. He could have been mixing her eggs with a whisk.

"OW! Stop scrambling my eggs!" she screamed, kicking him away and yanking out the invading object.

"I told you it was going to be rough." He wiped the instruments on his jeans, before placing them back into the bag. "Well, you're as barren as this here desert that we live in. No diseases. But your womb is hard as a rock, which means you won't get your monthlies. And there seems to be something magical stuck in your back. I've never seen it before."

"Something hit me as I ran," the woman explained.

"Well, the fact that this source is lodged so far in there makes me think it's a curse. And this cold that keeps spreading from here seems to also make me think that it's a curse capable of taking over you."

"Will she be okay? How do we cure this?" Sadie jumped in, as the girl was quiet. Sadie expected the girl to be full of tears, much as she had been after the news had been broken to her. It had been the end of her marriage, after all. Alas, the girl seemed confused, but no tears fell.

"I have never seen magic like this before." He was trained in the basics, apparently, but Sadie must not have thrown in the heavy coins on a more knowledgeable staff person. "You'll just have to manage the symptoms, or the curse will take over your body. Try to stay warm."

"That's the only treatment you have?"

"Unless I hear of something else, I doubt you'll make it through the next year. Welcome to your new normal."

Healer Frumo packed up his kit and walked out of the room. After he left, the patient burrowed back under the blankets and caught sight of the green-black shadow outside the window. The woman smiled back. She knew in her soul that those talons on his claws would not harm her. Those arms had been the shields to protect her as the wings swished the sweet breeze around her skirts. He had saved her from that brutal city, the selfish cold, and her impending marriage. Where she was now, she had no idea. Her geographical knowledge of Cosimo had never been encouraged throughout her upbringing as a valuable commodity. She did know that the dragon outside her room maintained her safety enough for her to fall back to sleep—which she promptly did.

The dark poured in through the windows of the large room that night. The lights in the saloon had been extinguished. Slewja slept down the street, but he would return bright and early the next morning. The woman who had been asleep all day, awoke to the rings squeaking across the curtain rods shutting the dark out. The lamps lit the area, softening the face of Sadie and highlighting the circles under her eyes. After closing the curtains, she looked at the guest on the couch, who gazed back at her. The madame walked over to a sofa adjacent to the couch and sat down, placing the lamp on the table next to her. She propped her feet up on the table between the furniture, and bent over to untie her boots.

"One order of business. In this house, I'm Sadie to the girls, but to the clients, I'm Madame Sadie. We all have our own pasts, and we can choose to keep them secret. What name would you like us to call you?" Her voice spoke surely and carefully.

"You can call me Grace," the dragon girl said, truthfully.

"I'm Eve," piped the girl who sat in the chair in the corner, knees curled under her, as she peered up from the book that she attempted to read in the flickering light. She closed her book and moved in closer to Grace, now that she was awake.

A coal-haired woman not much younger than Grace sashayed into the room. If she heaved too deep of a breath in her yellow corset, Grace would learn if her nipples had hairs growing around them. Come to think of it, hers were daggers forged of ice protruding from her skin. Below the blankets, she ran her finger over them, testing to ensure that the half-priced medic had not missed that her nipples had actually turned to ice.

"I brought some whiskey. Figured it might help our mysterious dragon girl warm up a bit!" The new entrant set the bottle down in the middle of the table where Sadie and Eve had their feet up.

"Are you just getting back, Britt?" Sadie gave her the motherly once over.

"Yeah there was an intense game of cards going on at the saloon. Some guy brought in enough money to buy half of the town and he lost it all." She cracked her neck and stretched her back.

"I hope you had Annie put that bottle on my tab." Grace's stomach turned at Sadie's sentiment. What was she going to do about money? She couldn't live off the charity of people to whom she used to provide charity.

"Nah, I got this one with my tips from tonight. I helped her serve the swarms. People were just clearing out this morning." She yawned and pulled her shoes off. Grace could not stop staring at the holey tights that this lady wore. So when she was caught ogling them, she had no response to the mischievous smile.

"Explains why tonight has been fairly quiet," Eve chimed in, standing and rubbing her eyes.

"Are you off to bed?" Grace hoped she would say no. She wanted to know more about these women and their lives. Nothing they did or said reeked of pretense.

"No, I'm going downstairs for glasses. I'm not putting my mouth on anything that Britt uses without her seeing the healer first." Britt threw her fishnet stockings at Eve who evaded them, laughing as she bounced downstairs.

The quartet drank as the morning's haze diluted the sun's orange brilliance. With each shot taken, new secrets were revealed, forming strong bonds of trust between them. Grace could not be any more vulnerable than in those hours; she placed her own gamble that these people valued a backbone and persistence.

"My husband kicked me out when he found out that I couldn't have children," Sadie added into the conversation with heaviness in her voice. "I wasn't serving Mother Maker well enough, he said, and he wouldn't have me holding him back from making it to the fourth staircase." She swirled the contents of the shot glass over her crossed arms. "So I took every valuable item he'd purchased with my dowry and used it to get out here. Set up my very own home with my own family. Hope he's got a passel of brats and a shriveled dick."

"I was meant to be married," Grace chimed in. "I darted from that bastard, though. He was pure evil."

"Here's to the women who realize it's not their job to fix a man!" Eve stood, raising her shot glass and downing it in one. The three others downed theirs in solidarity.

"How do you feel, Grace? Are you warm yet?" Sadie broke the conversation with a hiccup, citing that she rarely drank anymore, on account that she stayed awake while the women worked.

"No, in fact, I might be growing colder." She had snuck her father's whiskey enough in Hamber to know that her double vision was not due to the cold. She would have thought that she had contracted the cold sickness if she had not survived an entire city's pandemic already.

"I think you should use your fingers to warm yourself up."

Grace did a double take at Sadie's advice that the others quickly agreed with. Sadie's face remained flat, as if it were the simplest solution in the world.

"You mean... like self-sex?"

These women astounded her. She had never heard women so openly discuss how to create friction between her legs. When she had let men invade her, she had enjoyed it. It made sense that she might enjoy the same sensation if she were to bring it on herself. She looked at their faces again; no one seemed disgusted by this idea in the slightest.

"Do you think it'll work?" Grace asked with trepidation.

"Will it hurt if it doesn't?" Britt supplied. Grace mulled over the pros and cons. No, Britt was not wrong. So when Sadie showed Grace to an unoccupied room, Grace set her fingers to work. Much to her dismay, only her bottom half received any warmth. She elected to try a different manner as soon as she was fully up and about.

Once Grace could walk out of the brothel, she immediately set out to the clearing to thank her rescuer. She needed to see the dragon. Clinging to her borrowed shawl around the used sundress, she welcomed the warm sunlight that penetrated the threadbare outfit. The dust slipped through her worn slippers as she shuffled to the end of the street. There the dragon stood as if he had been waiting for her. As she drew closer, she realized that he stood about twice her size with his knee coming up to her hip. But he had seemed so much larger as he hovered outside her window. His yellow amber eyes, the color of liquid gold, stared straight at her–unfaltering, unwavering. She stared back, caught in the trance of his steadfast gaze. She did not know what she had expected. A conversation? A thanks and his departure?

He tilted his head to the side, and she placed her hand on his head, closing his eyes at her touch. Smiles spread across their faces as if they were each other's mirrored reflections. A connection between the two pairs of eyes that solidified their acknowledge-ment of each's importance in the other's world.

The dragon shrugged a shoulder, then, beckoning Grace to hop on. Her blue eyes looked back at him with trust. He had saved her from certain death before. He would not let her down. She searched his scaled body, analyzing the best route to take. She was ready.

The one thing her parents got right was her name. Grace was nimble and light on her feet, thanks to her years of private dance instruction with the best tutors in the city. She bore herself with clear and confident movements, gliding, almost floating when she walked. Despite her surety of her movements, she could not place how best to climb aboard the creature. She returned to his front.

"I don't know how to best do this," she explained, feeling as though the opportunity was about to slip through her fingers as she admitted to this shortcoming. The dragon crouched down, lowering himself onto his forelegs. He flipped his tail from side to side, drawing her attention to the spikes on his back.

Grace started climbing from the bottom of the tail towards his head. When she reached his back, she straddled it, resting her bottom against a spike. Though it was a more rounded spike, she could see how it would intimidate his foes. But as for her, she found them comforting, for they had protected her when she could not protect herself. Her body was close to his neck but she did not want to hold him there and choke him. The wings stretched just behind her, fanning out from where she sat. At a loss for where to hold on, she tried holding the spike in front.

He took it easy. He wanted her to ride him, to give her that feeling of flying and freedom. She seemed so lost and helpless the first time that he saw her, as she crawled out of the forest maimed by what smelled like an old dragon's magic. He could help her as he could not help the other. Maybe that would be enough for forgiveness.

The dragon moved and her hands spread to gently grab the scales just jutting out to the sides. He began with a slow walk. Never before had she felt this feeling of complete trust in another living soul.

"Slewja, Sadie called you. She said it meant *big-hearted hero.* You are definitely my hero. Thank you for choosing to be there when I had no one left."

His back straightened, the praise bringing him joy in the appreciation that he had not heard in some time.

"I only wish that I could explain to you enough how you have helped me grasp my own life between my hands."

A tear dropped, and she wiped it away with her hand, finding that at this pace, she did not need to cling on for dear life. Pulling her shoulders back and tilting her head to the sky, she took a deep breath. The air was drier than she had become used to back home in Hamber. Years had gone by that she had not basked in the warmth of the sun. It felt like the hug that she had always wanted to receive from her mother. Her nannies had hugged her, but nothing could replace the endorphins released from a mother's hug.

She wanted to feel it all upon her skin. She wanted to be free.

"Slewja, I don't want to disrespect you, but would you fly with me?" She had heard tales of dragons out in these parts. In fact, she often read books about them in olden times, choosing their own adventures and flying across the sky. Knights and princesses would utilize them in times of warfare, which was a sacrilege to the freedom of these magical beings that had been around since before the time of writing. She refused to objectify him as only being useful, much as men did with her. Old texts lauded their hearts that were filled with an unwavering, unconditional love. They believed humans to be adorable pets to care for in this world of treachery. He had cared for her. The two would never be objects to each other in this place that sought to make them so.

In response, he turned his neck back so she could see him bare his teeth at her, which she inherently understood to be a smile, nodding his head up and down. He flapped his wings, and she returned her hands to the two jutting scales. He started out close to the ground, though not low enough for her to bend over and touch the tops of the tall grass that was dry and yellow from sucking up the sun too long, or for his hind legs to scrape the crumbled grey dirt. She closed her eyes, resting her head on his long neck, now parallel to the ground as he flew. Despite the exhilaration of being in the air, the steady calm breathing stoked a sense of tranquility within her.

"If you're okay, then let's go higher," she said after a few moments of sharing the space and the moment together. With that, he flapped faster and they flew up into the air above the plateaus around them. From above, the dirty, dry land looked like crumbled pie crusts scattered for the scavengers to peck upon. She held on to him as he soared above the ground. The wind blew her hair behind her, billowing her skirts, and she squeezed his sides tightly with her thighs. She did not worry–she was born to be in the sky, to feel the air swishing around her, challenging her grip on life. The adrenaline surged through her veins. She did not know if he was flying as fast as possible–she did not need that. She just wanted to fly. And Slewja sensed that, keeping her up in the cool air. She would need to wear leathers next time or at least trousers. And for that, she would need money.

Grace approached Sadie in the office as soon as the sun rose. "Let me work with the girls, Sadie."

Sadie's eyes widened in incredulity. "But you've only just finished healing!"

"I will not live out my days in the shadow of a man who wants to control me. At least I am making this choice for myself," Grace retorted.

"He's coming for you, you know that, right? Even if he hasn't shown up yet, he's on his way. The man you ran from will come for you. No one shows up the way you did without a tail on them. You should be lying low."

"What should I do? Even if I'm able to leave this town, now that I'm moving around, I have no money to go anywhere. I'm not scared of using what I have to get me ahead in this world, Sadie. Mother knows I have little else."

Sadie noted the persistence in the woman's eyes and recognized the same trait within herself. She slowly nodded her head, relenting. "But you work the parlor, and you let me set you up the right way."

Grace beamed, "Oh thank you! I'm going to be the best time this town has ever seen!"

Whispers of the new dragon girl turning tricks floated around town that morning. In the afternoon, she sat in a corner drinking wine and reading a book at the saloon, not facing anyone, as a way to garner interest. Any time a man would come near her, Britt would intercept him and invite him back that night. No one saw her face until she held court in the parlor that night. More men than normal showed up that evening. While they were perfectly content to wait, many became distracted in their waiting and went with other girls.

She chose a man in his twenties, wide eyed yet worn down from life already. Taking his hand, she led him upstairs to her room. Maybe she could cheer him up for a few minutes; everyone needed to have a bit of fun.

She closed the door behind him and motioned for him to sit on her bed. He awkwardly made to take off his boots, but she shook her head. He was already hard. His sallow, hollow look indicated that this enjoyment might be the only one he received this week... or month. She accepted the twenty-five gold coins that he shakily placed in her outstretched hand. Placing it into her bedside table drawer, she climbed onto his lap. Leaning over to the bedside table, her fingers curled around the small bottle, smoothing a bit of lube onto her hand. With a sly smile, she undid his trousers, leaning close to whisper the lie, "you're so big." Guiding him down onto his back, she straddled him, angling herself just right, a flicker of warmth building inside as he moved. The sensation grew, her breaths quickening, until that warmth blossomed, rippling through her, her release coming with a deep, shuddering groan, one she hadn't experienced in too long. He tightened his hold as he followed, his grip so strong that she knew faint bruises would be on her hips the next morning. The heat lingered, spreading all the way to her shoulders, leaving her breathless and stunned by its intensity.

She couldn't believe the amount of warmth that seemed to radiate to her shoulders. Maybe the others had been onto the right idea about the internal heat. Before the client could catch his breath, she was off of his lap, needing to try this warming method again.

"See you later, big boy," she said with a smirk, as she tossed his pants at him. Pushing him out the door, she peeked out and sent a wicked smile at Sadie. "Send in another!"

She sat waiting for him with spread legs, freshly toweled and lubed. This guy liked it fast and hard, the next liked it slow and possessive. Madame Sadie seemed to be curating a lovely client list for her, full of men with individual needs. Grace's insides were toasty warm by the time the sun came up. She fell asleep having been appreciated and having much more money in her drawer. For a time, she hid it in her boot during the day, never having known any woman to have her back.

This group, she learned though, was trustworthy. They each made good money and looked after one another. Britt would leave books out for Eve. With Sadie's extra money, she would leave out bottles of champagne for Sunday brunch. Eve tended to do the dishes, even when it was not her assigned day. Mutual respect blossomed through them based on Madame Sadie's lack of favorites and caring approach. She distributed clients out fairly, ensuring her ladies had enough to pay rent. But you did not need to look too closely to realize that Grace was one of her fascinations. Perhaps she saw herself in Grace: well-bred, independent, and alone. Perhaps she just found Grace entertaining. Either way, the group quickly adopted Grace as their own. Britt taught Grace some fighting moves for kicking a man off her. Sadie explained how to not only keep the books, but how to charge interest and collect debt. And daydreaming Eve demonstrated that you could hold people to your ideals. To be a woman of the world meant you owned your place in it.

As Grace became more comfortable, her voice began to come through stronger. Living in this place of support, she could say whatever was on her mind. In fact, unlike her time growing up in high society in the city, here in the diverse town of Grogtown, Grace received encouragement to voice her thoughts, needs, and desires for survival. And she learned that she could contribute to the group, as well. She was quick to act, always ready to throw out a client with verbal and physical lashings. Grace provided a constant shoulder of support in the way that she had always dreamt of having herself.

The sun shone brightly through the gaps in the drawn curtains, casting a triangle dance across the hardwood floors. Lounging Hour had brought in "two overly stuffy men with stuffed pockets," as Madame Sadie had put it. Eve and Britt were entertaining the men when Grace ventured up to the pianoforte that stood derelict in the corner.

"When was this last tuned?" she asked the room's occupants as she sat on the shoddy stool.

Britt turned her face from the man's crotch that had been occupying her. "The tuner died during the last cholera outbreak."

The man attached to the appendage smashed her head back into himself, adding, "Last Juu-uuune."

So, recently enough that the instrument might have some life, she deduced. She sat at the keys, some missing–wasn't that life? You just learn to play without them; they always sound missing, and it never quite is the same song without them. Other times, you just learn to play new songs that take into account those missing notes. Her fingers tested the keys out.

"Don't play anything too fast, or ol' Blowjob Britt will have me finished in two minutes."

"I really don't see the problem with that." Grace smirked. She looked outside at the sun, remembering how it felt to run away– that feeling of desperation. She started pairing some notes together in memorized progressions in the key of D minor. Outside the french doors, Slewja appeared, hovering closer so that he could listen. When Grace finished to silence, she decided to look around. The room was in tears and Madame Sadie stood in the doorway with her arms crossed to survey the landscape.

Britt's client looked both sad and satisfied as she sat on the floor in front of him, now looking at Grace. Eve's client, on the other hand, looked pretty miffed that his money had been wasted on a less than enthusiastic session.

"Next time, maybe try A major?" Madame Sadie suggested in a too knowing voice.

"Whoops." She grimaced. Looking at Eve's twenty-year-old client, Grace told him, "I'll make it up to you." Getting up from the stool, she walked over and grabbed his hand to lead him to her room. "Just make sure Eve is paid."

On her way out the door, Sadie held out her arm to grab Grace's attention. "I'll have a new spot for you tonight," she informed Grace. And that was how Grace had ended up next door at the saloon, tickling the ivories and advertising wares with the ladies.

That was where Sao found her the night that he walked in and lost his heart.

THREE

The piano melody drifted from the saloon to the dusty street, entrancing the twenty-eight-year-old to make his entrance. Sao remembered hearing his mama's singing of this melody to herself as she hung the wash on Tuesdays in his youth. The tune called to him, reminding him of his family back home that he would not be seeing for some time. Not until he recouped his losses from a few weeks earlier, at least.

He entered through the swinging doors, noting the bar on his left with wooden stools lined up neatly in front of it. Round tables with chairs positioned around them bedecked the right side. In an alcove, opposite the door, sat a woman at an upright piano, her sandy brown hair tumbling down her straight alabaster back. Feathers fringed a blue bodice and trailed off her bottom, sweeping the floor as she turned back and forth on the spinny stool to reach the different registers of the keyboard. He had seen similar outfits on the showgirls who worked on the riverboats on Lackluster Lake, near where he was from. Between songs, the brown-haired pianist turned to take a sip of her wine from the glass tumbler that stood on the side next to the tip box. She caught Sao's eye from the side with ice eyes that sparkled like diamonds and contrasted with the raised eyebrow of contempt.

Raising her glass in echo of her eyebrows, she took a sip of her wine.

"This one's for you." She toasted Sao in an invitation to stay. She returned to face the keyboard, and started playing a slow song that lamented the loss of innocence. Short but heartfelt. A yellow-corseted girl sitting at the bar started singing along. Sao pulled his hat off and walked to the bar where he sat, never taking his eyes off the musician. Her dexterous fingers danced along the keys, the only part of her that seemed to move. Without tearing his gaze from her, he held up a finger to the bartender who responded by pouring him a beer. He knew this song well, as his father would hum it to stay calm while shooting.

"Always keep a steady beat and a sure head," his father had taught him as Sao shot at various objects in target practice outside their homestead when he was a teenager. Sao knew nothing about music, but he knew to cock the pistol on the count of one and to pull the trigger on the count of three. Inhale and cock, exhale and pull. This woman had already made him lose one requirement.

All night, he listened to her play, watching as the natural curve of her spine led his gaze to the floppy chandelier with half-mast candles that swayed above her every time someone walked across the creaky floorboards to leave her a tip or touch her back. She would raise her shoulders to her ears in response to the touches, as if to protect her back that was exposed to the patrons. The barkeep caught a few of the customers getting handsy a few times, and would respond by pointing to the rifle that hung on two metal hooks next to a large chalkboard. This chalkboard, as Sao had learned his first time in the fine establishment, held the names of everyone who started a tab at the saloon. Those who purchased drinks on credit would have their names added to the board. Each drink thereafter that was delivered without payment would earn a tally on the board. At ten tallies, the barkeep would cut the patron off until payment was received.

The next few nights, Sao watched the woman's performances and added tallies to his name on the board. Each night, he drew the courage to move a seat closer to the piano. By the fifth night, he occupied the yellow-corseted singer's spot at the edge of the bar from the first night, earning himself an earful of profanities and slurs from her against everyone from his mother to his nonexistent cat. He ignored the spit on his face as he viewed the pianist's profile as she worked. She played with feigned emotion, as if she were used to entertaining under a facade of pleasing others. Every once in a while, she would glance behind her, under the guise of shifting in the leather spinning seat so that it did not stick to her bare thighs exposed by the bustier. The cheap cigar box that an old man had left at the brothel next door sat on the right hand side of where the music would typically stand. Except she did not need any sheet music. Every night, the box would be half full of coins, and every night, the set would be different.

On the seventh night, when Sao was all but next to the piano with his beer, she turned to him after a particularly happy jig.

"I swear that Daughter Dreamer didn't take this long to come out of Mother Maker herself. You've finally made it near me. What do you want to hear?" She sipped her wine and batted her big blue eyes at him, as she would any other admirer. Sao nearly choked on his beer, his own eyes bugging out of his head.

"I want to hear your story," he told her.

"Ah, don't you all," she lamented with a sad smile, playing a lighthearted ditty as they spoke. "I'm a woman on the run with only her skills and body left to guide her through this world. Maybe you can help a poor girl out?" She started trilling the keys, waiting for his response to her physical innuendo. Taking another gulp of liquid courage, he nodded slowly. At the close of the night, she grabbed a bottle of wine and took his hand as she led him out the swinging doors. The weather was warm and her tenacity was enticing.

That night Sao and Grace whispered over the bottle of wine in her room.

"I was on the run from a bad situation and an even worse man, but he seems to not have followed me," she quietly divulged as she swirled the red liquid in her glass. "His name is Dimin Greystock, you ever heard of him?"

Sao shook his head in denial but immediately felt compelled to protect this woman.

"Well, he wanted me to marry him, but I didn't. And that's how I ended up here. Well, not in this brothel. I ended up here, because I'm no spring chicken. I've had my share of romps in the broom closet, and I had hoped to ruin my reputation enough not to be marriageable material. But apparently, dirty goods are a commodity for that man."

Sao quickly downed his glass which Grace filled without his asking. Feeling the liquid courage flowing through his bloodstream, he inhaled deeply.

"I'm probably the best gunslinger in this town right now, you know," he boasted. His arm movements caused the glass to fling out of his hand and to crash into shards on the floor.

"Oh really?" She batted her eyelashes at him, trying to cast the spit off of them that had flung from his lips. She bent over and picked up the pieces quickly, throwing a towel on the spilled wine to sop it up.

"Yes, ma'am! In fact, on my way up here to Grogtown, I held off a gang of outlaws that tried to steal my money. Would've made my old man so proud. My pops was a real vigilante. Could shoot an owl between its eyes in the dead of night in the middle of a forest in June. I could protect you, you know."

Grace's eyes lit up at this admittance, bolstering his courage to kiss her. He assumed that she had been sexed up a few times at the brothel where she earned her keep, and her tongue did not disappoint. That first night, he had asked her how much she would charge him; instead, she presented him with a quid pro quo arrangement.

"Teach me to take care of myself," she pleaded with him when he came up from drunkenly thrusting his tongue down her throat. His less than discerning eyes could only read the desperation in her countenance.

"Sexually?" His eyebrows raised to his hairline as he wondered how she managed herself at Madame Sadie's if she could not even pleasure herself.

"No, dimwit! I know how to do that!" She playfully hit his arm. "I meant from predators."

"What are you? Meat?" He laughed at the idea that she was nothing more than a slab of salted ribeye, hanging from a smokehouse hook. He raised the bottle of wine to his lips, but she took it from his grasp.

Looking him straight in the face, she deadpanned, "To most men, I am."

She took a deep swig of wine. He guiltily realized that he had done no better than other men when he had sized her up as she sat at the pianoforte. He did not even know her name.

"Well, I'm not most men." Sao puffed out his chest. "I'm Sao Rollins."

"Grace," she said, eyeing his holster on his hip. "Grace Wesson."

"Ha! That's funny. My gun's a Smith and Wesson!" He grabbed her arm and pulled her into him. "I'll be happy to teach you to use it."

"Your expertise will be appreciated." She grinned at him. Sao leaned his face in and successfully closed any remaining distance between him and the girl at the piano. As time went on, he prided himself on being special enough to her that she did not charge him for their nights together. He never knew that she made very good money from her other clients.

⚘

Grace tucked away the leftover money from her payments to Madame Sadie for groceries and rent, then set off toward the saddle maker's shop, passing the empty carpenter's shop on her way.

No one else was in the shop. She expected to be waited

upon quickly, especially as Madame Sadie had informed her that Walter was the best in the nearest three cities. Unfortunately, she found after clearing her throat for five minutes that she would need to engage the white-haired man's attention. Walter, whom she recognized from her nights at the saloon, directed her to try another shop when she explained what she wanted.

"Is it because of what I do? You won't take my money because of how I earned this? Because some of it is from playing those lovely tunes on the piano for you the other night, Walter, for which you so eagerly tipped me to play so you'd forget that you spent your day alone." Her indignation began to rise.

Another customer, a male unknown to her, had entered the shop as soon as she had approached Walter. He decided to join in. "Aw, c'mon, Walter, why don't you just take the little lady's money. She works for it fair and square like we all do." She wanted to take that man's cravat and shove it down his throat. She wanted to tell him that she could handle herself, but apparently, she needed another man to intercede upon her behalf. At this observation, fury rose within her.

He looked around at the wares hanging on the walls. "I'll tell you what. I have a nice little side saddle that I've been working on that I'll give to you cheap, for thirty-five gold coins."

Her heart sank. She had the money, but that was more than twice what she had intended to spend on a saddle. "Cheap? Martin Doxworth got a saddle off of you for fifteen yesterday, I heard him bragging about it."

"Well, that was cheaper leather that a man can handle. For a lady like you, a nice worn leather side saddle will do perfect, but the worn leather costs extra. It's a good price. You won't find another like it around."

"I'm not stupid, Walter. Worn is just a fancy word you snakes uptalk for used. And I don't want a side saddle. I want a proper straddlin' saddle."

"I don't have any of those in your size, I'm afraid."

Throwing her hands up in the air in exasperation, she exclaimed, "I'm the same size as Martin Doxworth!"

"Thirty-five, missy." With that, he turned to the man behind her. "How can I help you, sir?"

"I need a new pommel for my saddle."

"I have a new pommel, but it'll cost you twelve gold coins. You'd be better off just getting a new saddle for fifteen."

"BAHHHHH!!!" Grace stormed out the door and ran straight into Sao.

"Howdy, why what's going on, Grace?"

"That man." She pointed at the building behind her. "Is a crook." She started stomping towards the brothel. She could not contain her fury which erupted in words from her volcanic mouth. "He charged Martin Doxworth fifteen gold coins for a new saddle. He's refusing to sell me anything but a worn side saddle for less than thirty-five."

"Well, maybe he just didn't like the tone you were taking with him, Grace." She walked around the brothel to the back of the house. "Listen, you stay around here. I'm going to go see what's up."

"Oh, sure, you'll believe his side of the story, but not mine."

"I just want to be fair." He shrugged and hurried over to the saddle maker's shop.

She had a hidden scarlet letter, except hers was a punishment for refusing to let the patriarchy dictate her next move. It haunted her with all men. Those gunslinging lessons could not come soon enough. Seemed to her the only way to get through a man's brain that she had power was through a phallic firearm. She walked through the cemetery behind the brothel, looking at the different headstones. How many of the women in this graveyard had been fucked over similarly? Annoyance tumbled in her lower stomach with anger. In an attempt to release the churning feelings, she slammed her hand on the Maker's Mark at the top of a grave-stone. A power surged through her hand, casting frost over the mark and knocking it off.

Taking a step back, she looked at her hand. Only slightly tinged blue, the hand bore no marks from the stone it had just struck.

"What the fuck?" she murmured to herself, glancing around her. Had anyone seen what had just happened? Slewja stood at the entrance of their resting place with wide eyes and mouth ajar.

She mouthed "did you see that" at him and he shook his head as if to say no idea. Her eyes bore into the corner of the headstone as she wondered if she could do it again.

"Grace! I straightened it all out." Sao jogged up next to her, saddle over his shoulder. She resigned herself to this conclusion of the saddle-purchasing saga as she pulled her eyes quickly from the headstone.

"How much?"

"I got it for twelve! It was a steal." She reached into her coin purse, pulled out twelve gold coins and tossed them to him. Though she had looked forward to making the monetary exchange for goods herself, evidently this transaction would be the closest that she would get.

She plastered a fake smile on her face. "Thanks, Sao."

"Anything for you." He pecked her cheek and put the saddle on the ground. "Now, if that'll be all, I'll be back on my way to doing what I was doing when I needed to rescue a fair maiden." He left, whistling a melody from a ballad she had played last night.

Turning to Slewja, she admitted to him, "I know absolutely nothing about saddling up a dragon." Slewja motioned at the saddle then patted his back. He knelt on his back legs and Grace tossed the saddle on. She recalled seeing colored blankets under other riders' saddles and she mentally noted that she should bring one out the next time. Slewja used his claws to secure the straps across his chest.

"Oh, it seems that you've done this before," she observed. Eagerly, she climbed onto his back. The saddle was a major step up from clinging on for dear life to his smooth scales. He looked back at her and she assured him of her readiness, then he lifted off to the sky. "Let's find somewhere that I can blow shit up." She smiled.

Slewja landed them five minutes later at the base of the mountain range. Tilting her chin to the sky and looking upwards, Grace could discern the city sitting amid the peaks. Grace wondered who would ever live on such a hill. And if you died, did they just lower your body to the base of the mountain? Disembarking from the saddle for the first time, her foot caught on the side, so she was left hanging upside down.

"Hey, Slewja, buddy, help a girl out." She stole his attention from scanning the skies. When they flew, he would make it a point to fly through an arm of a bird "V" with his mouth open, hoping for a snack. She learned to keep her head down or feathers would fly at her eyes like knives in a kitchen fight. Because she dangled just below his left armpit, he had to sit up and use his right arm to cross under the left and extricate her without seeing her. Placing her gently onto the ground, her hand-me-down dusty brown boots landed flat and then he brushed her off.

"Thanks," she chuckled as he tried to right her shirt and trousers that had twisted and undone from her dangling upside-down. Her attention drifted to their surroundings. Trees spotted the path around the grey rock that stretched high above her average height. Placing her hand on the smooth stone, the warmth seeped into her cool touch. Green winding tubes peeked out of the cracked dirt path, calling out to the sunshine and rain for sustenance. Birds cooed in the distance, teasing her that they could play a better ode to the moment than she. She tried to memorize the melody, but as soon as she named the note, it would change. Another bird would harmonize, or the song would halt, and get picked up by a bird in a different key.

As she looked around her in awe, her foot snagged on a stray rock. Her body careened forward, but Slewja caught her. He gave her a nudge towards the rock. Yes, that rock needed to be chastised, she agreed. With her hands outstretched, she reached into her abdominal area, a bit as if she were trying to vomit from a late night drinking session. Instead of moving the power out of her throat, though, she moved it through her shoulders, which hunched forward before ice flew out of her hands, immediately changing the rock into a snowglobe.

Once again, she met Slewja's curious eyes. He brought some sticks over and set them into a pile. Grace held out her hands and in a moment sooner than last time, the sticks dripped icicles. Slewja grinned at her. As she was about to turn her back to find some more objects to test, he inhaled greatly through his nostrils. He pursed his mouth together, as if he were about to whistle, and blew a small stream of fire at the sticks. They instantly thawed and maintained the flame. Steam danced in the air, the only remnant of Grace's magic.

She marveled at Slewja's power, having thought that dragons only used their fire in extreme circumstances. Perhaps the cold magic that dwelled within her was a more dire case than Healer Frumo had made it sound. She decided to counter the dragon's move, pulling out more of the ice to douse the flames. He merely exhaled more fire. Back and forth they went, each one-upping the other's previous move.

Finally, Grace could not pull out any more. The pile of sticks had frozen the flames from the bottom of the sticks to where they licked the sky. She sat on the ground, her head feeling light with the head rush from the last use of her magic. "I'm out, buddy."

The duel had exhausted her energy and lethargy devoured her body. Placing her hand on her head, she reached out for an anchor to steady herself. Slewja's body arrived below her fingertips. He lowered himself so he was prone to the ground. The cold had begun to spread to her stomach and lungs. She hiccoughed and hugged herself, willing her legs to move, but they could not. She needed to be warm. Slewja's taloned claws scooped her up, placing her on the saddle. She maintained just enough internal warmth to hold onto the pommel while Slewja sped them back to Grogtown. With a kiss of his snout, she stumbled up the steps, jumping with her hiccoughs the whole way. Eve, on her way out the door, abandoned her plans so that she could help Grace on her pilgrimage to the interior room that she rented. Tucking her into bed, Eve asked Sadie to heat a bed warmer.

Grace snuggled into the heat, waiting for Sao to show up as he inevitably would, thinking that the cost of the power was her ability to freely move about. It would not provide her the power for independence–it would cripple her freedom to move as she would be in bed recovering from its use. She vowed to herself that she would emulate the dragons and only use her powers should the situation absolutely require her doing so.

FOUR

As three months passed, she gradually grew into a state of comfort in Grogtown. Any fear of Dimin existed as a mere thought that would surface only in the moments before Grace fell asleep. That quiet time between the nightmares of the day and the reveries of the night.

While contemplating the previous night's escapades, Sao sat spread across his wooden chair in the saloon. His glass, still shadowed red from the wine that had dubbed its spaces earlier, questioned him.

Sao raised the glass slightly, making eye contact with the barkeep who brought over a fourth glass of wine and then promptly added a tally next to his name on the chalkboard. Two lines remained before he would reach unlucky ten, when Annie the barkeep would cut him off until he paid in full. Fuck decisions, they would be made tomorrow.

Across the pub, next to the hearth, only aglow with warm welcome on chilly nights, the girl called Britt toyed with her lips as she absentmindedly waited for more possible clients to wander in. She looked lazily at the barkeep, perhaps waiting for her to point out her next client.

Sao sat in the corner waiting for Grace to show up. As typical, she took her sweet ass time. He hoped that she had been successful in eliminating the orange-eyed lumbugs at the Hurley house. Those fuckers still gave him nightmares from the time he had tried to help at the Murphy stead. Sao's stomach had made the decision to take on that work. He had brought Grace along in order to test out her gun skills in a less high stakes situation before she attempted to use them in a life or death situation. The second a gun came out, blood pressures and the stakes could be counted on to automatically rise.

He missed her presence in the place. He thought about starting a game with three of the unsuspecting folks passing through Grogtown, until he noticed he had met them two nights ago. Tipping his head, he angled it away from them so his dirty brown hat blocked their view of his face. He had not considered that he was in the same outfit, but Sao never was good at thinking an entire situation through completely. He had taken two hundred coins off them that night, unbeknownst to Grace. And then he lost it last night to Henry Hurley; but rather than the truth, he told her he was working to help restore the sheep barn that the dragons of the town had broken into like thieves in the night.

Those lumbugs, as tall as his kneecaps, creeped him out. Shooting each one with a bullet straight at the orange eyes was the best way to rid a place of them. They would instantly burst like the seams on a dress after a feast. Given that Grace was a much better shot than he, despite being a novice, she was the best choice for the situation. She once explained that she could separate herself from the emotions of shooting and see clearly, whatever that meant. Also, Sao just did not want to do it. He wanted to look around for a game to try to win some money for dinner. He had not anticipated that his previous night's co-players would be visiting the saloon again so quickly. Hopefully they left before she ever learned the details of what had happened.

Unfortunately, his hopes were quickly dashed as the swinging doors almost flew off their hinges. In roared Grace, gun in her right hand aimed towards his head, left hand on her hip. The perfect mesh of society impertinence and western impatience.

"Fuck you and fuck that bitch you rode in on!"

The dust from the street swirled around her calves as their eyes met, hers glaring, his lusting. Despite the wine, his mouth watered for a taste of her.

"Lovely to see you Gra-" a shot hit the wall to the right of his head "-ace."

He did not flinch.

"What the fuck, Grace?" Annie chastised her from behind the bar as she threw the tap off from filling the mug with beer. Grace had turned Sao on to the nuances of wine, even if it was almost vinegar, he could at least classify it as red wine vinegar, apple, or balsamic. Sao, in turn, had taught her that immersing one's throat in a cold beer topped off a rough day of manual labor perfectly. They agreed that whiskey was for special occasions.

That day was not a special occasion, unless Sao had moved, and then it would have been his funeral. Little did Grace know that Annie had heard throughout the day what Sao had bet in the card game last night; she was not even going to ask Grace for money for that beer, so she put it towards her always clean tab. In the town, Grace held the record for most clean spot on the chalkboard. She drank what she could pay. She never owed anyone anything. She came by her money fairly. Unlike Sao.

Sao sighed, running his hand over his square face. "What did Raikka do now?" His grey female dragon had a habit of getting excited and attempting to make new dragons with Grace's black-green-scaled male. Who could blame her? Slewja was beautiful and majestic, with a heart that could melt the mountain caps of Puntos.

Ignoring him, Grace grabbed the beer and threw down the unsolicited coin onto the wet counter. She did not even want to deal with his bullshit tonight. Reeling around without making eye contact, her unkempt, greasy, sandy brown hair shone more black in the dull candlelight. Beer in her left hand, right hand resting on her holster, she walked back out into the dust towards the brothel. She might be finished with the conversation, but Sao was not. He grabbed his hat and jacket from the hook next to the table, dangerously close to the new hole that decorated the already perforated plaster, and nearly tripped over his own worn boots as he scrambled out the door after her.

He knew she probably went next door to the Madame's. Banging on the door of the building next to the saloon, he hugged his jacket closer to his body, at least pretending to be chilly in the night air despite the four drinks he had imbibed while he waited for Grace to arrive. After five minutes, Sadie answered the door, a look of disdain painted across her face like he was a mangy dog on her doorstep.

He peered around her, scratching his face, the stubble reminding himself of the last time that he had showered. Eyes from the parlor glued to him, waiting for him to announce his purpose so the front door could be closed.

"Do I need to ask, Sade?"

Her crossed arms communicated that Grace had already spoken with her at the front door.

"Madame Sadie, to you." She had never liked Sao. He only thought of himself. Rumor had it that he had gambled away his family's money that he had been meant to invest. Instead, the guy had lost it all on red. The fool lacked street smarts.

"You need to pay if you're coming in." She held out her hand. Reluctantly, he put his last two silver coins into her palm and she opened the door, pointing to the stairs immediately in front of him. He bound up them, two by two. Sadie rolled her eyes at the trail of dusty tan boot prints she would now need to clean off the stairs and silently wished that he would trip up them. Grace would not be happy at his appearance, but at least Sadie could hand over the two silver pieces to her as a consolation.

The last room on the left had a cracked door open. He pushed it slightly and caught Grace in her naked glory. Lounging in the bath, left arm on the rim, with her right hand she cocked her gun at him. He rued the day that he had told her to keep it within arm's reach at all times.

"You are nothing but a liar," she accused. He put his hands in front of his chest in surrender and froze at the door.

"What did I lie about now?"

"You lied when you told me that you were working last night. Instead, I found out from Henry Hurley that you were really out with him playing cards. And, instead of gambling with whatever spare change you had remaining on your body from paying off your bar tab with Annie, you added into a bet that someone would clear his house of lumbugs. So, after I spent hours searching out and ending every last beady-eyed fucker, I waited for my payment like an idiot before he told me that no, I would not be receiving money for the work that I DID. And to deliver the message that you two were even from your game."

"Hmm, that sounds vaguely familiar." He rubbed the back of his neck. Shame was a foreign feeling to Sao. If he did not think of something, it did not bother him. Out of mind, out of care.

"Probably because it happened, you piece of shit. And then, to add to my dismay, when I trudged the mile back here from the house, I found your dragon harassing mine. AGAIN. And I'm tired of it. Now leave and go find yourself another game to lose. I would like to enjoy my bath in peace as I contemplate how many men I am going to need to fuck in order to cover my living expenses for the next ten days."

"I told you that you didn't need to do that anymore! I could cover you with the money from the games."

"Your whole life's a game," she retorted at him.

His face dropped, taken aback by the cool disdain in her voice and the harshness of the statement. He froze where he stood, contemplating the validity in her reply. Sao had never been one to work hard. When he saw an opportunity, he would quickly act upon it, much as he did with Grace the first night. When his parents discussed investing money in lands north of his town of Lakeside, he quickly volunteered for the journey. They trusted him to make it there, especially as his dad had trained him in shooting. Sao did arrive. And then he promptly lost the money trying to double it on a game of cards - red cards to be exact. Embarrassed and worried about disappointing his father, he could not return home to see his parents. They would make him work it off or return the money to them somehow, and he never did have a mind to work hard if he could find a quick way through a situation. Considering his dad had probably acquired the money through some unsavory means as he worked as a vigilante, Sao did not think he should be held accountable for his gambling losses.

"Well, it's not like you take your life any more seriously." He hoped that his rebuttal would one-up her and force her to quell her anger.

"Life's an adventure, Sao. I don't play games with people's money or their lives. Being adventurous differs from being reckless."

Sao's mouth hung open as he stared at her. He whirled around, leaving the house as quickly as he had entered. The door slam echoed up the stairs to the bathroom.

Grace uncocked the gun and put it next to her on the table that held her towel. Leaning her head back, she wondered how she ever got tangled up with such a sweet dumbass. She pondered what she had said to him. Was she lying and playing games with Sao? When she climbed out of the tub, the water was freezing and she was only merely warm. She grabbed her towel from under her gun and patted her suntanned skin dry. Throwing on the rabbit skinned robe, she opened the door and trudged out to the room that she rented.

The windowless, interior room stank of sweat from her clothes. She would have to do laundry the next day for the clothes that she owned, which included jeans, a shirt, a showgirl costume for performing, and a slinky negligee for at night. She smiled at the freedom of not having to change multiple times a day for multiple events anymore.

A soft knock on the door came as she was inserting her leg into her flannels. Sadie, hair piled high, shawl around her neck, popped her head in.

"I saw that Sao wasn't staying so I put a bed warmer in your bed, unless you want me to find someone else." Just as Sadie always knew what every person who walked through her front door needed, she instinctively had a clue as to what her girls needed as well. Grace, like always, needed to physically warm up her body.

"No, he's not staying. He needs to learn his lesson."

"Will you be okay?"

"I don't think the cold will take me tonight."

"What luck," Sadie commented. "He's just a boy, Grace, even though the lines on his face may say differently." Sao could not have been thirty yet, compared to Grace's thirty-three years. Grace had never bothered to ask him how old he was, though. With his charming smile and puppy dog eyes, he would have made a great third son in a big house. Mother Maker must have kissed him with some form of invincibility though, because with his lack of intelligence, there was no other way he could be heralded as an example of "survival of the fittest." His father had seen it fitting to teach him how to use a gun well, so he eked by. She had never seen him use it on another person, though.

"Boy or man, all males are the same and all are after the same thing, Sadie," Grace replied. Sao was a steady heat source, which was where her interest in him ended. She climbed into her bed lying flat on her back, though she had never rested well in this position. Madame Sadie walked across the room. First, she gently lined the bed warmer up below Grace's lower back. Pulling the sheet and three quilts over the top, she tucked the bed dressings into the mattress so Grace was tightly in with the heat. Finally, she placed the rabbit skin robe, Grace's Trinity present from her housemates, over her feet.

"Just try not to break your toy, dear. You'll be hard pressed to find another one." Despite being only ten years older, Madame Sadie had silver strands in her hair. The candle danced over them, as she raised it to her mouth and blew out the light. Grace heard the snort outside her window as the door closed.

"Good night, Slewja," she told him, smiling to herself about the one male she actually could trust and rely upon in her life.

FIVE

The morning brought new light to the situation at hand. If Grace wanted to ensure that her access to warmth remained guaranteed, she would need to remain on friendly terms with Sao. She missed him some days, but more like one misses ice cream on a summer's day.

Walking downstairs in her rabbit robe, she entered the kitchen where she started the coffee process. Before arriving at the brothel, Grace had never had coffee. Now, her brain enjoyed waking slowly as she drank the bean juice. The girls had had to teach her how to use the percolator on the stove. No longer a slave to her past instilled helplessness, she found herself wanting to pull her weight in the house. This dog was still capable of learning new tricks. She pulled a mug down from the cupboard, still thinking of the situation with Sao.

He would come back; and he had better be apologetic. And then they could have whatever makeup sex that he thought he would need to feel like she was his. The pattern would repeat itself next week, too.

A note with two coins awaited her on the counter with the coffee pot.

*Here's his last two cents. Now he's full of non-
cents. Maybe you can knock some cents into him. Love,
Sadie*

Dear Maker, the puns. She must have been half asleep when she wrote that, though it was damn clever. Sadie had a habit of getting quite silly between three and four in the morning. Grace figured that Sadie must have done alright last night, or Sadie would have pocketed the money, and she debated whether or not to give it back to Sao. Eve sidled in wearing her hair up, and an open silk robe over her bustier. She covered her mouth as she yawned, pulling an extra mug from the cupboard and setting it beside the one Grace had placed on the counter.

"Not quite cream tea, is it?" Eve joked while Grace measured spoonfuls of ground coffee into the pot.

"I would actually love a good tea time. Just sit all nice and clean while someone brings me hot tea with sandwiches." She had always delighted in eating the variety of finger sandwiches and cookies that could be expected during calling hours. The food had always trumped the conversation.

"And sugar," Eve added with a nostalgic look. In another age, Eve had also been quite accustomed to the finer things in life, until her father lost everything on a prospecting gambit out west near some place called Cliffside.

"Uhhhhh." Grace held on to the counter. "I think I just orgasmed on the memory."

The women laughed as the pot started boiling. Grace poured for the two of them. She had become accustomed to the strong, black liquid coating her insides in the morning. The heat helped the never ending struggle with the cold. Eve raised her cup in a toast. "Here's to men with big... incomes." She winked at Grace, and brought her cup with her upstairs. "Have a good da-ay," she sing-songed.

Grace wondered who was about to be kicked out of Eve's bed. Her coffee and book ritual came second to no man.

Several white rocking chairs adorned the raised back porch that delivered a panorama view of the town of Blatho, about a ten minutes ride away via Slewja. Heavy clouds umbrellaed the distant area. Less dreamy in the foreground was the town's graveyard. Sitting cross-legged on the chair closest to the door, she held the coffee between both hands. It was a precarious position, but no one was nearby to topple her balance. She thought about Sao. His gambling really knew no bounds, but thirty percent of the time, he hit big enough to last him a good turn. He was no different from those elitist braggarts that she used to be forced to socialize with back home. Well, not quite home. The home she remembered celebrated summer and rain and health. In its current state, she did not care for it. She had yet to find a hearth that would beckon her return.

As she sat silently ruminating on her problem, her problem sat himself down at her side, facing the side of her head. He leaned over, putting his forearms between his knees and clasping his hands. "I'm sorry," he said, wringing his fingers.

"Okay," she replied flatly, staring into her coffee.

"Grace." He tried again, a bit louder. "What do you want me to say?"

She had wanted an apology for throwing her to the dogs. For whoring her out without her permission. She wanted some semblance of realization to dawn upon him. Unfortunately, the only dawning to occur that morning would be the one she was watching.

"I want you to say that you're going to pay me for my day's work, if you're going to hire me out on a daily basis."

"Fine. And then we're even?"

He put his hands on his knees and stood up, holding his hand out to shake on the bargain. Grace looked at his outstretched hand. She placed her hand daintily in his, a vestige of her upbringing. He awkwardly shook it when she fully expected him to kiss it.

"Then we're even," she agreed. He pulled her upright to him, splashing coffee onto her hand and the ground.

"Kiss on it."

She leaned in towards his mouth, before pecking his cheek.

"Earn it," she whispered into his ear. Instantly, his hardness brushed her thigh.

She patted his shoulder as she walked back into the kitchen and put her cup into the sink. He stayed a moment, watching the sun come up over the foreboding clouds that seemed to never quite arrive. If he had paints, he would give them to Grace and ask her for a painting of it. Though he had never seen her paint, he assumed that her upbringing surely involved such a pastime.

Dragons flew towards the city, so he made his way to the post office, wondering if any inheritances happened to find their way to him. He would see Grace later that night and they would make up, just as always.

Grace had a day to herself, which meant she should do her laundry. It was Britt's day for dishes, or so said the chore chart behind the kitchen door. But all she wanted to do was look for Thalassa and get her advice. She passed Eve who was tucked under her covers in her room at the top of the stairs. Grace flung her rabbit robe onto her unmade bed and changed into a simple white button down, suspenders, and brown trousers. She ran a quick brush through her long hair before tying her gun holster around her waist and heading out the front door. Her legs took her down the street of their own accord.

Thalassa Charles had ventured to town one day, looking for work as a carpenter. Her father had trained her in wood. Yes, she realized all the jokes and made them whenever she could. She also pointed out the different woods to Grace when they would walk around new buildings, ridding them of pests. Grace had met Thal when she had needed to consult with her about how to rid a home of nurox without harming the wood. The pests had flown in and made themselves comfortable in what turned out to be cedar. She walked into the carpentry shop perfectly prepared to have to prove herself intelligent to the grumpy old tradesman, only to be pleasantly surprised by the dark-skinned woman's knowledge of trees. Later that night, Thalassa had entered the saloon to find a guy whose whistle she could whet, and Grace dedicated a jaunty song to her. The two chatted as Grace played all night. Grace stayed on a mat in the back of Thal's shop that night, both girls too drunk and giddy to separate. From then on, they rarely parted for long stretches of time. Grace had grown accustomed to walking to her friend's home in the mornings.

"Everyone can go to hell," Thalassa declared, tossing back a shot of whiskey in the front of her shop at ten in the morning.

"Who hurt you? I swear..."

"No one that I wouldn't maim right back, sweetie." Thal put her hand on Grace's forearm, squeezing it in reassurance. "You are freezing! When did you get laid last?"

"A day or two ago. Why is everyone going to the pits of hell now?"

"I have been working in Blatho on that temple that they're erecting..."

Grace giggled.

"Have another shot, you whore. You think you'd be numb to certain words by now." She pushed the bottle towards Grace, who took a swig. "I've been working on directing where the beams head in and the carvings. Oh, the carvings are incredible. A real masterpiece. They've taken me hours and hours. A real tribute to Mother Maker herself, guaranteed to at least get me past the second staircase when I die. And after the install, rather than pay me so that I could divvy up the funds appropriately to those that helped with the manual labor, the town made a big ceremony of paying the foreman. And that asshole gave me thirty percent of it!"

"WHAT!?" Grace replaced the whiskey bottle top. Her eyes had grown to the size of half silver coins. "Let's go."

"No, Grace, it's really alright." Thal's eyes grew big with Grace's impending impetuosity.

"Unless he gave you the money back, it's not okay."

She pulled up her trousers, straightened her holster, and strode out the back of the shop, suddenly sober. Motherfuckers like this guy pissed her off. They always had back east too. But she was finally in a position to do something about it.

Thal might not be willing to risk her business, but it was a risk to her livelihood to not receive the money she was due. They couldn't set this as an example to others. Whistling for Slewja, Grace motioned for Thalassa to get on the back.

"We can take Vim," Thal offered. Grace laughed.

"Your dragon? Awake before noon? I highly doubt it. Tell Slewja where this asshole lives."

With a smile on her face, Thalassa told Slewja where to find the town of Blatho. The dragon nodded, not requiring much direction. All her life, Thal had wanted a best friend, but moving from town to town with her father to find work made the prospect of long term friendship difficult. Not only was he a carpenter, but an architect as well. He went west to make his mark on the burgeoning expanse. Thalassa kept busy in the shop with her father rather than make new friends at every post. She learned early on that leaving them would only tear apart her tender heart.

Off Slewja flew to the next town over. Glancing behind her to see how far Grogtown was in the distance, Grace caught sight of Vim as he trailed them. So, he had been awake! She chuckled to herself and shouted in Thal's ear that the dragon had followed them. Thal shook her head in disbelief. The adrenaline flowed freely through the women, increasing over the course of the ten minute ride.

A chill cut across their faces as Slewja descended through the heavy clouds that she had been watching just that morning. Her visible breath reminded her of the weather on Trinity's Nighs when she celebrated back east.

Thalassa, in front of Grace, pointed to where she had found the foreman. Grace slid off the back of Slew down his tail, landing nimbly like a ballerina. Not waiting for Thal, she started stalking towards the back of the stable where she unhooked her holster and pulled out her gun, wiggling her left fingers to stay calm. She kicked the door open. Vomit and shit scented the air. Covering her mouth with the pale-green bandana that she had made from the tattered ballgown she had arrived in, she stalked the stable for her prey. A sallow-faced man used a feeding trough as a pillow. Maintaining her distance from this blight, she kicked the man in the ribs and aimed the pistol at his head.

"Wakey wakey, smell the bakey."

The man grunted with the impact to his chest and opened his eyes groggily. In his morning hangover stupor, he looked her over twice. When he registered that his waker held a gun to his head, he immediately raised his hands up.

Grace commanded his attention. "I want your hands to travel to the point on your body where the money you stole from my friend is hiding. Anything coming up like a weapon will receive a bullet."

Moving onto his heels, away from the trough, the foreman's hands went to his crotch with a pathetic grin on his face, like he was the only guy to have ever used that joke before. Grace rolled her eyes at Thal before she shot at his crotch.

"OOF!" The foreman doubled over holding his privates.

"Oops, it was so big, I thought it was a weapon," Grace said in mock stupidity. "Money. Now."

She held out her left hand while her right hand remained holding her pistol. The large man in the fetal position with the pain raging through his body began to pray to whatever religion's deity to save him. Grace had no patience for this man who stole from women and then prayed to be saved. The hypocrisy was the ultimate disrespect. The man's wails crescendoed annoyingly.

Thalassa left and returned a moment later, her hands full. She bent down and shoved a wad of sawdust into his mouth to keep him quiet. Her foot pushed into his stomach, forcing him onto the ground so he rolled around on his back like a lumbug.

"Nice touch!" Grace praised Thalassa's ingenuity and willingness to help solve her own problems. The two girls smiled at each other, enjoying their moment of camaraderie, together against the world. While bent over, Thalassa patted the man down, until she found the bag of coins. She opened it, counting the fee.

"Thirty percent is missing, that is what you gave me. Now there is about half remaining of that. So, I'll just take this. I'll let the boys know that you have their paychecks. Keep the extra five percent as a tip from me."

Thal stood and walked away without looking backwards.

Grace twirled her pistol back into its holster at her waist and saluted the foreman with two fingers.

"Nice doing business with you, bloodcrotch. Now you know how it feels to be a woman in more than one way."

SIX

The sheriff of Blatho flagged Grace down just as she was about to get onto Slewja. Behind her back, she waved for Thal to hide. Grace strode up to the rotund, tobacco chewing man, giving Thal time to dodge behind a wooden joist before the Sheriff could see her. Vim crawled around to the opposite side to pick her up.

"Ma'am, you are under arrest for harming a person outside of normal rights." He pulled the badge, secured to the left breast pocket of his pilled wool coat, closer to her as if she couldn't already see his authority.

"What the fuck does that even mean?" The words escaped her mouth as she was so dumbfounded by his incompetence with the language. Slewja started creeping away behind her.

He smacked his lips and spat on the ground as he took out his shiny pistol. "It means you've harmed a civilian."

"Pretty sure you've done that too at some point. Even outlaws are civilians. And you look like you're threatening to do that to me now with your gun out."

"Ma'am, it's best if you just let due process and habeas corpus do their magic and succumb to the law."

Still slack jawed at the sheriff's wrong use of phrases, she held out her hands, slightly blue without covering, and stepped towards the bombastic blight. The cool metal handcuffs slipped over her wrists. The short man seemed to revel in this action, as if it was the best part of his job.

"Ever play with handcuffs, sir?" she uttered in her best sultry voice as he snapped them shut.

He faltered in his movements and choked on his spit. She could not contain the smirk that thrust itself upon her face. It broadened as she saw Thal slip away on Vim, with Slewja following close by. Thal whispered to Slewja, and he followed her, though his eyes never left Grace. A slight breeze flowed through the alleyway and whipped wisps of hair around her sweaty face.

Thal kicked off, heading north to distract any that might be seeing Slewja's flight path. As she hit the sky, the sheriff's deputies scattered behind her, giving chase. Vim could maneuver, at least. And he took the two of them on a path, she knew not where. She just hoped the dragon knew enough to go around and fast.

Once he saw that she had distracted the posse, Slewja headed back the way they came, towards Sao. Thal did not have the gun skills to take on this many alone. Sao did. As good as Grace was, she had to learn from somewhere, and the smartass boy that he was could at least bust her out of the trouble she'd gotten herself into.

As Sheriff Shitbag trudged the manacled Grace across the dirty street, people popped their heads out of doorways and windows. She held her head high; no shame would paint her path. The man made sure that she tripped up the steps, hoping to take her swagger down a notch. She spat on his boots as she was on the ground and pushing herself back up. He ended her walk of no shame when he tossed her into the manky jail cell. No one else was in the cell next to her. Slow day at the office.

"Get in there, you whore," the gruff voice commanded her as he slammed the door of the metal cage behind her. "You're lucky that our healer could get to him in time, or you would be facing murder charges."

With a sugar sweet smile, she retorted, "You're just pissed that I'm not *your* whore."

She had learned early after her escape that even if letting out the thoughts that swam around in her head did not change anything, at least they were not pent up inside of her. It was a freedom she had never known before–this saying things that she wanted to whomever she wanted.

"You will be tonight."

"Why? Your arthritic hand can't keep up with your limp dick, old man?"

She sat on the bed in the corner, and put her handcuffed hands behind her head leaning against the wall. The sheriff had seen a lot, but he really wanted to smack the insolence off this woman's face. She should be at home under some man's thumb, pregnant so she couldn't make more trouble. Women like her needed to be controlled. Her father had failed her.

As he was thinking his misogynistic thoughts, Grace licked her lips at him. She pulled her legs up and out, spreading them wide into a V, as she moved her handcuffed hands above her head on the wall and bit down on her bottom lip. He could not stop staring.

"Well Sheriff, it seems you did need me to get a rise out of your limp dick."

She decided at that moment that she could use him for her break out. If he could get sex-crazed enough for her, then he might want to let himself in or her out. Either situation posed options for her escape. Snorting with disgust, he threw his water on her. The droplets landed on her chest like a burst of rain through a wandering cloud. While staring at him, she rubbed her nipples making them hard through her shirt. When he held his gun out at her, she started untying her trousers so she could show him where to put it. He shot a hole in the wall behind her and she told him that she hoped his dick was bigger than that in order to satisfy her.

"Are you married, Sheriff?" she asked him, doing her best

impression of Sadie buttering up a big spender. She pulled her hair out of her ponytail, shaking the ratty mess free. She looked from his eyes to his lips to his eyes, the triangular look.

"I bet your wife is going off tonight looking for someone else to please her. Especially since that foreman is out of commission. I bet he had a great time with her. I did you a favor, because he won't be inserting that large dick of his inside her and making her scream like a coyote at the full moon anymore."

Grace proceeded to spend some time in that cage toying with the sheriff's head. His hatred towards women, coupled with his arousal worked together to make the man take steps closer to opening the cell. His mouth had salivated to the point that a drop of drool dangled from on his chin. Her victim failed to notice that Sao slipped into the room where this dance was occurring between the black widow and her prey.

Grace knew Sao had entered; she recognized the sound of his footsteps from when he tried to creep around at night. Maintaining the sheriff's attention, she licked his hand that was grasping the bar. He was completely taken off guard by this move; so much so that he had no idea that a pistol delivered a knockout blow to the back of his head. When he woke, he would only know that he had been standing and then on the ground.

Stealing the keys from the misogynist sheriff's belt loop, Sao noticed that the guy had fallen sprawled out. Twisted with his belly up, the man's raging hard on caught his attention.

"Really, Grace?"

When she saw what Sao referred to, she shrugged with wide eyes in response, as if to say, *The fuck else was I supposed to do?* Did this girl know no boundaries? Sao's attention turned to unlocking the cell that she stood behind. The sheriff must have been quite organized, despite his lack of understanding of the law he had sworn to enforce, because he found the key labeled "1" just as Grace's cell was. Slipping the key into the hole, he turned it easily until it clicked.

Sao grabbed the handcuffs that she held out to him.

"I think I earned my kiss," he boasted, grabbing the chain between the cuffs and pulling her out of the cell.

He caught her in his arms. As much as she was bothered that he had arrived hoping to rescue her, she gave him a quick peck on his cheek. He turned his head, eyes closed tightly, and his mouth sucked her in, his tongue drawing her deeper. He wanted to remind her that she was his, not this sheriff's. In her handcuffed state, she could only put her hands on his chest. Half holding him back. The kiss had a strength about it, of him reminding himself that she was still there. What would he have done without her? She kept him honest. He needed her passions and ideas to give himself a sense of purpose. Without Grace, the melancholy of living would consume him.

"Let's go," she said, pushing back from his chest. "Wait, you go first to hide the cuffs."

Sao walked out front, tipping forward his hat. He surveyed the street, hoping that they would not be spotted and described by anyone within the vicinity. He blocked the view of Grace from the street as she headed to the back, keeping her handcuffs from direct view. Sao followed her once he knew they were not being tracked.

Once behind the jail, she tried to shimmy up the back of Slewja but it was rather difficult with her hands together and no way to pull herself up. Sao put both his hands on her ass and pushed. She went face first into Slewja's behind before she could army crawl up his back. Slewja snorted, finding the situation comical.

"I don't see you helping, mister," she said to him. "And we're in a time crunch if you don't want your ass next to me in a cell next time."

A sheriff would never put a dragon in jail. The dragon would most likely be sold to the highest bidder for town funds. The convicted human would be shit out of luck.

Sao pushed her a second time and she used her arms to crawl up towards the creature's head. Sao quickly followed, slamming his body over hers and holding on to the pommel. The dragon propelled off the ground and into the air before anyone could see the three of them leave.

Little did they know that the sheriff had a photographic memory that Sao had not damaged with that hit.

SEVEN

Though a short ride back to Grogtown, Grace grew bored with not being the pilot. Riding with Sao on Slewja was not the same as riding alone on Slewja. For one, he and Slewja constantly battled for control over how to fly. Sao, though decent, could not compare with Slewja's obvious mastery of the situation and his inherent sense of direction. Grace had learned through the weeks that she had spent with Slewja that he knew how to take humans into consideration. She deduced that in some part of his life he had been accustomed to co-existing with humans. His eye contact and expressions reminded her of a conceited older brother who knew more than she did, but was willing to keep her misadventures secret. She would have words with Slewja later about his bringing Sao into the Blatho situation. She could count on one hand the number of times that both males agreed to intervene in her life. Most of the time, they argued about her freedom restrictions. From her spot on Slewja's back, she noticed that the warring over control between the two males led to their straying from a steady current, so the amount of turbulence was making it difficult for Grace to hang on.

To get Slewja back in the driver's seat—whom she trusted more with the flying since he was connected to the mechanisms—

Grace quickly decided to steal Sao's attention. She maneuvered around to face him and threw her hands over his neck, so the metal of the handcuffs rested on his hairline. She shifted slightly, giving him the old triangular look that had driven the sheriff wild not long before. She had learned the technique from Sadie as a way to loosen up anyone. Sao's lips parted, his eyes darting from the view in the sky to the view in his lap.

"Don't you think you should be holding on?" he asked, distracted from looking ahead.

"I am, to you," she replied in his ear. Slewja hit a pocket of turbulence as he slid into an air current and Grace's pelvis slid forward, opening her up to Sao. She tightened her forearms around the sides of his neck. "That's better."

Now, Grace never had a great relationship with her father. But she had been taught to never owe a man anything, and to call a fig a fig. Her clit was positioned right at the place she could feel his hardness, and when they hit another air pocket, a moan escaped from her mouth. Realizing this sound had emanated from her, she giggled. She felt him growing harder. Smiling at him, she wiggled her eyebrows. This guy had no idea what she was about to do but he had better...

"Hold on," she directed him aloud. She leaned back and rolled her pelvis upwards and downwards, pushing backwards as she climbed to the head of his cock.

"Mother Maker and all that's in between," he swore as he exhaled. "You're not making this easy."

"It sure is to me, unless you have other ideas," she challenged him. His gaze darkened at her.

"Alright you high falootin' thang," he turned on her. "You want to play? I'll play. Slewja, you're in charge! Take us lower!" He shouted to the dragon; to her, he said, "I want people to watch this." He lowered his head to the placket of her shirt. With his teeth and tongue, he began unbuttoning her satin buttons. She felt her crease dampen. What else could he do with that tongue? Oh she knew all too well. Her dampness moved backwards as she slid forward more. Her legs wrapped around his mid back. The turbulence made her flush, and she stretched her lower back, willing the blood to descend from her head to his.

As her chest opened to the cool air rushing around her, she felt his warm breath over her frigid nipples. Her breath caught as he leaned forward at that moment. Her legs went further upwards, his body weight pressing her backward, but his cock went forward towards her so she could feel his length through their trousers. He just let it sit there, immobile as he nibbled at her tits. First licking, then nipping, before he made her cry out by sinking his teeth into her sensitive points. And as he bit, she ground up against him.

"Listen, you brat, you can move all you want, but if you come before we land, I'm going to keep you in those handcuffs until I have my way with you on the ground." His threat came as a growl. She never did like when he called her a brat, as she considered that knowing what she wanted in her world did not make her a brat, but he seemed to like it, so she did not care that much. At that moment, Slewja decided to swerve, with Sao's hands spreading out to catch himself on either side of her head. Grace could have sworn she felt a chuckle reverberate from Slew's stomach. There they were: her wrists behind his head, clit at his cock, with his arms barely holding onto the massive beast below them. In her peripheral vision, she could just see the greens of the leaves below. She moved her legs to a half up half down position, anchoring the two of them to the dragon's back, inner thighs squeezing him into the place she wanted him to stay.

"What makes you think I'm coming first?"

He bit her nipple, and the pleasure radiated through her body. Warmth, sweet warmth. It wasn't in her core, but at least her neck was warm. With her wrists, she pulled him in towards her harder. He bit on her neck, licking his way all around her clavicle, out to her armpit, sweet kisses to just where her chest met her full turgid protrusions. Everywhere but her nipple, which is where the pulsations in her pelvis seemed to cry out for him to go. And when

Grace thought Sao had heard her internal yearnings and was headed for her left bud, he breathed below her breast. Arching her back and gaining friction, she wanted to burn a hole through those leathers so her skin would be closer to his. She could feel the release as she moved her hips in bigger and faster arcs. She could hear Sao trying not to be affected as the buildup became too much for her to handle. Oh no, so she would get it twice? The precious warmth swarmed her body, tingling from her swollen pelvis to her head and out to her fingers. The bliss of feeling warm echoed her in her low moan.

"Always getting what you want, aren't you?" Sao chuckled as the dragon arrived at a standstill.

"Sao, just undo me," she begged. "Take me off here."

Sao bowed out of her hands and took a moment to spread the blanket that had been lying across Slewja's back onto the ground. He had been sitting on it, so as not to chafe between his thin trousers and the leathery skin of the dragon. Slewja huffed at Sao, also impatient for this to end. Grace had no idea where they had landed; she didn't even care if Sao knew. Here came her "punishment." He would not be able to inflict pain upon her even if she told him that it brought her immense pleasure. He undid her laces, and she relented. She had had her way, let him have his. Arms in front of her now, she was able to undo his laces. He inserted into her and proceeded to rapidly thrust. She reached down to her small bud of nerves and massaged it rapidly attempting to catch up to him. He didn't seem to mind the extra pressure that she provided as he tumbled over the edge. She followed quickly. He pulled out of her and she went to the nearby bushes to relieve herself of the pressure in her lower pelvic region. When she returned to what she now noticed was a spot between trees, five minutes later, Sao had made the tent and was groggily tucking himself into the blankets. The mosquitoes swarmed at the heat of Slewja's nostrils and the smell of sex. She opened up the blanket and licked her initials on Sao's back, hoping the mosquitoes would leave a lovely letter in bites for him in the morning.

"Mmm, thank you," he said.

She giggled.

He wouldn't be thanking her in the morning, but at least they would have something to laugh about at the saloon the next night. He needed to lie still and sleep if her prank was going to work, though. He deserved the karma for their romp and his not trusting her to take care of herself. She would need to visit Thal in the morning to cut through the cuffs, because she was pretty sure the dumbass had dropped the keys in a canyon that they had passed over.

He had actually left them in the door of her cell at the jail.

EIGHT

Back in the town of Blatho, the next afternoon, the crowd parted out of reverence for the esteemed newcomer to look at the wall of the post office. Along with a foot of snow, Dimin had arrived that morning, ready to start a local government campaign in a new location. He was now governor of the territory of Greystockton, mayor of the city of Bleak Harbour, and, as of yesterday, a founding member and donor to the town of Windhaven. The unsick members of the city had voted to rename the place known as Bleak Harbour as "Dimincity."

Making sure that he kept his team of "assistants" in check, he decided that he would stop at the post office to check out the wanted posters. For one, he wanted to determine which of his "loyal" supporters needed to be permanently ousted from his team. Secondly, he hoped to scout out the bad eggs, to get them to desist or cease forevermore.

Searching the wanted posters for familiar faces and typical MOs, his eyes fell on one. He pulled his glasses out of his inner jacket pocket. His eyes surely deceived him. He tore the wanted poster off the post office wall. His magic had killed her that day. Dimin Greystock took a good look at the paper. She had no new defining features; she had not even tried to disguise herself to hide from him. Grace Eastbrook, according to this drawing, remained a breathing member of society. Her contributions were gaining her renown, though her name was not attached to the image.

The sheriff walked in and saw him looking at the poster.

"That bitch done escaped my forbearance, and trial by error."

For speaking the same language, Dimin could not believe that the words emitted from this man's mouth meant absolutely nothing when placed together in a sentence. Yet he was curious about the female in question, so he decided against all better judgment to ask this man what he had meant.

"She was in a cell and then she got out. Whacked my head pretty good too."

"How long ago was this?"

"A few days ago." He lied in the conversation, thinking that he would not sound inept as a sheriff if he had managed to keep her locked up for more than one hour. This man in his navy pinstripe three piece suit with a gold timepiece looked mighty important. "I had her holed up here for a few days though. I let her go to get a head start to give my bounty hunters a way to make some easy money, you know, help them out. What's got you interested?"

"That woman is my wife," Dimin informed the sheriff, with all the surety of a schoolmistress singing the alphabet. The sheriff gasped with his entire body.

"Well, sir, then you are to blame for not keeping her under lock and key. Why is there no baby in her belly to keep her at home? Aren't you a mighty bit older than she? I should charge you instead of her for the crimes ceased in this territorial domain."

Dimin pushed his hand forward towards the man's jugular and froze his vocal cords to cease his obtuse ramblings. To the people around them, Dimin appeared to be fixing the sheriff's collar.

"Thank you, my good man, but I will handle it, as she is *my* wife."

With that, he left, cursing at himself for not having the

forbearance to persuade the man to divulge more information. No wonder she had tricked him—clever Grace's spirit would have run wild over this man's ineptitude.

In his distraction, he ran into a peddler with motley trousers who was hoping to use the crowd for his own financial gain. Their collision shook the merchant's cart, knocking a few items to the ground in a shattering demise.

"So sorry, here," Dimin absentmindedly reached into his pockets and thrust a handful of coins into the olive-skinned man's hands before he continued his dazed walk.

Now, he walked with a new focus. Now, Dimin knew that Grace had escaped him and dwelled nearby. A few days out from where he was, in fact. He had to find her before she could elude him; dissent in the ranks was never to be tolerated. He wanted to know how she had survived his magic hitting her. She should have been killed, which was why he had not looked for her. With this knowledge, he hopped into his transport, and headed back to Windhaven. He gathered a few of his loyal supporters back at the mansion, so they could devise a plan to bring her back to him.

Though she was making this difficult, very few people were immune to the cold sickness that he spread wherever he went. His curse did not allow him to become attached to anyone. He had hoped that he would be able to start a family and pass on himself to the next generation with her. He had not expected her to run from the altar. Of all the attractive offers that he had received when he made his plan for marriage known by the city, Grace's father delivered the best terms. Additionally, he thought she would be the most likely to accept his terms, given her seasoned years, especially since her father had all but gifted Dimin half of his property. When her old man, though he was the same generation as Dimin, caught the cold sickness, it all bequeathed to the Greystock family, namely him as the husband of Grace.

No one in Greystockton remembered that the two had not completed the marriage ceremony. No one remaining in Greystockton remembered that they used to refer to the town as

"Hamber." The beauty in the curse lay in the forgetfulness that gradually blanketed any area in which he dwelled, like snow that fell from the sky. He rubbed his chest from his wound that only worsened as the years wore on. He supposed that most people would have taken this curse to heart; however, it only made his thirst for power grow.

She would not be as lucky when he caught up to her this time.

NINE

One town west of Blatho, back in Grogtown, a chill permeated the air. Grace slipped out of Sao's tent, situated well outside the dragon clearing, happy to meander back to the brothel at the center of the main street. She tied her waist length hair in her tattered ballgown bandana, getting it off of her neck in a weirdly tied yet functional bun. A bath would be nice to wash off the scents of yesterday's occurrences. Still handcuffed, she made her way towards town. She thought of two options for breaking the metal constraints off her hands—Sadie might have a key, or Thalassa might have a saw. The town had not yet awakened, or its citizens might have had a few questions for Grace about her predicament. Slewja followed her.

Upon arrival at Thalassa's place, she thought it only slightly odd that Thal was not up and working. Holding her hand over her eyes to shield them from the sun, she checked down the street for Vim's maroon body lounging in the clearing. He was not around either.

"Thal! You up yet?" Grace announced as she tried the front door, but it was dark inside. She walked through to the workshop on the side of the house. Having deduced that Thal must have taken the long way and holed up for a night, she grabbed a saw from the wall. Her gaze cast between the cuffs and the saw repeatedly, imagining different removal scenarios. After several minutes of maneuvering, she realized that she could not remove the cuffs by herself. She peeped her head outside, looking both ways for the option of a person. No one. Slew waited outside the door. Stepping onto the front porch, she held out the saw to him.

"Slewja, hold this so I can rub the chain back and forth under it." She imagined that if he could talk, he would have something to say about the back and forth action on his posterior of the previous day. He lifted the saw in his clawed hand. She spread her hands, pulling the chain taut against the stone that read Thalassa's name outside of the door on the front porch.

"Okay now move the saw so it rests in the middle." He moved his head closer, in what Grace assumed would give him a better view to the small chain. Instead of moving the saw towards the cuffs, though, he moved his head, opening his mouth. Grace turned her head away, wincing. He slipped one of his teeth into the chain and bit, snapping it into two.

"Jury is out on the safety of that move, but it worked, so let's not think about it anymore!" She pet his snout. "Thank you!"

He snorted and wiggled his shoulders. Next, she needed to find a way to get the metal off her wrists. Her sleeves would hide the metal while she searched for a solution. Thal might have one when she returned. She left the workshop and headed out to the main street.

"Hey, sugar tits!" A voice from across the street interrupted her thoughts.

Grace's head quickly turned towards the familiar Fleckish lilt. Standing there, with his arms crossed over his chest and leaning against the side of the post office in a clean white shirt and pants in a motley of fabrics was none other than Verdis Uran, that topsy-turvy shit. A smile spread across her face and her pace quickened into a half-jog. He chewed on a piece of hay that he must have nicked from the area near the chicken coops–if Grace were to ask him, he would certainly tell her the truth. The man could not lie, which made her wonder how he survived on his peddling business. Scratching the letter V in the dirt with the toe of his boot, he waited as she crossed, evading a mother who was simultaneously juggling packages and her kids' screams for food.

"You smell like sex," he told her as he gave her a hug.

"Jealous?" She raised an eyebrow.

"Of your having sex, yes, not of the other person. Mother knows that I couldn't handle you."

She laughed a belly laugh. She had heard from the other girls at the brothel that this was true. He normally stumbled in when he was shitfaced, which meant his performance was anything but stellar. She had called him out on it early on in their friendship.

"My snake ain't your problem, your pussy ain't mine. Our pets stay out of this."

And thus, they lived in harmony.

Verdis had stopped by Madame Sadie's once during Lounging Hour as Grace was recuperating under a bunch of blankets. He had entered looking for "a quick sucky" from Britt. He lacked shame. But whereas Sao was shameless due to his stupidity, Verdis could not be shamed. He had learned that his unfortunate character flaw of honesty led to what some would term as off-color discussions. Every once in a while, he tested his family's curse of truthfulness, bequeathed to him by his mother. He got into a card game with Sao, once, on purpose to test it out. Because he could not lie, he lost. The banter between Verdis and Grace that night though, was the story of legends. People came in to listen to the two of them rather than watch the game. Annie ran out of whiskey faster than Verdis ran out of coins. The barkeep loved when he came into town, peddling his odds and ends.

"Let me buy you a drink," Verdis told her but raised his eyebrow asking if she was going to challenge him.

She half grinned, shaking her head. "Alright," he put his arm across her shoulders. "But I won't be held responsible for the shenanigans that you get into."

"Me?" he mouthed in mock surprise. "I do believe that you were the one to run out on the last check."

"It's not running out if they forget about you and never bother to check if you're leaving."

"Oh, Grace, Grace, Grace." Verdis chuckled, his green eyes sparkling with trouble. "What a selective memory you have."

"If I remembered all the shit that you've gotten me into, we wouldn't keep creating more."

"What's life but a bunch of good adventure stories woven together?" With that, Verdis held two fingers up to the bartender, who flipped two shot glasses onto the bar. "Uh uh," the ordering offender shook a finger at the bartender. "Two bottles."

"Shit." Grace scowled at him.

"Got something better to do? Sao still around?" He took a pull of the bottle, and she grabbed her own, replicating the action.

"Whoa." She made the sound not unlike telling Slewja to slow down. "Comin' in hot!"

She fake choked on the whiskey shot, before catching Verdis's sideways look and laughing. She reached into her hidden bag for some coins that she tossed onto the bar.

Verdis swiped them off the counter, returning them to her. He threw out his own. "You're going to need to save those," he said with an air of gravity. "Word's going around that a certain cold-hearted individual has leads on a lost wife." She raised her eyebrow at him, anxiety in her chest.

"And who might that be?" she asked the question, despite half knowing and all fearing the answer. Ignorance could only be blissful for so long.

"Does the name Governor Dimin Greystock mean anything to you, Mrs. Greystock?"

"He can eat it. And I'm not his wife." Pull of whiskey. How nice of Verdis to kill the peace that she had gathered around herself these past months.

"He seems to think otherwise."

"I ran out before the vows. This is old news for you."

"Yeah, well he's refusing to admit that you escaped. And he did away with anyone who did not come down with the forgetfulness from the cold sickness."

"That's exactly what I did." She punctuated her assertion with a pull from the bottle.

"I came from Orflux, which is about two cities east. They've got the cold sickness, and they're holding mayoral elections. I saw his platform speech. I followed his large crowd to Blatho this morning and the man himself nearly knocked over my cart after he saw your wanted poster."

"Oh no," Grace groaned at the mess she had gotten herself into. She needed to find a way to get into that city and tear the poster down before it could circulate beyond Blatho.

With that, Grace was pushed forward into Verdis, spilling some of the whiskey on herself and her friend.

"Sorry, ma'am." The man drunkenly staggered to hold himself on the bar. As she turned to wave off his apology as no problem, he gave her the once over. "No, I'm not."

In that moment, annoyance that she had been pushing down compacted itself into anger firmly in her chest. Grace was pissed that Dimin had found her. She was pissed that Sheriff Shuntdick had already gotten her face plastered on a wanted poster. She was pissed that undesired men kept throwing themselves into the small corner of the world that she kept trying to create for herself. This man bumped into the wrong woman on the wrong night.

She quickly searched them for any weaknesses. "Vote for Dimin" pins decorated each's jackets. In that moment, the taller of the two squinted his eyes.

"Hey, I've seen you somewhere." His head cocked to the side, and his left hand reached into the back pocket of his trousers. He pulled out a folded piece of paper, edges rusty-brown with the dust from the number of times he had pulled it out. The folds had worn so much that the paper simply flapped open.

"Well look at that, Morty, seems we've found the boss's little lady."

Grace's face betrayed her momentary fear, and in that vulnerable instant, Morty grabbed her elbow to haul her out.

"You might not have been sorry before, but you will be now," Verdis said, taking a drink, not advancing towards the trio. That vote of confidence triggered Grace's fight or flight response. And today, she was feeling the fight.

With full force, she stomped on the top of the manhandler's boot, who instantly let go to grab his foot in reflex. Taking a deep breath to center herself and remind herself that she was in charge of her own life, she wound up her arm and punched him square in the jaw.

Verdis's face lit up with a huge smile from ear to ear. He took his whiskey bottle and moved to the table behind the bar. Britt came up next to him and sat on his knee. "Best seat in the house for the best show in town," he told her.

"What's going on?" She took a swig from his bottle before handing it back to him.

"She's battling the bastards that are trying to return her to that guy that she fled. He's heard she's nearby so sent some goons to look for her. I'm looking forward to seeing her rage." He wrapped his arm around the girl and pointed with his whiskey bottle bearing hand. He narrated as Grace proceeded to wipe the floor with this guy.

"This guy is going to come at her, I'm sure you've had it done to you before, being good looking and all..."

Grace gave him an open handed smack across the cheek, just to watch it leave a mark.

"I taught her that one, brand the guy for the next girl," Britt piped up from Verdis's knee.

"Nice." He cheered her and returned to narrating. "Oo that one will hurt. Now she is grabbing the shot glass, a bit amateur to hit a guy with glass if you ask me, but oh wait, she smashed it. Where's that going? Ooooh, the ear! Really, Grace, the ear?"

She smiled at Verdis's comment but did not take her eyes off her current issue.

"She could've ended that with a slash across the throat," Verdis commented in curious observation.

"She's not looking to meet the hangman," the girl retorted. "Oh, there goes the heel of the hand to the nose. I'm surprised he hasn't gotten to her yet."

With that, the offending dick picked up a stool.

"Oh shit!" Grace yelled.

"Oh but here she goes, she's pummeling him in his stomach with a cue stick from the side wall, so the stool falls on the ground. This guy is doubled over. Stop smiling and END HIM, GRACE! Ok, I see you climbing on the bar, that light fixture isn't going to hold you much longer. Perfect jump release onto his back, and he's down!!"

Verdis and Britt high-fived.

When the offending male finally laid flat on the floor, stars spinning around his head, Grace picked up her whiskey bottle off the bar (safe from the melee), took a pull, and said, "I bet you're sorry now."

The door blew open and Grace's eyes flew to the door. Verdis stood at the back table, the girl falling off his lap onto the sticky dirt floor. The arrival surveyed the scene quickly before he put his hand to his holster at his waist, eyes back on Grace. In a minute, Verdis had thrown the whiskey bottle that was in his hand at the man's head.

"Why you—" he turned towards Verdis, that dark-haired troublemaker, seated to his right of the door and that gave Grace the break to come up behind him on his left and jump on his back, stealing his attention.

"You can't be serious," he gasped out as she wrapped her arms around his throat, squeezing the life from his lungs.

"As the undertaker, who you'll be meeting soon, I suppose, when you don't bring me in," she whispered into his ear. He lowered to the floor, inert.

The bartender stood up from where she had ducked behind

the bar. She looked around at the minimal damage, shrugged, and picked up a glass to dry.

"You've learned a few tricks, Grace," she commented.

"Oh Annie, you know I'm just a simple girl turning tricks." Grace batted her eyes, placed her hands under her chin and did her best impression of a Fleckish accent.

"I do not sound like that!" Verdis shouted at her. The women laughed and welcomed him into their conversation at the bar when he walked up to join them.

A man sat down at the piano and started plunking out the melody of some drunken sea shanty. "That's not music!" Grace yelled, pulling out her pistol and shooting at the lever on the side of the stool that she often sat upon.

The man dropped two feet, lowering his chin to the level of the keyboard. Smacking her hand on Verdis's shoulder for camaraderie, she laughed at the ridiculous sight. The man at the piano was bound, gagged, and determined to finish his song. The patrons were cracking up. It was a Friday night, and the room was filled with people who had been working all day on the water system.

Verdis, never one to miss an opportunity to egg someone on, elbowed Grace in the ribs. "You can't even dance to this song!"

"Maker Muck it," she muttered. She poured a shot of whiskey from the bottle and brought it over to the man at the piano. "Excuse me, but I will give you this shot if you stop playing." She tried to muster the sweetest smile that she could, but feared it just came off a bit creepy. "Please stop playing, I'm BEGGING you."

"This guy is flat out of order," Verdis told Annie. "Did you even give him permission to play?"

"Listen, I'm not stopping a free show," she said, picking up the whiskey bottle and wiping down where the shot glass had overflowed from Grace's pouring, then wiping the bottom of the bottle before placing it back on the bar.

"At least move over, new guy," Grace instructed the pianist. He did begrudgingly. "Okay, hit some C major chords. Do a chord progression down there. I'll take care of the melody up here."

And the whiskey flowed, thanks to Verdis coming over to her, tilting her head back, and pouring the brown liquid down her throat a few times during the song. When the tune drew to a close, Verdis was sitting next to her on the bench.

"You play?" She realized that they had never discussed their hobbies.

"Nope, but I need to tell you this before you keep going and before I black out." He looked at her very seriously. "I feel as if you brushed off my warning before, so I am going to give it to you plain."

He took her hands off the keys, ensuring he had her full attention as she turned her body towards him.

"You need to get out of here if you want any chance of retaining your sense of self."

"Ah, he won't get me." She shook her head. She did not want to let this information sink in and let Dimin dictate her life again. "I'll just keep fending the guys off. Plus, the sheriff is dragging those guys out now, so it's not like they're running back to tell him that I'm in this town." She nodded her head at the doorway where the badged man was instructing a few broad shouldered men in the rough handling of the instigators.

"Grace, you're leaving tomorrow. He's been making moves at Blatho, lately. He's on his way, and this night is just a small taste of what's to come for you. I'm leaving too, we're getting out of here before he can hurt us or the town."

"You're coming with me?"

"No, I'm going to cover your tracks after you leave. Give me something of yours so I can carry the scent with me."

Already a few shots in, she did not argue with him. She asked him for a knife. Reaching into her trousers, she made two cuts. Pulling the fabric out of her trousers, she smiled. She wrapped her underwear around the knife and handed it back to Verdis.

"Of course you did." He rolled his eyes. "If some girl finds this, how am I supposed to explain it away? I won't get laid for weeks."

Patting his cheek, she said, "Aw, it's so sweet that you carry your sister's underwear around with you." She giggled, turning back to the piano. "Well I've had a good run here. Cheers to what the sun brings with tomorrow." She clinked her bottle with that of Verdis. "What the fuck, if I'm leaving, might as well make this one memorable! Verdis, help me!"

He nearly collapsed onto the floor as he slipped off the edge of the bench. Annie rolled her eyes at whatever shenanigans were about to occur. Grace would have been making a spectacle of herself, except she had two traits going for her: her confidence and her big blue doe eyes. Men who had left their wives and sweethearts to go west for the waterworks job had not seen a woman in sometime. She could have been reading the tally board for all they cared; she had the attention of the saloon.

In fact, when Verdis had pulled himself back onto the bench, a feat considering half of his bottle was still full, he told her so, causing her to begin singing out the tally board to well known tunes. And a funny thing happened. Those drinking in the bar started throwing money on the piano. Verdis would bring the money to Annie. Over the course of the night, one by one the debts of those present were paid out. Except for Sao's. She wasn't going to let him off that easily. And if she were leaving, she wanted to run the risk that he would be held back by the debt. Half a bottle in, the thought made perfect sense; later, she would kick herself when she remembered that she would need some body heat to keep her alive. As much as she was friends with Thalassa, neither of them were about to sleep with each other.

So the two friends celebrated the moment, bringing in the rest of the saloon into their carpe diem spirit. For tomorrow, the temporary peace would end for Grace.

TEN

Empty whiskey bottles should never be used as decorating trophies. If one remembers the night, those memories should be trophies enough. The bottles only carry undeniable evidence of past acts and unsavory scents that can turn a stomach for months. But they did make great shooting targets for practice. So Annie saved them. But the scrap metal from the night, like the pins, would go to the blacksmith for melting down. She walked out back, cutting the two friends off for the night.

Grace and Verdis took the hint that it was time for them to leave. "You could always tag along," Grace said wistfully, afraid to disembark from her stable chair at the table.

"Nah," Verdis said, staggering out of his seat and clinking a few coins from the scattered locations of his boots and back pockets that he had hidden as a deterrent to thieves. With that too knowing grin, he told her, "You're a hell of a friend, Grace. You run like the wind and let the world know what happens when they fuck with you."

She half smiled back, tears forming in her eyes at his departure. He two-finger saluted her, whispering, "Til the next, love," and stumbled out, ricocheting off the door posts as he left.

The image injected uncontrollable laughter in her belly as the saloon doors spanked her on the way out. When she went to approach Slewja, who patiently waited outside the door, she noticed she had laughed herself onto the ground. So first, she had to get up. She clambered to a post, put her hands on the base, and took a deep breath. Thighs propelled her upwards, so she was hugging the structure for support.

"You can hold me like that anytime you want, sweetie!"

On the drop of the hat, she reached into her holster and fired a warning shot at the ground next to the perpetrator. He fucked off. Sao had had the foresight to teach her to shoot in all sorts of ways: blindfolded, handcuffed, drunk. That handcuffed time was fun. She walked on.

One step, two step, three steps, she had this, step dooOWWNN.

And she was all the way down, ass first into the dirt ground. Small flurries made it slightly damp enough that the caramel dirt stuck to her leather pants.

"Slewja!" she called, tired of this game. That dragon was always on call to come to her rescue. Why, she had no idea. Maybe he was a glutton for punishment. It's not like she had helped him first.

Whoops, she stepped with her ankle onto the ground first, and down she went into the dirt again. Luckily, the whiskey had rubberized her bones.

She should have stayed at the saloon. Verdis had probably gone around the corner and spent the night in a comfy bed on the chest pillows of some voluptuous girl. If she had gone with him she could have at least crashed in her bed. Her spinning head was in no shape to be working a shift, though. Sadie worried about her establishment's reputation too much to allow for Grace to tarnish it. A girl had to make money.

"Slewja, go to Sao."

She pointed forward, dropping her head onto Slewja's back and holding on for dear life. She deeply regretted not returning to her room. The airborne feeling was not helping her sense of balance. As soon as Slewja landed outside of Sao's tent, Grace leaned over and retched up all that whiskey, wiping her mouth with her sleeve. Disgusting, but at least her stomach was somewhat more settled. She stumbled over to the patchworked tent, giggling as she held onto the pole.

A pissed off Sao came out without his shirt on.

"I'm baaaack!" Grace flung her arms out in a T, as if she were going to hug Sao.

He stood outside the tent flap with his arms crossed, blocking her entry.

"Aw, you look so serious!" She ran her finger over his lips and made a vibrating "brrrrrr" sound. Sao grimaced when he caught a whiff of her breath that close. Vomit and whiskey.

"Whiskey?"

"I brought some back for you. It's over there!" She pointed at where flies were congregating around her vomit. She doubled over in laughter before she realized that he was not joining in with her. "Why are you such a sourpuss? Come on, dance with me!"

She grabbed his hand and put it around her waist. Even three sheets to the wind, she could reel. She used to love reeling. She always knew she would have a partner for reeling–she would set out at the start of every ball just to try to fill that one spot on her card. Fuck the waltzes; the reels were where the fun was. And cooped up with her parents, balls were about the only time that she could have fun. She proceeded to move her feet around but he did not move at all.

"Why aren't you dancing? It's the Fleckham Reel!"

"Because, Miss Belle of the Ball, I do not know the Fuckum Reel."

"Fllllleeeeekkkkkmmmmm," she enunciated in his face. "Psh, I was never the belle of the ball. I was more like Betty who was good for a fun twirl around to make the girl you wanted jealous. Here, I'll teach you." Or that was what she thought she said. All Sao understood was "Betty twirl tsch you!"

"Who did this to you?"

"ME!!!" She stopped trying to dance with him and was spinning around with her arms wide out. And then she remembered that she had just gotten rid of the spins. She ran over to a new spot further away before hurling up what she hoped was the last of the bottle. She wondered how Eve and Sadie were handling Verdis's less strong stomach and bedroom enthusiasm that they often laughed about.

"You should see the oth'guy," Grace told him, thumbing behind her, which was not the direction from which she came. This girl needed to go to sleep. He needed to go to sleep. He had lost one hundred dollars that night and did not know where to find it. He was exhausted.

"Do you have fifty bucks?" He figured that he would try her while she was drunk.

"Ah, go fuck yaself!" She swatted her hand at him. Then, she frowned at him and tried to sit on a rock with aplomb. She missed the rock and fell on her bottom, which she attempted to play off as lying on her side and holding her head up with her right hand.

He shrugged and went back inside the tent. Thinking that he did not want her to hurt herself, he came back out.

"Who were you out with?" His curiosity got the better of him.

"The fuck does it matter to ya?"

It did. He did not like it when she went out with just anyone. It killed his soul when she took on other clients. One day, he would be able to protect her so that she did not have to work at Madame Sadie's anymore. His expression remained stoic as he waited for her response.

"Verdis," she said.

"That sonofabitch—" Sao started.

"—just told me that Dimin's coming. So fucough."

Sao went back inside the tent and started tying it from the inside. Drunk as she was, Grace still did not understand why he was so miffed. Sao had stumbled to her bed unable to stand more times than she could count. Why was there a double standard?

"Hey! Lemme in!"

"Go sleep with Slewja and Raikka. You've done it before!" he called from the enclosure.

"But I'm so coooold!" The statement was true. She was still shivering despite her intoxication level.

He undid the top two togs and stuck his head through.

"You'll be fine. It won't kill you."

He noticed Slewja and Raikka already near her so he closed it up. Little did he know about the magical cold possessing her body.

"But Sao, you're so warm, and I'm so coooold. And I'm cute!"

"Handle your business!" he shouted through the tent.

Well, now what was she going to do? The dragons could only compete if they started blowing fire from their mouths, which was likely to set her hair on fire and send people running for cover. Dragons did not blow fire every day of the week, these days. They really had no reason to anymore.

Teeth chattering, Grace sidled up between the two dragons. She prayed to the Granny, Mother, and Daughter that the two creatures would not get any ideas in the middle of the night about having some fun. At first she had thought she was next to only Slewja and she was really drunk. But now she was seeing four dragons. Whatever. In her drunken state, she reasoned that Sao must have kept her out solely for the sake of being with another girl in his tent. Good for Sao that he found someone with whom to expend some energy. Goodness knows Grace was anything but warm.

While she tried to heat up next to the dragons, she wished Sao a sarcastic good luck at getting through the dragons when they were pissed off. She buried herself into Slewja's tail. Slewja did not seem happy with this situation. Though he did not mind that Grace sought him out, Sao continued to drop in his esteem. He wrapped himself around her further, positioning his backside towards Sao. As far as he was concerned, Sao failed at being a protector of Grace in the simplest way possible. Grace never told Sao that she needed his warmth, though. He supposed that she was a female, and therefore quick to be cold. Again, not the brightest candle, since they were in the middle of a desert.

She wished that she had just gone back to her room next door to the saloon. Shame on her for assuming that Sao would be delighted to see her. She neither understood nor appreciated his jealousy. What claim did he have on her? So he had taught her gun skills. She was the one practicing daily and paying for her bullets. In no way was he her world. Her world was still waiting to be seized and explored.

Did he think that because she was a steady fuck that she had feelings for him? All she did was give him freebies here and there in order to pay for her tutoring in the art of gunnery. Always a fair trade with others, never owe anyone anything. But she never told him that the sex maintained the cold at a manageable level. He probably would not have cared. Sao really only cared for his own hide. Yet she would not risk telling him.

Despite his indication otherwise, Sao regretted his reaction as soon as he had shut the tent. He could not stomach the idea of Verdis and Grace gallivanting about town drunk. What if she left town with Verdis one day? She repeatedly spoke about wanting to explore the great unknown, which was everywhere to her. He had less of a desire to roam. If he saw one town, he had seen them all. This Grogtown was no different than Lakeside where he had grown up. Same physical layout. Same types of people. The only difference was that he could not go back to Lakeside. Not yet anyway.

When she had first introduced the two, she mentioned that Verdis had been at the brothel not long after Slewja had brought her into town. Grace held that nothing had happened between the two of them, but he could not see how. Verdis was objectively good looking, with his olive green eyes and suntanned skin. He wore a henley with a navy blue jacket that cut at his hips and a popped collar like an imbecile. Their friendship predated Sao's entry into her life.

Where had Verdis been when Grace wanted to learn to shoot? Where had Verdis been all those nights that she did not want to be alone? Sao had been there for it all, and he would continue to be. She was all he had, as close to family as he had these days. He was not going to let her go. What was Verdis but a peddler? As a peddler, what could he give Grace?

As Sao reasoned himself out of his overreaction, he considered inviting Grace back into the tent. Then, he heard her retching in the background. On second thought, maybe it was best if she were outside. He rolled over and fell asleep to the sweet rhythm of whiskey the second time around.

ELEVEN

A hangover of epic proportions rattled through Grace's body. She would never drink again, she remonstrated herself for not the first time in her life. Groaning, she wished she were passed out again. Though the sun shone overhead, a strange frost clung to the desert ground. Ugh, Dimin. She had to leave, but her body did not seem to comprehend the speed with which she needed to accomplish this feat.

Teeth chattering and arms folded over her chest, she tried to enter the tent again. Sao had untoggled it and he lay under the blankets. She dragged herself under them, curling up. She needed warmth and she needed it fast. Two days was too long to go. Additionally, the chilly breeze had transitioned to an icy breeze overnight. As she cozied under the warmth retainers, Sao lost his coverings.

"See? The cold didn't kill you," he ignorantly told her as he caressed her icy face.

She needed heat.

She began unbuttoning his shirt, but had trouble with her shaking fingers. Hopefully, Sao saw it as desperation for him. If he ever found out that she had no feelings for him besides friendship and meaningless sex, he would probably stick around, but she could not imagine what other possible consequences would follow. Funny considering he never demonstrated that he cared for anyone other than himself, as evident by his actions the previous night.

Grace moved her leg to scramble atop him, not removing her pants fully so she could keep whatever warmth she had. Sao swung her over and pinned her underneath him, taking the lead.

"Please, I need you." Her hands trailed over his shirtless chest, smooth and lean. He smiled at her and undid his trousers. He pushed inside of her and she proceeded to grind against him. Grace pulled him in closer for warmth as the blankets had fallen to the wayside. She needed his heat and she needed it fast.

"More," she moaned to him.

He quickened his pace. She let herself go and the warmth rushed through her like warm water. He followed with a stupid grin on his face.

"We're so good together, look how fast we come," he told her as he pulled the blankets on her. Grace rolled her eyes at him, playing it off as "oh you're silly," but in actuality she could not believe his insight. Shaking her head rather than correcting him, she burrowed into the blankets. She enjoyed the warmth, feeling a bit soporific. He got up to start the day and departed the tent to go who knows where. She did not really care.

After Sao's departure, Grace yawned and stretched. She stepped outside to relieve herself, fixing her disheveled outfit in the process.

A dragon screeched in the distance. Raikka jumped to her feet from where she had sprawled out sleeping. Next to her, Slewja raised his head and called back to the sky in response. The wind picked up as the dragon came in closer. Grace shaded her face from the sun with her hand to get a better look. Vim landed quickly in front of her and nearly deafened her with his screech in her face. On his back, Thalassa barely held on to the pommel of the saddle to which she had tied herself.

Grace's adrenaline cured her hangover in an instant. She untied her friend, pulling her down onto the ground. Running to the tent for anything to help, she noticed that Sao had left the camp in shambles. Now that it was day, she did not need him mooning around anyway. Grabbing a canteen of water and a blanket, she darted out of the tent, knocking it over in the process. Further disarray remained in her wake. She carefully helped Thal onto the blanket that she spread onto the dirty ground. Pulling her hands away from her friend, Grace noticed the blood painting her palms. Frantic, she searched for the wound with her eyes and her hands. When Grace pressed on her thigh, Thalassa winced, the pain oozing out her forehead in sweat. Grace tore open her friend's trousers at the thigh. She gently turned Thal over onto her side to see if the wound went straight through before she rested her back on the ground.

"We have to close the wound," Grace told her with trepidation.

"Alright," she said through clenched teeth. "There's a needle and thread in my bag."

"Do I look like a fucking tailor to you, Thal?"

"Weren't you trained in the domestic arts, Grace?"

She snorted. "They tried." She looked at the gushing wound. "I can't embroider your damn leg shut!"

"Just get the damn needle and thread. You'll figure it out."

"Thal, wasn't your mom a seamstress? Can't you at least talk out what I need to do?"

"Just because she gave me the needle and thread doesn't mean she taught me to use it!"

"Oh Good Granny above. Why carry it then?"

"Sentimentality." An ashen matte was replacing Thal's sweaty red-splotched skin. Their arguing only shortened the distance for Thal to walk to those gates in the sky. Thal's breathing shallowed. Grace needed to fix this situation before it got worse.

"Listen, I think the bullet is out, right? Or do I need to go digging?"

"I don't even fucking know."

"Well then hold on to Vim, shit's going to hurt." Grace dumped some whiskey on her first two fingers.

"Bet Sao does that every night," Thal winced through the pain. She grabbed onto Vim's outstretched claw.

"He does not get my pussy drunk, thanks."

She plunged the two fingers into the gaping hole in her friend's leg. There, buried right next to the bone, about three inches in, sat the small round bullet. Squeezing her forefinger and middle finger awkwardly together, she pulled the shrapnel out of the wound. Blood gushed. Thalassa's chest stood still.

"Shit!!" she cried out. "Thal, hold on!"

Mustering her strength to her fingertips, she surged a winter compress into the wound. The blood stopped. She could see it through the crystal clear ice. Thal lurched forward, gasping for air. Heaving a sigh of relief, Grace sprawled out on the ground. She patted her friend's foot. "You're going to be okay."

"What the fuck happened?" Grace asked, now that her friend was out of imminent danger.

"That sonofashit sheriff's goons went after Slewja. I tried to lead them away from him, which worked until they started shooting at me."

Footsteps crunched loudly across the dirt. Through their exhaustion, both Grace and Thal could only raise their heads to look in the boots' direction.

"I went all the way into town, haggled for everything that we might need, and you two are just lying around taking a nap? Nice to see you by the way, Thalassa. Missed your familial contributions."

"Fuck off, Sao. I just contributed that piece of metal from my body. Go get Raikka to melt it down while I nap so we have some coins."

"She and the other dragons need to do a flyaround to find a meal before we head out."

"I'm not going anywhere," she laughed at him, motioning at her leg.

"No, I am," Grace said sullenly. "Dimin found out I'm alive and he's on his way."

"Well, fuck, we better get going then," Thal conceded. "Just tie me on Vim, and I'll nap along the way. Come to think of it, you're going to need a nap too."

"In that case, gunslinger Sao can stand guard while we pass out here for a bit."

And so, for the next few hours, the women slept in the embrace of the dragons and the protection of an inept gambler.

TWELVE

With a heavy heart and heavier boots—having not quite replenished her energy from healing Thal—Grace walked to the brothel. The funeral march for the friendships that she had made played through her head. Verdis was right; action needed to be taken.

She stopped off in the saloon, which of course was bustling this Sunday. Taking a visual survey of the occupants, she decided that she needed to warn everyone. Having spent enough time here now, she had grown to care for some of its residents. Once Dimin arrived, it was only a matter of time before the town fell.

Annie waved a bottle at her from behind the bar, asking if she wanted it filled before some of the others in line. Grace shook her head in refusal; she needed to be clear headed to say what she was going to say. She considered going behind the bar to Annie to tell her that she wanted to make an announcement, but she decided that she would use her perch at the empty piano to do it for her. As she sat on the keyboard, the cacophony jarred people's attention from their drinks.

"Howdy, y'all," she started, uncertain of any etiquette for giving a rousing speech. "Many of you remember when I was brought here by my dragon friend. Well, I'd actually been running away from quite a few things. But most notably, I ran because there was a cold sickness that overtook my town out east. I didn't get it. But lots of folks did. And they forgot things and died. I just found out that the purveyor of the cold sickness has been making his way west slowly. And now that he's close, he's heard it through the grapevine that I am here. So he'll be here any day. I suggest we either prepare for a stand or we evacuate the area."

The audience erupted in laughter, calling her "dragon mad," and alluding that she had been "suffering so long from the venereal disease that it reached her brain."

"Play us a tune!" One man called from where he leaned his forearms on the bar.

"I'm dead serious!" she shouted in frustration. "He will take over this town and you will have nothing."

"Sounds like he's a'coming for you, so why don't you just leave on that dragon o' yours that brought ya in?" An old man from the table next to the piano locked eyes with her, but Grace broke the stare down.

When she looked around at the audience, they had started nodding their heads in agreement. A chorus of whispered "you go" or "leave us alone" made its way towards where she stood. Grace took a deep breath and scrutinized the people's faces. She could see that convincing this group of the evil that was approaching was a moot point. She remembered the deathly cold air and the droned clicking of teeth chattering in the hospital where she had volunteered. She had hoped the cold sickness would claim her before Dimin could. She was one of the few to make it out untouched. Who in this saloon would make it out alive?

As she walked straight through the bar to the front swinging doors, the patrons laughed at her, spanking her as she walked past. She had no fight for these people that would not fight for themselves. A beer splattered her back before the glass hit the wall beside her head.

From her right, Annie shrugged at her, cleaning the inside of another glass. The women nodded goodbyes to each other. Saying a silent prayer to Mother Maker for these people's souls, she turned and walked out the door.

Madame Sadie opened the door for her, as if she had been waiting for the woman's return. "I saw Verdis at the general store talking with the storekeeper. He told me that you were heading out, too." Commenting on the blood that covered Grace, she asked, "Who did you teach a lesson to?"

"It's Thal's. Had to deal with a situation." Grace made her way up the stairs. "Hey Frumo! I know you're around here. Can you clean me off?"

Healer Frumo poked his head out of Eve's room, his hands holding a book and his pants undone.

"I was just borrowing one of-" he stammered.

"I don't really care what you were doing. Just suck this red up please, it's a bit of an eyesore." He tucked the book under his arm, and closed his eyes, holding his palms out in front of her chest. As he slowly moved them downwards, the blood popped off her clothes in droplets. With a final snap, they disappeared.

"Anything I should know?" Frumo asked her.

"Yeah," Grace said, knowing he meant about how she wound up covered in blood. "Dimin is on his way. Mother Maker only knows what he will do to this town. I tried to warn everyone in the saloon that his power is a plague. It infects some then eventually all, just spreading through the layers of the earth and the society."

Sadie followed behind her. "I still can't get over that you were the only one the sickness didn't affect."

"That's not true. There were at least five citizens that I knew of that sensed that something was wrong and that it was related to our sacred mayor Greystock." She said those last two words sarcastically. "He was nothing but an overgrown set of testicles, too puffed up with himself and his abilities."

Sadie looked at her calmly, in her best motherly side-eye. "We both know that that isn't true."

Sighing, Grace asked her, "But can't we pretend?" Her eyes, half full of salty water from the time she entered yet another home doomed to forget her, continued to fill and threatened to spill.

"I wish."

"The people next door seemed to be of one mind that if he was coming here, he was coming after me, so I should leave this town."

"You don't need to. We can protect you here."

"I won't stay. He'll turn everyone. In fact, we should all go."

"Where Grace? What skills do we have? Most of us almost died to get to our home here. How would we survive roughing it? We all don't have a Slewja to rescue us by flying us away to safety."

Grace fought back the tears; Sadie was right. Many of the town's occupants had given their all to make it to Grogtown. As Grace racked her brain for other ideas on where they could go, she turned to walk into the room that had become "hers." Her one safe haven in Cosimo, filled with her thoughts, prayers, and dreams, would become but a moment on her timeline.

She could hardly bring herself to look into Sadie's eyes as she watched from outside the door. Grace threw together the few items that she had acquired in her stay. Flinging her rabbit robe over her, she held her head up and her shoulders back. The makeshift cape surrounded her in the embrace and hope of the people that she had learned to care for, and who in turn cared for her. Slewja waited outside the balcony where he had originally deposited her. She could not promise that she would see them again, as much as she wanted to make that commitment. No sense in lying to each other, they never had before.

"I feel like I'm abandoning you when you never once abandoned me," Grace said, reluctant to leave with Slewja.

"You asked us to come with, and I think I speak for everyone when I say that we won't."

Evie and Britt entered the room with a brown paper parcel wrapped in twine that they handed to Sadie. The house matriarch handed it to Grace.

"We all thought you should have one, since hopefully you're heading towards sunnier times." Pulling back the stiff paper revealed a white wide-brimmed hat. And not a Sunday bonnet decorated with flowers and ribbons either. The type that men wore to keep the sun out of their eyes. She twisted her hair up so it rested on the top of her head. Placing the hat over it kept the sandy brown mess off of her neck. Sadie nodded in approval.

Grace lamented hugging each of these strong women who didn't mind supporting the other. Life had never been a competition here, vying for the best man. It was as close to a home as she had known, though to her it still felt like a stopping off point. A rest stop on a path where you don't have any idea when the next one is arriving.

"Don't become so hardened by the world of men that you forget that women labor to bring life into this world," Sadie told her.

She put her hands on the smooth balcony, standing on it. She opted to not go out the door. Two goodbyes in a day stretched her emotional limit. She was not nervous about what would come. She would persevere. But what would she preserve?

Turning around at second thought, she said, "Nothing that I say will be enough to capture my feelings of care and gratitude for you both."

"Just go, Grace," Sadie laughed through the tears. Her eyes had become faucets between the door and the balcony, with each footstep recalling a different occurrence at each floorboard. How fitting that this force of nature would exit their lives as she entered. Sadie, hugging her shawl around her, shed a tear down her cheek. Eve and Britt looked sadly on as another person in their lives abandoned them.

Grace jumped off the balcony and onto the saddle that was laced up Slewja's back. Blowing a kiss to each of them, she guided Slewja away from her comrades.

"Take care of her, Slewja!" Sadie ran to the balcony balustrade after them and called. He turned his head to look backward, making eye contact and nodding once at the kindhearted woman, before he flew back towards the meeting location.

The women would quickly forget Grace within two weeks, when Dimin arrived with the cold sickness to establish Grogtown as a new stronghold.

The silent first few hours of their flight were punctuated by birds squawking as they dodged the paths of the dragons. They were headed west. Away from the storm, away from the torment, once again away from the home that she could have had. Behind them, the thick snow clouds loomed over Blatho, still, but they would not for long.

Grace broke the silence after flying for a few hours. Thal had woken from her nap. Outwardly, her clean clothes hid her recent wound. Her body still demanded recovery, though. Grace replayed the emergency in her head.

"Thal, I've gotta ask you. I had to rip off your trousers to get the bullet out. Why the fuck do you have a tattoo on your ass? What is that, a brand?"

"This guy would only let me ride him if he could brand me first."

"So you let him?"

"Pain and pleasure baby. Plus, if I get lost, please send me back. That was a great night." She sighed and closed her eyes, reliving the sweet memories of orgasms long ago. They continued flying, making camp at nightfall.

Thal, Sao, and Grace laid around the campfire, having eaten rabbit that the dragons caught for them. Slewja, Raikka, and Vim, full of his usual vim and vigor, encircled them looking outwards, both keeping watch and guarding. Grace laid spread out on her back, her new white hat perched over her forehead.

"Hey Grace?" Thal broke the silence.

"Hm?" The hat remained over her face while her arms were propped behind her head.

"Remember that time that you sat at the piano all night, and then rather than pay you, the saloon owner wanted to pay you in kind." A low chuckle reverberated in her chest.

"Thal, that was only a month ago. Hope the asshole's sitting on the second staircase wondering where he went wrong"

"I think he would've paid you with venereal disease."

"Or some extra mouth I'd have to lug around." She was not dismayed that the magic that had hit her lower back had made her infertile. One less obstacle in this world or way for a man to control her. Two nights after the proposition, the saloon owner had suffered a heart attack while with one of the girls at the brothel. Annie had been his second-in-command; the town didn't protest when she assumed control of the saloon, having practically run it while the owner was alive.

"Oh shit, we forgot to pay our tabs!" She curled her left hand in and out of a fist.

"I did," Sao said softly. "I sold a few items and paid it off. My name had zero tallies for the first time since I arrived." He smiled to himself in silent pride.

They fell asleep under the stars, wondering where the next day would take them. Slewja kept leading the other two dragons in a V formation towards the west. They all could tell by the once tundra land turning drier into more desert. Before long, they came upon a river. The three dragons slowed to a walking pace as they padded through the water. Sao had tied himself to his saddle and fallen asleep on the back of Raikka. Vim and Slewja snorted and huffed at each other in their own private discussion. The women figured they discussed tactics for hiding and locations to land; the two males actually chatted about females and the best meals they had eaten recently. To pass the time, Thal and Grace started to play "What if."

Grace posed the first hypothetical question. "What if a magician somewhere said, I'll give you a dick, no strings attached. What size would you want it to be?"

"Hm, probably down to my knee," Thal responded quickly.

"That's a fucking liability, Thal."

"Yeah, for whatever person rode it."

"I'd want mine to be the size of a thumb. I don't need a dick getting out there and in my way. It can't be comfortable while in a saddle. Imagine the amount of chafing. And I wouldn't want to get into a dick measuring contest with Slewja. Would I, buddy?"

He tossed his head grinning, snorting over his shoulder at Raikka, who was trailing them as she cared for the sleeping human on her back.

"Oh that's why she likes you."

From atop him, her saddle shifted a bit as his belly jiggled in a laugh. He stepped a little higher, splashing her in the river, and she laughed at his playfulness.

"What if some guy bought you a house and said here you go, do what you will?" Thal asked her.

"I wouldn't even know where to start. Also, why would anyone give me anything, much less a house?" Grace countered.

"Let's say he loved you," Thal surmised.

"If he bought me a house, then he wouldn't know the first thing about me, so I doubt that's love."

"Ha! No man can tame you!" Thal paused, considering her own hypothetical. "I'd take it. I'd just make sure he paid the taxes on it in perpetuity."

"Let no one say that you're dumb, Thal."

"If some guy gave me a house," Sao added his thoughts to the conversation, "I'd set it on fire, then collect the insurance money. I'd take the insurance money and put it all on black to buy a bigger house."

"I have no doubt that you would, Sao, no doubt in my mind."

Grace reasoned that he had put it all on red and lost it before, so perhaps he felt like he was learning by choosing to put it all on black in this hypothetical. Whatever fresh look he had given her by admitting that he had paid off his bar tab before departure completely reverted to her old opinion. He was still the same old Sao.

THIRTEEN

The six beings landed near a copse of trees. A dull fog had landed with them, as if they had brought it with them from the East. Through the fog, though it was night, torches were visible from about a mile away. Grace wanted to go and see the town immediately, remarking that they were setting up camp in the dark already so what was a little more. Sao wanted to set up camp, and to keep Grace nearby. He had no idea what trouble she would find this late at night and he wanted to keep her under his thumb. They could not afford to attract any attention. Thalassa, as she had been declaring for the last two hours of the trip, was hungry. He had nearly thrown his shoe at her and told her to eat the leather. She reiterated her gastral needs and nearly growled at him when he had threatened to do so. With that, she told Vim to go grab her something as he roamed with the other two creatures. He brought her back rabbit, which he speared on his tail and held for her over the fire that she had started.

The tent that Sao carried was designed for two. The three of them agreed they would sleep Thal, Grace, Sao across. After much negotiation, they further voted two to one that everyone would remain clothed while sleeping. Sao attempted to justify his vote, noting he liked sleeping naked, not that he wanted a free show.

When Thal awoke in the morning, she felt that Grace was not in her sleeping bag. She hoped that she was not on top of Sao—some things were better left unseen. She stepped out of the tent, looking out of her peripherals quickly to see if Grace was with Sao. Sao slept on his side, blissfully unaware of Grace's absence. Pulling the flap aside, she saw Grace crouched over a pit, stoking a fire beneath a pot of coffee and boiling water. How long had she been awake?

"Morning." Thal yawned. "Coffee?"

"Yeah, I started that, then I realized that we don't have cups." With a twinkle in her eye and a sideways smile, she added, "Oh darn, we're going to have to go into town." Thal noticed that Slewja stood at the ready for an expedition.

"Alright, let's go, my adventurer," Thal motioned with her outstretched hand for them to get onto their ride. Vim opened an eye to watch Thal get on Slewja with Grace. The latter had been insistent that they would not be gone long at all. Vim tended to not be a "let's go now" dragon anyway. The friends took off for the bustling town.

The town of Rockdale was all abuzz with the wedding of the century that was due to occur in five days' time. Amidst the people bustling and conversing, Grace found them a bathing house that catered to women. In other words, Grace found a brothel where she paid a whore to fill up the bathtub with hot water. And as there was only one tub, Thal was off scouting around while Grace luxuriated in the hot water. In a show of female solidarity, the woman had added some lavender oil and offered to wash her hair for an extra three gold coins. Considering she probably made ten coins for fifteen minutes of spreading her legs, three gold coins was a steal. She pulled the money out of the satchel she wore around her neck. For all intents and purposes, the hand sized leather satchel looked similar to the prayer scripts that devouts of Mother Maker wore. For her purposes, it kept her money safe, especially from Sao who had no idea the amount of money that she hid from him. Someone in the group needed to be the financial planner; and planning did not include throwing all of the cash on black and letting it ride. She had ridden too much for that investment, she chuckled to herself.

"Yah needs tah wash yah hair more," the woman said in her thick, lower-class eastern accent, as she leaned Grace's head back and poured warm water over her hair.

"Yeah, well, I can't say that I have had access to a warm water supply, or oils, or non windblown forms of transport."

"Yah needs tah take cahe ah yourself. Catch a husband. Have children."

"Like you did?" Grace bit back. The woman answered by using her nails on Grace's scalp which had the opposite of intended effect and felt positively blissful. As she relaxed, she continued in her conversation. "I don't hate men, and I don't hate children. I just want neither to define my identity."

"A lady es many identities. In a world whehe thehe es nah ah space fowh a lady, she must have multiple ways tah make heh way."

Grace pondered the counterintuitive statement. Beatrice, her mother, would only half agree with this woman; though she would be encouraging of the marriage and children part. Did Grace herself want that? She had never had the moment afforded to her to stop and contemplate. The water sloshed down her back, sweeping the suds out of her hair and into the bath water. She knew that she did not want anyone telling her that she needed to be a wife or a mother. She popped the bubbles in the tub. After rinsing, the woman, Celeste was her name, combed out her hair.

Thal had returned to the building after her jaunt. She was leaning on the door frame with her arms crossed at this point, waiting for her turn in the bath.

Celeste looked her over as she towel dried Grace's sandy

brown hair, now picking up a natural wave without the two weeks' worth of grease.

"I can do your beautiful black hair too. Out east, I was a lady's maid. Only hair I can't do es bald."

"Why did you leave?" Thal asked her, as she ran her hand over her braids, suddenly hyper aware of what her hair looked like.

"I'd ratheh be my own hoodsie than someone else's," she told Thal with a tap on her nose. Grace stood and grabbed the towel that Celeste handed her. Wrapped in the towel and out of the bath, Grace went to pick up her clothes off the floor and noticed that they were missing. Searching the floor, she remembered scattering them all over in her haste to get in the tub but now they were nowhere to be found.

"Yah needs new clothes."

"No, Celeste, noooo," Grace whined at the woman, placing her palm on her forehead. "Please tell me you didn't throw away my clothes." Celeste could wax poetic all that she wanted about life, but if she decided to start interfering in her actual life, Grace drew the line there.

"I should have. Nah ah, they ahe hanging out tah dry. Vanna washed them. Nah ah chahge." Grace supposed she would just hang around the brothel, waiting for her clothes to dry. If the place had been bustling, she would have asked if she could take on work; the place was moving pretty slowly for first thing on a Monday morning. Apparently no one wanted to whet their whistle after scourging their soul the day before. So noble.

Grace walked around the house as the well intentioned woman drained the tub and refilled it for Thalassa. Thalassa had just settled into the bath, when she heard an out-of-tune piano clunking. She wanted to yell out a request for something relaxing, but she held the shout in, lest she wake up a whore who had been working all night. When she realized that Grace had probably woken everyone already, she shouted down her request. A pretty little etude drifted up the stairs and danced through the hallway to the bathroom. The path could be marked by doors opening one by one throughout the hallway for a clearer sound.

"She plays well," noticed Celeste. Thal nodded. She learned something new about her friend daily; how she had learned to play piano was the first thing that she had asked Grace. Though it was not her story to tell, she found she needed to clarify her friend to this woman, even though her friend never answered to anyone.

"Grace is a woman of many talents. She was raised for a different world. One that many only dream of. When Grace dreams of that world, it is only nightmares." She quieted, listening to the etude, which quickly turned into an upbeat sonata, mimicking the mood of the town and the sun. A few of the workers came downstairs to listen; the more clever ones opened the windows. The music brought in a few stragglers, all taking their hats off and nodding to the women before staring at the scantily clad woman playing beautiful music at the piano.

All this occurred behind Grace's back. She was much too lost in her own present sense of freedom to care about anything, much less that she was naked in a worn bath towel with wet hair in less than hot weather. What did she want next? All she could think of was holding autonomy over her own destiny. As much autonomy as she had to play whatever note she wanted during this song. Maybe she stuck to the sheet music as she had memorized it. Maybe she played some trills or things that were not original, yet still fit in the scope. Maybe she modulated to a different key and started a whole different song before returning to the original opus. Any option she went with was still her option, not that of someone else.

Someone cleared their throat as she was about to hop into a more meditative nocturne. She noticed that she had garnered quite a gathering in the front. The workers were taking advantage of the crowd and were pulling clients upstairs one by one quietly. The piano invigorated the whole business. The person who cleared his throat went by the name of Saturday Rein. No one wants rain on a Saturday, but in this case, his momma absolutely loved to laze on a Saturday without any callers or things to do because it was raining outside. The man had acquired quite a similar personality, except when it came to the woman he was about to marry. Listening to the music, he decided that his wedding that was to take place that weekend (on Saturday no less) needed to have beautiful music. And this woman would be the perfect present to his fiance. No solemn, out of tune hymn sung by a half inebriated congregation would do for her. He could picture his girl, Red, walking down the aisle, all decked out in wildflowers to a pretty little ditty played by these dexterous fingers.

Red, not for her hair, but her fiery temperament and the way her face got all red when she had a bone to pick with someone. When she was born, she came out head first, screaming at everyone in the world, red-faced til someone threw her onto a breast. Saturday took one look at her at church the day of her baptism and knew his way to the fourth staircase was fraught with Red.

She was his trial and his redemption. His everything and his sweet Mother Maker. She never knew a day in her life without him; his momma delivered her from her momma's womb. Life-mates, they would joke to each other in the stolen moments at night between pants, hands in various places holding skin as teenagers. Their marriage could be defined as common law; however, her daddy had a shotgun and a rather good eye. So the two would be getting married in the church under the loving eye of Good Granny, Mother Maker, and Daughter Dreamer.

Red had planned all the details and her mother had filled in the blanks. His checkbook had paid for it all. He didn't care. But when he heard the music enchanting him to enter from outside on the street, he was lulled into asking this half naked woman if she would play at their wedding. He did not care about the cost. She said she was open to negotiating the price and to set a meeting date and time when she was more disposed and a voice called down the stairs that Grace would do it for free.

Grace sighed and rolled her eyes. She would not have done it for free, but Thalassa's bleeding heart made her survival techniques feel selfish. She smiled at the man and reassured him that they would be happy to meet him at a place of his choosing.

As soon as Thal got out of the bath, they made their way over to the assembly hall where Saturday had said he would wait, blushing at the mere thought of waiting in the parlor of the brothel. Red would call off the wedding if she even knew that he had considered that move. The ladies arrived, clothed in borrowed dresses, each pulling awkwardly at seams attempting to line them up with different crevices. One seam cut clear across Thal's tits, dividing the two in half. She didn't have melons, but her pleasant little apples never looked so disfigured.

"Apples or oranges popping out?" Thal asked.

"Girl, it's a draw either way. It's a meeting, not a night out on the town." She grabbed Thal's hand, dragging her across the street to the assembly hall that was connected to the place of worship.

"Oh, the things I would do to this place if you gave me a tool." Thal discerningly eyed the ceilings and walls. Grace elbowed Thal in the ribs at that louder than a whisper admission as they both looked around. The place was basic framing; Grace had definitely been in more ornate barns out east. This fact drove her desire to help even further. Thalassa jumped in before even consulting Grace.

"Do you have a juniper arch?" Juniper arches, abundant in Mother Maker's scripts, were known to withstand even the colds of Below the staircase. The intended couple stood underneath one and said their vows to one another. At one point it had started as an arch, now it was more of a rectangular structure. After the ceremony, the newlyweds would use it to construct either the doorway to their new home or their wing of a multi-family home. This construction symbolized the doors opening to the staircases, and how close marriage was to the perfect afterlife.

"I'd been planning on doing it this week," Saturday revealed.

"I'm a carpenter. I'd love to do it for you, as a wedding

present," Thal said, ignoring the look that she knew that Grace would give her. As expected, Grace gave her the wide eyes, hoping that she was telepathically communicating "What the fuck? We need the money."

"A woman? Doing carpentry? That's man's work!"

"Oh, shut up, Saturday," a high pitched voice that would grate on anyone's nerves for a lifetime chirped. "You're a piece of work of a man." In sashayed the voluminously bosomed, tar-haired girl that the town knew as Red. "You yourself don't know how to carpenter, so how could you judge another?" Her blue dress, cut low to let her breasts breathe, brought out the cerulean hues of her eyes, which set off her rosy red cheeks. So red was her face, that if she had started coughing blood, Grace would not have been surprised in the least.

"We'd love an arch, please. And if you're in town, I hope that you'll stay as our guests for the wedding."

"We'd love to!" both Thal and Grace said in almost unison. It had been so long since either of them had been to a good party.

A worried voice from behind them made them both jump. "What would we love to do?"

FOURTEEN

They had gotten too relaxed with their baths and the overall friendliness of the town; in doing so, they had let down their guards and forgotten that Sao would probably freak out when they were nowhere in sight. When he spoke, they remembered that they had left him that morning. It seemed so long ago, because they had packed a lot of punch into the past couple hours. Now, about midday, he must have set out looking for them. Neither of the women wanted to turn around and address their companion first. Red and Saturday excused themselves with made-up wedding tasks.

"Thal here volunteered to build the arch," Grace tattled as she angled her body towards him, attention still on Thal.

"That's alright, Grace said she'd play the music," Thal retorted, mirroring Grace's movement.

"At least I'm getting paid!"

"It's an investment for future work?" When Grace's face did not accept that response, Thal added, "So what? I like helping people out!"

"It's going to be your downfall one day, Thalassa Charles." Grace shook her finger at Thal, and found herself all of a sudden channeling her mother.

"Where did you get the dresses?" Sao asked, softly touching the puffy sleeve of Grace's dress.

"We made new friends," Thal boasted. "And they want us at their party."

"Ever stop to think that maybe we shouldn't hang around here and we should keep going as far as we can go away from Dimin?" Sao suggested.

"He thinks we're in Grogtown. He didn't come after me for months last time. He'll be too busy taking over the town."

"Didn't you say that Verdis told you that he was after *you*?" Sao pressed, gently putting his hand on her back.

"Fuck off, Sao. I've had a great day and I don't need your shit right now," Grace snapped at his attention. He drew his hand back quickly like a hurt puppy. He walked away, tail tucked between his legs.

"Yeah, you might want to go after him," Thal remarked. "It's going to be a cold night and you don't know what kinds of diseases are around this part, so you won't wanna be trapping unknown cocks in that elitist pussy of yours without a healer around."

"Ugh!!!" Grace threw her hands up in disgust. For once, she would like to not have to worry about where her warmth was coming from. She had had a bath, but it would only last so long. Out on the road, Sao was her most reliable source of heat. Thalassa was right. Flicking her off, she turned and marched out of the house of worship. She caught up with him outside the general store. He was chomping on a peppermint stick. He held out the bag to offer her one.

"I haven't had one of these since I was a little girl," she remembered with a sad smile, accepting one.

"My mama used to have them on hand all the time. Whenever I would get nervous, my stomach would start turning so she would give me one." Grace sucked on it, trying not to think about the music that she would play at the wedding. "Does it turn now?"

"Worrying about you makes it turn all the time," he said, kicking the heel of his right boot onto the toe of his left as he leaned against the siding with his hands in his pockets.

"Why do you worry about me?"

"I worry that I didn't teach you enough to keep you out of trouble," he said slowly, cracking the stick as he chewed on it. "I worry that one day you won't come back and I won't get to see your face smiling like you just played the biggest joke on the town. Your eyes twinkle with mischief and that gets me worried about what trouble I'm going to need to bail you out of."

"You don't need to rescue me, Sao. I'm not some damsel in distress." She slid her mouth around the stick, letting the taste linger.

"I know. I don't let you be in distress."

She choked down the words "No you don't," and forced out her best version of a kind smile. She hoped it did not look as though she pitied him as much as she did. One day she would tell Sao. For right now, she should just apologize and make it up to him. Like Thal had said, he was reliable and she did not know how long they would be on the road. She figured that if Rockdale's sheriff did not receive a wanted poster in a few days, then Blatho's sheriff had not wanted to admit that he had let a girl out of his grasp. Quickly she hoped, she did not want to forgo whatever good that bath had done.

Sao watched as she distractedly slid the peppermint stick in and out of her mouth, the nervousness quickly slipping away. Without warning, she tossed it into the dirt road. She took Sao by the hand and led him to the dark alley next to the general store.

The sun was high overhead and most people would be in a shady situation. She pinned him up against the wall.

"I'm sorry that I made you worry," she whispered into his ear. She put her hand on the front of his trousers. "But you do such a good job of looking after me." She unlaced the front and slipped her hand inside. Sao let out a groan. "Maybe I can help ease–" she gave him a stroke "–that worry a bit."

She kissed his neck, bare of any hair. Goosebumps raised through the perpetually smooth skin of his baby face. She put her left knee to the side of his legs leaning on the wall, blocking any view of when her right hand pulled his cock out. With a challenging look, she proceeded to stroke him. He was a decent size, though Mother knew she had played with larger. She looked down to see her handiwork.

"You like what you see?" he asked gruffly, holding onto her left leg below the knee. She bit her bottom lip in response, stroking faster. "Fuck this," he said, reaching down to grab under her right leg as his hips smashed into hers, smashing her back into the wall. Her legs clung around him for balance. In this dress, she didn't have to untie any of her own trousers.

"You need to wear dresses more often." He pushed up her skirt to her hips where he held her steady. He pushed aside her underwear and shoved his cock into her. She gasped with his entrance. He got closer and her knees pulled him into her. With fast and long thrusts he gave her no relief. She tore at his shirt, clinging to his neck as he impaled her again and again. She could feel herself clenching around his throbbing fullness. Her breathing quickened.

"Fuck me, Sao, fuck me like you were eye fucking me when you saw me in this dress." He picked up his pace, his breathing getting faster with his movements into her. With his hands on her hips, he could feel her lower back beginning to arch, and the thought that he could bring this wild thing to this point made him harder. With another thrust, she pushed back from the wall taking him the deepest she ever had and she cried out with her release. He followed her, moaning into her shoulder as he shuddered. He remained inside of her while they regained their normal breathing patterns and readjusted to their surroundings.

That was when they noticed the man in the apron that read "General Store" on it staring at them with his hands on his hips. "You knocked the teacups off the wall," he said when they noticed him.

"Sorry sir, I'll be right in to take care of that," Sao apologized, kerfuffled, trying to pull down Grace's skirt over where he remained inside of her.

"Take care of yourself first." The man's eyes moved to Sao's crotch area. He walked away, shaking his head. Grace burst out laughing as she pushed Sao off of her and grabbed the handkerchief that he kept tied around his belt loop. She wiped herself off, then tossed it at him, shaking her skirt over her knees.

"Have fun with clean up," she said. "I'm going to go relieve myself to clean off and then you can find me back at the tent with Slewja. You know, in case you find yourself any further distressed." She blew him a kiss and then sauntered away. Sao redid his trousers and went to pick up the pieces that she left behind.

FIFTEEN

The warmth from their tryst tingled around her core, making her feel soporific and calm. Sao was visibly embarrassed to have been caught. She wondered how long that clerk had been watching them screw in the alleyway and if she should go back to demand payment for his voyeuristic intake of the show. Pulling up her skirts behind the store, she relieved herself. *Always urinate after sex,* Sadie had told her after her first client. She had handed Grace a bedpan and challenged her to fill it by the end of the night. The result of that evening caused her to retch right on top of it. But Sadie had been right; she was no worse for wear the next day.

Grace had a smile on her face thinking about the fun that she had just had with Sao, and what she could coax him into next, when Slewja came up next to her, sniffing. He huffed at her.

"Oh, and you think I can't smell Raikka on you? Tsk tsk," she told him. He rolled his eyes in response and walked alongside her quietly for the rest of the trip outside of town.

"I wonder if we'll be able to stay here long." She caught herself debating aloud. "I didn't hear from Dimin for a couple of months last time. I'd ask and ask and ask everyone who came through town. I thought I'd gotten away and he'd have forgotten about me. Y'know, I thought that for the first time, I actually did not have someone breathing down my back. Boy, was I wrong." Grace patted Slewja's flank.

On Thursday, though, she woke to a chill in the air. When she mentioned it to Thal and Sao, they both reassured her that it was just a temperature dip for the day. Slewja seemed more on alert though. They all set off for town together, and the morning's bustle quickly erased any anxieties from their mind. They spent the next few days preparing for the wedding with the town. The piano from the brothel she had bathed at was wheeled down the street to the worship house. Red had decided to pretend it was just on loan from a friend, lest anyone try to associate the "virginal bride" with whores.

Thal and Grace were back in their traveling clothes; however, Red told them that she would lend them dresses for the wedding.

"Every girl should be in a dress at a wedding, or it's bad luck for the bride," she recited to them. The women snickered about it at camp that night, but reluctantly accepted that offer. One did not mess with Red's will and efficiency. From all the details the bride had worked out, Grace had no doubt that Red had been planning this wedding since she was twelve.

On Thursday, Grace and Red sat in the middle of the assembly hall with a blue wedding dress spread across their laps. Each woman embroidered sentimental touches onto Red's wedding gown.

Thal sat in the corner hammering pieces of beams together for the promised arch. "Do I look like a fucking tailor to you, Thal?" she said in a mocking tone at Grace, recalling when she became injured.

"Shut up, Thal," Grace warned her. "Or I'll call Slewja to burn your work down."

"You know it would need to be some life or death situation for that to occur," Thal retorted. "He wouldn't waste his breath on me. Plus, he would probably side with me."

"Who is Slewja?" Red asked.

"My friend, well, he's a dragon, so I guess my dragon friend?" Grace tried to come up with a better label that encapsulated their relationship. When words failed her, she remained quiet.

"I've always wanted to ride dragons, but my daddy would never let me."

"Maybe now that you're married, you'll be able to," Grace offered brightly, hoping the girl would have time to feel the wind on her face. Her mother had always told her that once she was married, she would be able to make her own life choices. For most of her twenties, she had dreamed of saying the marriage vows, merely for the freedom that marriage seemed to offer.

"Oh I don't reckon so," Red lamented. "My husband won't let me."

Thal dropped the hammer, missing her foot by an inch. Grace stabbed her finger with the needle, and sucked on it, hoping no blood stained the dress.

"I'm sorry, won't LET you?" Thal repeated.

"Good thing he's not your husband yet," Grace said, hoping to simmer Thal's boiling blood down a notch. The room grew silent as the three picked their work back up.

Red put her work down after a beat and said, "I don't mind giving up everything for him. It's my duty as a good wife."

"Yeah, but don't you have wants? Needs?" Grace asked, trying to keep the conversation calm and genial. She had heard the pitch in sitting rooms before, but hearing it this far west of the civilized cities surprised her.

"I need to take my place in society. I will be a respectable wife and we will be very happy together."

"Your vows literally say that you will obey him and the Maker and may you die if you do not." Thal could not contain her disdain for the misogyny.

"I hope to make it to the fourth staircase one day. Then I shall have my just rewards."

"Yeah, but what if denying yourself limits what you can do for others?" Thal prodded.

"'With love, comes eternity,' says the Mother," quoted Red. "And I love Saturday for eternity. I have been waiting for this moment all of my life. I trust him to do what is best for our family, and I will go along with all decisions he makes."

Thal started, "Yeah, but—" and Grace shook her head, cutting her off. People did not often change their minds on things that they had come to believe for the duration of their lives. The trio would be staying for a bit so she did not want any hard feelings on any side.

It was Grace's turn to choke on her spit when Red added, "He can have everything. Mother Maker molded men to be smarter than females, so they can care for us in this scary world." Thal shot her a look that said, "I could've said something." Rolling her eyes, Grace returned to sewing the red rising sun.

After another hour spent small talking while Grace and Thal avoided the subject of males, they left to go meet up with the others. Walking outside to the pub, Red eyed the dragons that lazed at the end of the street in the late afternoon heat. Grace noticed her longing look at them.

"Red, do you want to ride a dragon?" She took a chance on guessing Red's desires.

"What?"

"You can ride Vim!" Thal added excitedly. "It'll be our wedding present to you!"

"Full of presents, aren't you, Thal?" Grace reminded her of her promise of the arch as a present and not a commission. Thal ignored her friend as she watched Red's face. Five different emotions passed over her visage before she could reply.

"Yes, I do, but no I won't." Red looked longingly at the dragons.

"What if you rode him through town on your wedding day?" Grace prodded.

"Oh, that would be so regal," Thal said, glossing over the fact that Vim was anything but regal. "I think you should. Who could stop a bride on her wedding day from doing what she wants?"

"Her husband."

"He's not your husband yet," Grace shrugged. "Just think about it."

And so, two days later, Red rode into town on Vim's back. She sat side saddle, of her own insistence, clinging to the pommel with white knuckles. The only white on her body. Her bridesmaid cousins walked alongside carrying her simple bouquet of wild daisies that they had found amongst the trees in the cemetery. Vim let the ladies put a bow tie of greens around his neck and ankles to mark his participation, and the accessories made the dandy's back a little straighter, his head a little higher. As they approached the worship house, Vim decided to give her one last taste of single life and took off into the sky. Thal yelled for him to come back, but he had disappeared into the sky.

"She'll be fine. He's super gentle," she reassured everyone standing there though not quite sure of it herself. Thal's father had bartered for Vim when he was a young dragon. Its previous wrangler had been beating him when he had been a young dragon who accidentally set furniture around the house on fire on a regular basis. Her father, ever the compassionate soul, which was one hundred percent where Thal had learned her loving ways, traded a new doorway with Granny Good markings on it for Vim (who had been called, "Shitgrin"). Because of the nature of the Charles family's work, the dragon needed to remain outside until he learned to control his breathing habits. The little guy roared and grew around the open spaces, and Vim, named for being filled with "vim and vigor," developed a cozy relationship with Thal. They allowed each other their own space, but he would not hesitate to burn the world for her.

The maroon hued dragon landed after the longest two minutes of Red's life with her yelling strings of obscenities on his back. Her face was red but full of life. As he slid her off, she took a moment to recoup herself.

Patting him on his shoulder, Red smiled. "Thank you. I won't ever forget that." And she gave his wing a kiss. He opened his mouth into a giant smile and flapped his wings in response, sending her grandmother tumbling to the ground with the gusts of wind that he conjured.

One of Red's bridesmaids grabbed some hairpins from where she had hidden them at Red's mounting of Vim, when this crazy cockamamie scheme unfolded. She attempted to throw the wisps that had escaped Red's updo into various positions, continually whispering to the pieces "Back, go back" as she worked. Thal gave Vim a thumbs up and with a grin from ear to ear from his antics, she found her spot next to Sao inside the worship house. Grace sat at the piano, which was now even more out of tune from its trip across the road. Despite the flatness, she still managed to make the room echo with a serene beauty. Her fingers wove the story of the couple's love, from birth to their eventual death and reunion with Mother Maker.

Not a dry handkerchief remained hidden in pockets as the bride walked down the aisle, red faced yet glowing with happiness. Grace did not understand it at all, but she would support this woman to do whatever she believed she needed in this world. And if Saturday Rein was what she needed, then Grace would not stop her from obtaining him.

SIXTEEN

Grace did not have a view of the bride's walk down the aisle. She zoned out as her fingers took care of the music, drilled into her by the expensive music tutors her mother had employed to make her more appealing to men. Like trimming the fat to make cuts of meat look better at the butcher's. She remembered her day walking down the aisle, pale green silk dress accentuating her long sandy brown hair that her mother had directed her maid to pile atop her head in some sort of puffy and twirled concoction. Her small bosom was displayed to the whole world, as if it was some telling of her fertility; obviously, her only value to those who were present. She could smell the death emanating from the top of the aisle foreshadowing the end of the existence of anything she had hoped for herself or cultivated herself to be. The man waited. Sinister schemes stretched his smile into a sneer. She was not the sacrifice, but the lamb, fully marinated and delivered to the wolf on Daughter Dreamer's Day. When she excused herself, feigning upset stomach and nerves, she knew she would never be the one to be put on his spit. No one expected her not to return. Hence why she ended up running through her family's mangled estate as she "played" "The Demon's Gonna Get You." Yes, marriage was traumatic for her.

Grace realized that she had been playing an extra verse or two when she popped out of her reverie and back into the present. She played it off as if she had been intending it before she hopped off the seat and filled the space next to Sao.

While Grace had been thinking about the wedding where she had jilted her parents' intended for her, Sao had been dreaming of his own future ceremony. He figured that he would reconcile with his parents; maybe they would welcome him as their prodigal son or maybe he would have to earn it. Either way, they would miss him by now and thus be there at the ceremony. He hoped they would have forgiven him for losing the money they had charged him with depositing. Oranges would deck every hall with their bright optimism. And down the aisle would walk the girl of his dreams. The one who would wake up every morning and make his life worth living. Obviously one person fit the bill. Only, how long would it take for her to see it? He glanced next to him at Grace who was fidgeting nervously, probably due to her being on display. He placed his hand over hers and she pulled it away. Looking down at her left hand while she stood on his right, he wondered when she would realize what a good team they made.

While his face was betraying his internal strife, Thalassa put her hand on his shoulder. She could see it. Everyone could. One day, she hoped to find someone with such a level of devotion as Sao had for Grace. Yes, she enjoyed constructing, building something from seemingly nothing; but wasn't that what creating a child was? She always imagined herself in pale purple, walking across a field. All of her family and people that she cared for would be there. She would feed them and give them such a party that they had never seen. Everyone would have a good time and be talking about it for years to come. Until her child's birth party, at least. A nice light purple, a lilac even, so a wedding during the spring months would be best. A time of rebirth and when animals were being born. Maybe she would meet him one day on a job, or after a job at a saloon. She just hoped it would be one day soon. She tired of watching Sao and Grace, who were in two different places in life. Though Grace needed Sao now, he would never be her true complement and champion.

All three reveries were interrupted by the Trio Adoration. Grace had been brought up attending services, as had Sao and Thal. All three knelt for Granny Good, stood with hands behind their backs for Mother Maker, and put their arms to the sky for Daughter Dreamer. She looked around, coming to the odd realization that for all their respect for males, her brethren still worshiped a trio of women. Trinity's Nigh was the high point in the year for celebrating a time of past, present, and future joining together around a table. Men would sit reverently as women traded stories filled with morals and traditions. The next day, all would return to daily business and women were expected to once again simper quietly as men boomed about daily life.

After the Adoration, the chaplain guided the couple through the vows. Thal and Grace exchanged looks, both recalling their conversation with Red about these words.

"Do you promise to obey Saturday and the Maker and may you die if you do not?"

"I will obey everyday and if not, may she take me away," Red chanted the rhyme she had been pretending to say since girlhood.

"Saturday, do you promise to care for Red and help her mind the words of Mother Maker and Granny Good?"

"As her man, I will stand with her, beside her, in front of her, and never behind."

"With these vows, Red, you leave behind the care of Daughter Dreamer and enter the sweet protection of Mother Maker. May you bear children to please her."

Sitting there in the quiet of the ceremony as Red placed the ten rings on each of Saturday's calloused fingers, a similarly calloused hand slipped onto Grace's lap, covering her hand. Grace raised her eyes from looking at the hand on her thigh to its owner next to her. Sao turned his head and looked searchingly at hers. His brown eyes glistened with hope. A questioning grin was on his face.

With a tight chest, Grace removed her hand slowly, pulling each finger out of his grasp. His pinky held onto hers, and she made a show of shifting and wiping her hands on her pants before placing her weight on the right hand side of her body. He placed an arm across the back of her chair. Thal, who had seen it all, ignored their antics. The two as partners seemed a given. Whereas Grace was quick to move, Sao took his time. Grace's sure financial head offset Sao's money faults. She could balance him, and he would keep her warm. They fulfilled one another's needs.

As Red and Saturday clasped hands and kissed, Grace darted up to the piano, evading any more of Sao's advances. She put a happy face on, and mustered up the concluding song that was in style at the time of her fleeing. She had heard it at so many of her peers' weddings, and her mother had planned for the stylish tune to herald her daughter's beginning as Mrs. Greystock. Now, the tune sounded melancholy to her soul, reminding her of the person she used to be and the future that she had been nurtured to believe was correct for her.

She plucked out all four verses of the song. When she finished, the room was empty. Grace pushed the makeshift seat, a workbench covered with someone's heirloom lace, underneath the piano. She would help deal with returning the instrument the next day with the other townsfolk. They did not expect Red and Saturday to make any appearance for a full week after the party. The flower wreath with which Red had adorned Grace's long hair decorated the top of the piano. Grace reluctantly pulled it down and replaced it upon her head. As she turned around to go next door, Saturday entered, holding a beer and searching the aisle.

"Can I help you find something?"

"I dropped the rock pin that she gave me for my lapel. I'm just retracing my steps to find the damn thing."

"Why don't you just tell her that it accidentally dropped?"

"The things I wouldn't do for her," Saturday said, lifting his beer to his lips.

"Oh, like let her own her own land? Let her start a business?"

"Why would she do that?" He was bewildered.

"Why not?" she asked in a friendly low-stakes manner.

"Well, it's just not proper," he replied without giving his response any thought.

"Mhmm," Grace said with an eyebrow raised.

"Well it doesn't seem to be here. I'm going to check outside. I'll see you at the reception, Trace." He walked out the main entrance to the worship house as she took the side door to the assembly hall, shaking her head the whole way. He had hired her and he couldn't even keep her monosyllabic name straight.

As Red had put it, what a piece of work was man.

SEVENTEEN

At the sit down meal, where wild beasts adorned the tables as the main entree, Grace and Thal commented on all the occurrences to each other en sotto voce. Tittering and whispering about the colors and the beautiful decorations, a mixture of fabrics, ribbons, and wildflowers. But not gossiping. Grace never understood how to gossip in society; also, she tended to be the object of the gossip, so she knew the uncertainty of wondering if you were the scourge of the room. This town had befriended her, and in doing so, had earned her loyalty.

Once they had had their fill of the meats and salads, the two drank their way through the blessings and circular family dances. Across the table, Sao quietly watched the friends. When the band, comprised of the bride's father and his friends, played the opening bridal dance, Sao could not help but look longingly at Grace. He yearned to hold her in his arms and whisper to her that they had eternity. Through the bottom of her empty wine glass, she caught his glance. She placed herself in busy mode, hoping it would deter him.

"What if," she whispered to Thal, "you married a man, but you could never sleep with him?"

"Ugh! Really, Grace?! What's the point?"

"What if he had lots of money?"

"Mehhhh, I guess I'd have to find my fun elsewhere? That's a hard one." She sat in thought for a few moments watching the attendants that had joined the dance floor to form a ring of joy around the couple. "I don't know," she said softly. "I think I'd rather be broke and free than rich and unhappy." Turning slowly, in a moment of realization of her friend's plight, she whispered to Grace, "I would run away, too."

Grace's heart filled with empathy and understanding that passed between the two of them. Thal had never before seen her this way; she had not expected her to ever truly comprehend the feeling of entrapment from which she escaped. Sao cleared his throat, breaking the silence. He had come around to stand behind the women's chairs. He held out his hand. "Grace, can we dance?"

She put her hand daintily in his, another reflex from her days out east.

Standing up from her chair, she punctuated the conversation with Thal in a joyous exclamation, "I would rather not marry him and just love sleeping with him!"

Sao's face revealed nothing in reaction to that declaration. He would sway her thoughts. All women were fickle creatures; Grace often changed her decisions about meals and snacks multiple times during the day. He was glad to hear she had been considering the idea of marriage.

As soon as they reached the dance floor, the band modulated from a slow song into a much faster dance song. Grace's eyes lit up, her mouth opening in an excited inhale.

"The Fleckham Reel!" she shouted, scrambling to find a position. Out of luck for this tune, Sao exited the floor. He regretted not letting her teach him when she came home from drinking with Verdis. As another partner swept in to replace him and to dance with Grace, he sullenly headed to where other men were tapping kegs and slapping backs.

The music called her back to her days at her home in Hamber, before maps labeled it as "Greystockton." Ballgowns swishing around. Her feet seemed so much freer in these boots than they ever had in those damn stupid debutante slippers. The first time that she had made her appearance at one of the "deb dances," as she called them to aggravate her mother, she had stood on the side and waited to put those dratted lessons to use. Boy after boy asked girl after girl to dance some archaic dance routine that her grandfathers' grandfathers had probably devised while in their cups.

From the spots on the wall, she attempted any way that she could to demonstrate that she was amenable to leave her family. She smiled demurely at any boy who caught her eye. She waved the fan back and forth. She flirted with half open lips. She wanted to fall in love, to learn someone else. She would have compromised whatever beliefs her twenty-something self held. The longer that she sat and waited, the more time she had to observe her peers and form her views. The views her parents had never wanted her to have, lest they interfere with a man's.

More than once, she wished to herself that she could just approach the boy in the blue coat who kept to himself in the corner of the room. But that would have been dubbed "unseemly" for a girl let alone one in her position. And so it would go for three years. Until Byron Macavall, freshly out of debtors' prison, decided to waltz with her and then immediately propose marriage to her father. Her father promptly casted the prospectless man out of his presence. In a booming voice, he dared anyone that had less than generational wealth to ask for her hand, thus ending the line of men that her mother had been cultivating for her.

At one point, yes, she was excited about the prospect of marriage, house-managing, and child-rearing. As she spent more time waiting, her friends eventually became pregnant and stood near her once more. She overheard the horrors of the marital bed, the terrors of debt, the frights of childbirth. And the longer time rolled on, the closer she became to spinsterhood, which seemed to embrace her with open arms.

On the eve of her thirtieth birthday, a dark messenger arrived at the house. He bore a letter requesting her presence at the presumed empty Hilstrom manor up the road. A new player had entered their pleasant town. Glamming up once again in her patched ball gown from two seasons ago (her parents had all but given up on her), Grace rode alongside them in the coach to the evening's community activities at the manor. Greeted at the door by a leering valet, she bit her tongue rather than ask him if he enjoyed the view. Moving into the parlor where the familiar faces stood round discussing politics. A greyish skinned man in his early sixties with a black goatee and dark as death eyes lorded over the crowd. He seemed to drift between groups, and as he passed by Grace, she felt a sudden chill up her spine. Death, decay, and funereal roses perfumed the air. The rest of the ball went fairly normally, aside from the valet catching her father on the way out to request his presence at the club with the master of the house later that week.

Thus began the swift takeover of the city by Dimin Grey-stock. He was not the finest dressed in all of the land, nor was he the best mannered. He seemed to never worry about money and in eavesdropping on her parents' conversation, the mayor seemed to be in his back pocket. Where he had come from, no one knew. But the longer he stayed, the longer the chill in the air seemed to last. The air in the city, once fresh with ambition and ideas, took on a stale beer smog that blocked the sun's brightness. Clothes dulled from the smog, and the overall blasé feeling curtailed peoples' needs to peacock. Winter cloaks went on that winter, and three years later, they remained on bodies that mingled in the streets during the typical summer. The entire city seemed to die in the grasp of Dimin the Dreary, just as she almost had allowed herself to.

But today, she felt alive. The bright music vibrated off the walls of the assembly hall that had been turned into a reception room. Laughter cast light waves on the ceiling from the flickering candle flames. People around her smiled at her, tried to catch her eye, and did not even care that she was in a dress that looked like it was sewn by an eight year old. Grabbing the first person who caught her eye, she lined up for another reel. That night, she would dance. And dance she did. The center of the room felt so open and inviting. All she needed to do was step out and a partner would quickly fall into place across from her. She had no desire to garner any attention past each song. The ambiance infected her with a prideful joy as she triumphed against her past self.

When the band took a break, she left Thal with a well-physiqued male who was spreading a mischievous smile across her face as he whispered in her ear. That would not be the only area he would be spreading by the end of the night. She chuckled thinking about Thal's ass tattoo. She grabbed a tray of meat that had been sitting out for a few hours and meandered out to the meadow, where Slewja lay watchful.

"I'm sorry everything has gotten so complicated," she lamented to him, holding out the tray of meat that he quickly inhaled. "I bet you wish you were back in that clearing where you found me."

Slewja snorted, shaking his head, and wrapping her in his wing. They would be safe soon, she wanted to promise him, but she could not stand to lie, least of all to him. "Hmph," Slewja made a noise towards the outside of his wing. He moved it just enough so she could see a figure coming across the field. She knew that gait, strong enough yet still unsure. She tucked herself further into Slew's wing, hoping the darkness would conceal her.

"I know Slewja's hiding you."

"Hiding and hugging are two very different words that start with 'H,'" she told Sao. He raised an eyebrow. "You know, like the alphabet?" He guiltily looked down. "I thought you were paying Britt to teach you to read!"

"There, um," he cleared his throat, "wasn't much teaching, on account that there wasn't much money."

"Oh, well done," Grace said sarcastically to his guilty face. He could not bring his eyes to meet hers. He knew that he had fallen a notch in her book, and was ashamed that he could not meet her standards. He had never had a mind for reading; numbers, yes, letters, no. She always seemed to be looking for him to fill in the blanks for what she needed in the world, and he always felt downtrodden when he came up short. He searched for something to say to light up her face again, which had turned outward towards the west. She seemed to be contemplating her next move.

"Do you think he will ever stop following me?"

"I don't know, Grace. I don't know, " Sao uttered in an almost whisper. He wished he could tell her that he would hold her forever and she would be safe in his arms. He wanted to scream at Dimin and tell him to back off in a way that would tear a hole in the universe for him to fall through. He wanted nothing more than to go back to the peaceful days they had grown accustomed to in the last few months, the easy rhythm they had fallen into: work, banter, play, sleep. As the moonlight reflected off her face, illuminating her serious countenance, he desired her. Anything she named at this moment, he would do for her. And he would for the rest of his life.

"I do know that you don't have to do this alone," he started, taking her hand.

"I have Slewja," she said, trying to sound dense. She was not naive. A pit in her stomach knew the direction he was steering this conversation. And once they had it, she predicted she'd definitely be alone—who knew how long she'd last without heat then. She could not go back to Grogtown; she could only go west.

"You also have me," he said, trying to catch her attention.

"And Thal," she added, turning to rub her hands on Slewja's bumpy skin. Doing so calmed her. Thal constantly blocked Sao's goals. He wished that the two women had never met so that Grace could rely more upon him. He longed for the mornings that she would wake him up, bright-eyes and determined. He would rapidly grab his pistol and belt following after her. He relished those nights that they slept under the stars, passed out with exhaustion from work and their time together. He happily passed on the gun techniques that his own father had taught him. With pride, he beamed when her shot first hit the target. He just about jumped and screamed when his pupil hit the same spot twice in a row. He yearned for more of those days of Grace's hours belonging completely to him.

"Oh! The music has started, again!" She grabbed her skirts and ran across the grass, her white boots a reminder of how she had accepted what he had gifted her. Sao took a heavy breath, chastising himself for missing his opportunity. Once again, Grace had dodged a bullet.

And as Sao watched her whirl around the room, her smile stretched from ear to ear, gliding from partner to partner, he realized he needed to take his chance. He would not be able to sleep that night if he did not have one dance with her. Upon stepping into her sphere to claim the next dance, the music slowed to a waltz. His mother had taught him to dance the waltz, his tiny feet on top of hers in the dirt cabin that they shared in his childhood. She would have encouraged him to pursue Grace. No finer woman than one you can dance with, as his father would say, stealing his mother and dipping her. Grace's starry eyes twinkled, her face flushed from her evening's exertions. If he hadn't known summertime, he would have dreamed that she was the season incarnate. Aside from the fact that she was as cold as winter. Her chilly touch did not seem to stop his hand from clamming up the more that he thought about the possibility of dipping her in the kitchen of their own dirt cabin while their children looked on.

"I love you, you know." The words blurted out of his mouth, as if he were channeling what his father had said to his mother all those years ago.

"I never asked you to." Grace's verbal response and physical stiffening popped him out of his reverie. Her eyes stared at a spot behind his shoulder. Their feet seemed to be out of time with one another. He was a half second faster than she or maybe it was the other way around. So he had decided to end this, whatever this was. Her twenty-year-old self would have probably blushed and directed him to the corner of the room where her father colluded with the other fathers of the city about how best to sell off their female burdens. Now, she was just sad for the party to be over. They had had a good run.

Spinning her and narrowly avoiding another couple, he told her, "We make a good team. We should keep doing this." They made a team, for sure, like a group of dragons flying packages across the sky- each with their own destination, but their routes overlapping for a moment.

Pulling her hands out of his and taking a step back she said firmly, "Just stop, Sao." Looking into his heavy-lidded brown eyes, darker than mud after a downpour, she pleaded with him. "Stop, before you get hurt."

"I can't hurt any more than now. I ache for you. My head aches as it races with images of you throughout the day. How I can better help you. My heart yearns for you, beats just to make you happy. My arms feel empty when you are not in them. I want to fill your days with laughter and follow you on every adventure."

Tears welled up in her eyes and she mentally said goodbye to the good times. Too bad she had never had much practice at letting men down easily.

"I don't feel the same."

"You might grow to." His eyes beseeched hers.

"And if I don't? Will I be trapped in a loveless marriage forever, regretting empty promises?"

"We can start a family and I'm sure—"

"Have you heard nothing that I have ever said?" she interrupted sharply. "Trees will not grow from these seeds." She motioned around her lower abdomen. "And I am okay with that. I do not want that."

"Grace Wesson!" He could not believe that she would give up on something so easily. Didn't every girl dream of being married?

"That's not even my real name," she said, adding mentally, *dumbass*. But she did not care enough to fight that one out and deal with the conflict. Better to move on.

"What do you mean?"

"I mean, you don't even know my real name. Why would you assume that I would want to marry you? You have some weird dream girl version of me in your head that you think would be happy to be dirt poor and in love with you. I am a woman with wants and needs of her own, many of which you don't even know. We share nights together, Sao, but not the same dreams."

She slipped off the dance floor, walking towards the pasture where she had deterred this conversation from occurring just a couple hours earlier. Thal leaned against Vim as they shared a roast chicken that she had managed to cajole out of a very trusting drunk woman. She could see Sao as he leaned against the door frame and watched Grace walk away. His dejected stance betrayed the conversation that her two companions had just finished.

"Care to break the wishbone?" Thal held it out to her.

Grace brushed the dampness off her cheek that she had not realized was there. Her dry eyes were not the source; the sky seemed to be lightly misting.

"None of my wishes are being answered tonight, or I would be on that dance floor with a bottle of wine in my hand and not a care in this world."

Thal tried another tactic. "Maybe I should ask Sao if he wants to break it?"

"Mother Maker ain't answering his wishes, either."

Thal waited a moment before clearing her throat to ask, "Where does that leave us?"

"You and me will always be you and me. Fuck the man that tries to come between us. But, it leaves him without a partner on the dance floor and me with an impending sense of doom that I am going to freeze in the middle of the night."

"And me?"

"That question is for you to answer."

Thal left the pasture to go check on Sao. Tossing the chicken's remains in the air, Vim swiftly maneuvered below it and caught it in one gulp. Grace laid her head down on her arm, belly on the ground, running her fingers over the damp grass blades. She wondered how many seasons these tiny fronds had seen, how many lovers' quarrels, how many soured friendships. A breeze wafted through, blowing her long hair into her face and sending a shiver down her spine. She had not expected for the night to be so cool here, or she would have borrowed a shawl from one of the bridesmaids. She would need to find someone inside to warm her for the night–she doubted that Sao would want to be near her after her refusal. She contemplated the best course of action as the rain turned to freezing.

⚘

Sao leaned on the door frame, staring out at Grace, lying beautifully wild in the grass, surrounded by the dragons, her eyes greyed by the darkness.

"She will never be mine," he whispered in agony to Thal, running his hand through his hair. She passed no judgment on either of them. Would they work well together? In this moment yes, but as well as she knew her best friend, she could only grasp the past pieces of her that blew past, like tumbleweeds bouncing down a dirt road. Grace constantly forged ahead, forming herself with each new day. Thal only ever knew the ever-changing Grace who constantly revealed a new piece of her soul.

"You can't own people any more than you can own dragons, Sao. They fly their own routes." Thal patted his back. "Come on, let's get you a drink. It won't solve anything, but at least you won't look like you're the sad sap dragging down the mood of a much anticipated wedding."

The two turned and walked out of Grace's field of vision, though they were not far from her thoughts. She contemplated if Sao and Thal would ever find comfort in one another and settle down. A pleasant thought, though Thal would run that bedroom.

She stood up from the ground to search for some cover from the freezing rain. Dimin must be getting closer; she would need to leave in the morning in order to maintain her distance from him. Roses wafted to her nose from the assembly hall, inviting her into the party.

She stopped in her tracks.

But Red had not used any roses in the decorations. She had been specific that if she saw any rose, she would tear it up for the bees. A moment later, and the scent of death and decay blew in, burning Grace's nostrils. She noticed the snow dusting the rooftops of the nearby buildings. Her eyes grew wide, and her heart sped up. No tomorrow would welcome her in Rockdale.

She needed to run and fast.

<h1 style="text-align:center">EIGHTEEN</h1>

"Where is she?!" a voice from nightmares bellowed. The magical minions spun around the city. They swarmed the atmosphere. Guests dropped to the ground, avoiding the colorful air sprites.

"I've come to claim my bride on this happy occasion. I would like to relive our joyous nuptials."

Fuck, Grace mouthed to herself.

"Slewja," Grace whispered loudly. "Vim, call Slew," she ordered to Thal's dragon that was closer to her. With a head toss and soft snorts, Vim beckoned over his companion. Slewja silently strode up to where moments before she had been contemplating a suddenly much more minute problem. "He's found us," she explained, hating the words that came out of her mouth. Hoisting herself onto the saddle on his back, she wished that she hadn't dressed up and let her hair down. Thankfully, she never went anywhere without the holster on her hip and her trusty boots. Her hat had been draped on the pommel of the saddle, so she put it over her hair. They would find time for her to change; now was the time to fly.

"Vim, your choice. You can get Raikka, you can help, not

135

help. Any way you decide, may the Mother Maker bless your days, friend." She blew him a kiss before Slewja turned around and trotted to a clear spot. Spreading his majestic wings, he beat them strongly, thrusting himself with Grace on his back into the night air.

Sao and Thalassa darted out of the assembly hall, clinging to the shadows, and immediately headed towards the meadow with the dragons.

"We thought you would have left already," said Thal. "You need to go. NOW." She said this more to Slewja who hovered above the ground.

"Okay, let's go." Thal did not move. Droves of chaos erupted from the assembly hall. She looked back at the screaming town. "Slewja, land." The dragon reluctantly touched down. Grace did not understand why her friend was delaying.

"Hey, Grace, what if," Thal quietly posed, "a community of people that embraced you as their own needed help?"

"I'd run," Grace said with a lump in her throat and a pit in her stomach.

"Only because the threat is after you, so you would try to lead it away."

"What if, Thal?"

People ran and scattered in all directions. They did not have time to have the discussion but the chaos bought them a moment they might never have again.

"I'd stay and do whatever I could to help," Thal asserted.

Grace nodded, giving her friend a sad smile.

Thal beamed in response. "Gotta go, girl. Come on Vim!" As Vim passed, the two dragons knocked heads in a brotherly farewell. Slewja quickly walked away, flying under the cover of the darkness.

"I love you, Thalassa Charles!" Grace yelled to her friend's back, strong from woodwork and her own convictions.

Without turning around, Thal flipped her off.

That moment was the last she saw Thal, because her vision of the ground was occluded by mist and smoke. And Grace had no choice but to move forward, not thinking about the fate of the only other person who had ever delighted in owning and holding a man's ass.

Thalassa refused to admit that her one stable entity, Grace, actually ended up being unstable as far as a permanent home. She held no ill will, as she loved her friend enough to understand and not judge Grace's choices. With Vim at her side, Thal fought against the crowd to get herself and Vim towards the epicenter. Pretty soon, flames spewed out of the windows at the north of the hall. People kept running out, with flames seeming to replace where they must have been standing as they chased them out. Vim lit that place up like a barbecue. He had always had a bit of a crazy streak in him, a little too energetic about everything he did. Thal wanted Dimin to burn, for what he was doing to others, but more importantly, for what he did to Grace.

And Vim delivered, taking that building down. The top crashed down when the bottom's walls disintegrated. Thal made it out last and made it out safely. That was when the mist started to replace the smoke. The hall was frozen, flames stifled by the cold that Dimin was throwing down at it. As the mist rose from the cold, Dimin's smile grew bigger. As she ran, following Vim out of the hall, a bullet hit her in her back. Thal hit the ground. Thal, that big hearted girl who befriended Grace and never questioned her life choices. Thal, with her zest for helping others, even to her own detriment. Thal, with a dream for her future and how she could improve society. The cold touch froze her to the core, solidifying her prostrate stance on the ground.

All Grace wanted to do was to turn around and help her best friend. But Thal had made it clear that Grace must depart rapidly. Dimin's laughter echoed across the hills. Grace told herself that she would be okay. She would persevere.

Slewja beat his wings quick enough to escape, yet not fast

enough to create a wind that would attract attention. Sao yelled at her from Raikka's back, catching up to her. Of course, Raikka tracked Slewja's movements and scent. Trying to discern his words pushed her out of her grief for Thal. The adrenaline coursed through her body, in a temporary surge of warmth and invincibility.

"Go faster!" he urged.

"Two hours ago you wanted me to stay, and now you're telling me to go. You don't get to order me around."

"I do when it concerns your safety," he said, attempting to stick his boots in the mud. Grace's eyes blazed with defiance. Normally, she would have made a huge to-do over his assumptions, however he was not wrong. Slewja and Raikka looked at each other, sniffling and snorting and then they sped up. Below, the desert quickly turned to tundra, which faded to drifts of ice and snow. They made sure to urinate in two spots and then they flew back in the air in the direction from which they had come.

"West," Sao said. "We're going west. The dragons set a trail to the north to try and misdirect. They won't fly over the town now." As they approached the north side of Rockdale, Grace could see the burning building in the distance. She grabbed tighter to Slewja for strength to not turn around.

Sao could see the determination on Grace's face — both to get through the grief and to make it through the escape. He could not see how they would do it, though.

"Grace!" Sao shouted next to her. "I'm going back!"

"WHAT!? You are not!" Raikka flew above Slewja and Sao jumped down next to Grace.

"My turn to come up with the plan. You're going to go west, as far as you can. You're going to get away from this demon."

"And you're coming with," she told him with raised eyebrows. He smiled sadly at her, pushing a hair behind her ear. This pistol would forever astound him with her resilience and determination.

"No, Grace. I'm not. I'm going to go and distract this guy for a bit so you have a fighting chance."

"Sao, that's stupid. We already led him away. Let's go right now. You don't know what he'll do to you." She turned to Slewja, about to tell him to tell Raikka to follow, but Sao captured her chin, tilting it to look at him. He leaned his head in and kissed her like it was his last. He lingered on her bottom lip, with his eyes closed, memorizing the taste. Slowly, he opened his eyes, which were filled with tears.

"I loved you Grace. You were my best friend. And I need you to know one last thing." He slid so he was sitting sideways on Slewja. "I might forget you with the cold sickness, but my heart will still remember the ache of loving you."

He slid off Slewja's side into the air, and Raikka picked him up below before quickly curving. Sao pulled out his pistols in his holsters and blazed glory as Raikka dove towards the chaos. Dozens of tiny flying minions hit the ground in a clump rained from the sky around her as they fell out of her dragon's path. Like a dying ember, Sao disappeared beneath the smoke.

Once more, Grace was left with no one, and once more, Slewja took the lead as if he had been born with an internal compass. Grace frantically searched for a way to turn Slewja back towards the melee, but he had sped up on his way west. He seemed to know the way. She looked back, and as she did, she saw Sao running through the mists, guns blazing, in a way that would have made his father proud.

"Noooo!" she screamed. Grace's torso twisted while she held onto the saddle, but Slewja remained on course. She could not tell if he had been caught, could not tell if she had been his undoing, if he had landed on his own feet.

Once again, Grace fled Dimin and his minions. This time, she flew on the back of a dragon. Adrenaline surged or she would have been short of breath reliving that first escape. She pulled her gun and cocked it back. Luckily, the evil sprites remained in the area of the chaos. She pushed Slewja on their path.

The green-black dragon flew as if he knew the terrain and where he was headed. She trusted him to lead the way, away from danger. When they arrived at the mountains, Slewja merely flew higher. At one point, he perched on the peak of the tallest one. Grace could see for miles. The smoke in the distance from where they had traveled was but a small dot now. Whether that was due to their elevation or the fires had dwindled, Grace knew not. She had not seen any trace of Dimin or his minions for hours. Exhaustion crept up, obscuring her vision.

"Slew, I'm about to fall asleep, buddy. Let's find somewhere safe to stop. You need to rest, too." They landed and she curled up under Slewja's wing that he spread out for her. Next thing she knew, she awoke to that familiar feeling of being held as they flew. He must have sensed some danger or wanted to get out of there, so he had picked her up and held her as she slept so they could continue on their way.

On and on they flew west. His pace was less speedy than it was at their departure. Had they finally outrun Dimin? Could they take some time? The distance between them was so difficult to estimate. They could never quite escape the cold front that followed them.

Slewja finally conceded to rest. They found a hidden spot between multiple trees. His body could find more camouflage in the darkness of the small forest's floor as he slept there. While he slept, Grace looked for food. She could only find berries. Her background in the domestic arts had prepared her very little for roughing it in the wild. Yet another lack in her practical education that she had her overbearing parents to thank for.

She knew mint though, so she picked that. She chewed on the leaves for a little while, hoping that it would calm her gurgling stomach. She pondered what Slewja was going to need to eat. They would only find vegetarian meals here in the forest. He needed some sustenance.

She went looking around for wild game. When a rabbit darted out, she popped her pistol out of its holster and shot at it too late. Slewja appeared at her side almost immediately. When he saw the movement of the rabbit, he knew what Grace had been doing.

They were a few days out from safety, yet. But still, he needed a moment's rest. She needed it as well. The surprisingly quiet night was echoed by the noise dampening power of the light snow. When Slewja nuzzled her awake, snow had frosted their bodies and continued to fall swiftly around them.

NINETEEN

She awoke, once again with the dire need to get out of there. Instead of a sandstorm in front of her, a swirl of white precipitation occluded her view of the ground. Dimin must have figured out that she had gone west.

"Hurry, Slewja!" she leaned and called to the top of his head, right above the eye. She never could quite figure out where his hearing orifices were, despite having spent one afternoon searching. It seemed to work though, as always, because he gave her a quick jerk to prepare her before throttling forward. She sprawled out on her stomach, low on his back, holding on to the few raised scales he had acquired throughout his life.

This position took her back to the times that she had learned to fly with Slewja in the air. Those times in the mornings after Grace had had her coffee and basked in the morning sunlight reveling in setting her own schedule, accountable only to her friends because she chose to be. As the two flew together more often, they learned to communicate while in the air. Slewja learned how heavy her body would become when she became too relaxed as they flew. Grace could feel his wavering up and down as he grew tired. They would listen to each other and each set one another down to rest when that would happen.

For Trinity's Nigh, Sao, who had been on a one month ban due to his gambling away nights with the girls at Madame Sadie's place, snuck into the house and left Grace a present. Two brand new white and brown leather boots, stitched with flowers and dragons, sat on her windowsill when she walked in from the party at the saloon. He asked for nothing in return for once. She met him at the edge of the main street where he was camping under the stars. That night she spent with him kept her warm for a full day. It also ensured that he would be around her for a while longer. The boots made a difference in her riding, as the heels hooked into the stirrups of her saddle. With these additions, she was on her way to becoming a daily fixture in the sky around Grogtown, flying to and from different odd jobs to pick up money. They flew through all sorts of precipitation, in and out of the sun, through different times of day.

Nothing then had ever been as difficult as flying through this weather. They both could neither see forward nor backward. The blind leading the blind. Grace knew from their takeoff position that they were flying west. Certainly they would get to a point where the warmth was too hot for Dimin's minions to handle it.

She could feel Slewja's energy draining. "Come on, big guy, we got this!" The minions started falling away as bits of sand hit them.

"We're going to make it, Slewja, just a few minutes more, then we'll figure out what's next! They're falling away!"

She could see mounds of snow and sand on Slewja's eyelashes. Her hat and bandana sandwiched her own eyes into a slit of flesh so even if the air weren't a sandstorm blizzard, she would not be able to see much as she looked behind her.

All at once, the snow stopped. Nothing. No snow, no minions, no Dimin.

"I think we're good!" she propped herself upwards. "I think we made it!"

Slewja grunted in response, shaking the snow out of his face.

He'd just taken a deep breath of gratitude for being with Grace, when...

A massive wall of dense sand and snow appeared out of nowhere, blocking their way. Grace was lost for what to do. Should she tell him to move up or to the side? She couldn't see enough to make a split decision. It stretched across miles. They were moving too fast. He reared too late, flinging his underbelly at the wall. Grace had no time to reposition herself to hold on. She was falling mid-air and had no idea of what was going on. She closed her eyes, bracing herself for impact and the subsequent meeting with her Maker. She had had a good run.

She felt those leathery claws wrap around her like such a similar moment when she had made an escape from Dimin before. Slewja always had her back. She felt his smooth body at her back as he braced her for impact. He thudded onto the ground. They both lay motionless for a moment, staring up at the sky, catching their breaths.

Moving to her side, she slipped, putting her arm down to hoist herself up, hitting the side of her face on Slewja's body. She pushed herself up and wiped the lingering dirty precipitation off her cheek. Her wet back would have to wait until the next stop. She sat up and swung her legs in front of her. Bending her knee and placing her hand on it, she began the standing process, but couldn't gain any traction. She put her hand behind her to help. That's when she noticed the bloody handprint on her knee.

Adrenaline surged through her body. She would have to figure out where she was hurt and fast. Maybe Slewja could help her solder up her cuts until they could find a spot with a healer. She fully stood up this time, testing her faculties. As she looked over her body, she looked down at her feet.

A pool of blood bubbled across Slewja's stomach, where several dusty icicles were protruding and melting.

"NO!" she cried out at her hero. She scrambled, slipping multiple times, up to his head. "Slewja no!" His eyes were open and a tear appeared in their corners.

"I'm going to save you."

She mustered up the small amount of strength that she had inside her and crept over to his belly. Putting her hands on him, she called forth the cold. Ice plastered over the top, but still she could see beneath the clear veneer. The wounds were deep. She immediately felt tired. The ice bandages melted and she did it again. This time, the crevices held together. But her energy was drained.

"We're going to get around this wall and we're going to get better," she told him in as motherly of a voice as she could muster, trying to mask her exhaustion. She slid down his body and ran to his head, giving him a kiss on his snout. "Where else does it hurt?" His shallow breathing left no room for his response.

"It's okay, I'll find it, buddy," she reassured him. His neck was scraped and infected. She zapped him with some cold there. He grunted. "See no problem at all!"

"Being friends with you just leads others to their demise," a voice boomed out of the white. Fifty yards away, Dimin's form gradually became clearer through the diminishing whitestorm.

Slewja's eyes flew open. He rallied his strength to his arm, picking up Grace's form and placing it behind him, between his body and the sand ice wall. He breathed out a ring of fire, tearing down the wall and encircling them both. Looking to the wall, he cried out loudly, almost wailing in a way that Grace had never heard before now. He had exhausted himself. He looked at her with sad and sorry eyes. Tears made his amber eyes look like golden pools.

He would not survive this day, and by the look of it, neither would she. Dimin approached closer, taunting her. Slewja nudged her, rubbing his snout against her back and arm. His once glistening green-black scales had faded to an ashy grey. How could she let Dimin near her friend?

"You never once left me. I am not leaving you." His exhales pained him. She could hear the choking in his throat. A tear ran down from his eye. She began crying in frustration. Reaching into her back, she pushed her power in a stream that parted the flames. Dimin merely laughed her away.

"Your magic is my magic, darling. It won't hurt me at all. If you come home, I can show you how to best use it to work for me." In anger, she pushed another gust of power against him; again he swatted the stream of cold away. Each time drained her of more power.

"That dragon looks familiar. I do believe that I have met him before," he shouted through the flames. Slewja did not even stir through his deep breathing. She could not bear to have him linger in this.

"Slewja, buddy. You've done enough." The tears started to fall. "Call me selfish, but after everything you have done for me, I cannot let you dwindle like this. I cannot save you, but I can relieve your misery."

He opened his eyes halfway, and nodded slowly. Her eyes blurred. "I love you, my big hearted hero. We'll fly together in the clouds someday soon." She kissed his snout. Slowly, she moved towards his chest. Laying her hands above his heart, she reached in for the last of her power and pushed the cold in. Slewja went still as his heart froze, the final tear from his eye freezing on his cheek.

And Grace was once again alone in the world, struggling for survival against a man.

She was pretty drained. With Slewja's body protecting her, she noticed the flames around her dwindling. She slouched behind Slewja's curled posterior. Absolutely done. Parched. Exhausted. Grieving. Out of adrenaline. The wall disappeared into a puddle behind her. A sandstorm appeared from the west. She would rather go through that sandstorm than have Dimin get her. Did she have enough energy to make a run for it before the flames completely disappeared?

The sandstorm swirled forward in a twister, passing her and heading straight for Dimin. From a distance, she could barely make out a stranger walking forward, rope in hand. The rope lassoed the twister, the stranger compelling it to launch ahead. Grace closed her eyes, hiding her head in the tail of Slewja for protection from the elements attacking one another. Cold overtook her chest, darkness consumed her thoughts, and she knew no more.

147

Part Two

TWENTY

The dragon's screams traveled the distance to the large manor. Though faint, Ignacio Fuentes's ears perked at the cry that he had been waiting to hear for months, though he had not expected it to carry as much distress. He immediately sat up from the Adirondack rocker he'd constructed for Esperanza when they had found out she was pregnant with Marjorie.

At the fireside outside his manor, Ignacio was whittling a stick into the figure of the Trinity. Marjorie would be certain to love it - or love throwing it into the fire before dancing around it in some weird plea to the universe for her mother to come back. Since his wife had died more than a year ago, Naz's daughter had wished upon every star, blown away every dandelion weed, jumped over every crack, all in the hopes that Esperanza would return. Hope was lost to all but the six year old. Naz visited Espe's memorial behind the house every Sunday after worship. Marjorie refused to go. He told Espe about that, hoping that the wind would whisper words of advice to him. Dragons, he could handle–human children, he had no idea. Maybe his dragons could handle her. Jeb would have been great with her handling the news, but Naz had not heard from him for months.

Until now.

"Tara!" he called toward the dragon enclosures. "I hear Jeb! Listen for Marjorie!"

"Do you need Agrippa saddled?" Tara responded.

"Nope, he's still saddled from earlier, since I was hoping to take him out to that new land." He went to the field and whistled the birthday song for the maroon-purple dragon. The feral male strutted up to him and put his snout towards the sky, waiting for Ignacio to stick his hand out in greeting. Also, he sought to smell any meat on the ranch owner.

"I don't have any and you're going to have to deal, because we have to go now."

The dragon looked like he was going to prance his way towards the end of the field, where he would wait until he was enticed with a freshly feathered chicken. So much for behaviorism. "We don't have time, we have to get Jeb," he told the dragon. Agrippa moved forward and lifted the handle of the enclosure with his snout. Snorting, he motioned with his head for Ignacio to jump on his back quickly. Once in the saddle, Naz yelled, "Alright towards the crescent! Be wary!"

Agrippa flew faster than he had ever flown before that day. He could sense Jebediah nearby. And while he was not a wayfinder like his herdmate, he let Ignacio guide him based on his memory of where the sound had originated.

Further ahead, Ignacio saw swirling snow that stopped at the magical wards. Lowering himself to the ground, Agrippa slid Ignacio off his back via his tail. Though not chosen fellows, they still had an understanding: get Jebediah back to the herd. Maniacal laughter sounded through the distance. Who the fuck was that? Only one way to deal with cold snow though, he reckoned. He stooped to the ground and picked up a handful of warm sand. Standing he raised his palm, flicking the sand around and around in circles before he spun it towards the ground. He raised his palms from his hips to the sky while focusing on the whirling dervish, and it grew. It surpassed his own size. It became a tornado in the dust. Naz wiggled his fingers, curling them and uncurling them repeatedly, as he spun the twister fast and faster. As it started spinning out of control, he looped a rope and wound it up over his head. Saying a hope to Granny Good, Mother Maker, and Daughter Dreamer, he cast the loop over the top of the funneling air supply.

"Let's ride!" He smiled at Agrippa next to him, who merely rolled his eyes. Laughing, he threw his stance into the heels of his boots, and stood diagonally to the ground. As he stared at this uncontrollable force of nature that he had spawned, he realized that he had no idea what his further plan was.

"Yee fucking haw, bitches," he whispered to the world ahead.

Dimin moved closer to his prey as the fires diminished. Through the flickering orange flames, he could see the large scaled beast that he had floored. The creature was turning a blue grey after being affected several hours ago by his power. Something else must have happened. From his stance fifty yards out, he could not see the girl. He would have her–he had never been denied anything. Why would this insolent brat be the first? With a fist in the air, he called his ice demons back to him. As they grew closer he opened his hand and they absorbed into his palm. He smiled to himself as he could feel them find their homes throughout his corporeal form. Some took to his armpits and some to behind the place that he once called his "knees." Other sprites reveled at returning to their homes in his toes, causing him to wiggle them to settle their energy. He took a deep breath, inhaling any remnants of energy in the air, reminding himself of where inside himself his power came from.

As he approached and the flames dwindled, he was able to step over the circle that had protected her. He set about searching for the girl. She raised herself from behind the monster's tail, pushing cold air out at him. Surprise and the force of the impact spurned him backwards, until he fell on his rear. But how? How could she have this power? When he had seen her last, she was a mopey, insignificant little debutante, too long out in society with so little to offer except an unpoxed face and hips made for child bearing. She would have made the perfect accomplice to his plans to expand his empire. Her carrying his child would ensure that whatever he did would be for a reason. And whatever he did would be ensured to remain in their power. He reached out with his hands and absorbed the power that she cast at him.

Some breed of magic had attempted to trespass on the family territory. Ignacio saw the wall, where the magic had been stopped by the magic protecting the borders, refortified not long ago. His magic could be sent out through it, so he focused on the sun with the hand not on the lasso outstretched to the sky. Whoever was behind that ice wall was about to face a surly opponent. He moved his hand in an arc from the sky to the wall. The massive structure began dripping water, melting down into a puddle of dirt and liquid. As the water molecules separated, the forms of a large creature and another upright bipedaling creature could be seen through the glass. When the wall had been sufficiently thinned, he pulled out his pistol and shot through it.

CRACK!

Shattered ice glass rained down in front of him. He could see that the great big creature was actually two creatures: Jeb and a woman hiding behind him. No, not hiding. Using Jeb as a barrier. Jeb was down? Without a second thought, he threw the dust twister at the creature who was standing up. He pushed back who he could now see was a goateed older man, with dead eyes and grey skin. The older man changed his focus to the twister and the middle aged man before him. The debris in the twister reacted with some of the embers from the fire circle that Jeb must have made. The twister became a swirling cone of fire. As the old man threw out his hands, smoke flew from the spinning hell cone. He was attempting to extinguish the heat with the cold. But Ignacio's heat could not be extinguished. It could only burn out. It was the same fire as that which Jebediah blew, born under the same sun.

The twister gained speed and the tail swept under the old man's feet, knocking him up and sucking him inside the twister. There he spun around and around in the center, as the twister tightened its grip around him. And then, with a push of his hands, he sent that twister back east, away from his lands.

"And don't fucking come back," he yelled after the inferno. Naz had sent him days backward. And it had drained his energy.

So when he saw his friend, sprawled lifeless on the ground, his tears easily flooded his amber eyes. He motioned for Agrippa to grab him by the tail or legs and to pull him back across the border. As Agrippa unfurled his comrade's tail, he exposed a woman who had been tucked away. Adrenaline surged through Naz's body. Who was this woman that Jebediah had sought to protect? He ran to her and shook her body. She was only slightly warmer than Jeb, with purple extremities and lips. She needed to be warmed, and quickly, or else this old man would have claimed two victims that day.

Thinking quickly, he called over Agrippa, who did not want to leave Jeb's side.

"It'll be okay. We'll come back for him. We need to get her home as quickly as possible. Jeb would want us to." The dragon's eyes remained staring at Jeb's form on the ground. "I promise you, Agrippa, we'll take care of Jeb. But there has to be a reason that she was wound up in his tail, and maybe we can save her to find out what happened out here."

After a moment, Agrippa nodded his head and trudged over to where the woman now lay flat on the ground. He picked her up in his hand, and waited for Naz to climb upon his back. When both passengers were secured, he took off. Reluctant to leave, he understood the logic that Naz presented. He would find his brethren and return with Jebediah's body so they could say farewell in proper dragon fashion. He was tired from the ordeal, but he knew the code. Protect the humans. So he extended and flapped his strong wings, remembering the course he flew so he could return to Jebediah.

When they arrived at the manor house of the ranch, Ignacio yelled for Tara. He lifted the unconscious woman so he carried her in his arms, her neck held up by his chest, while his arms were under her arms and her knees. Rushing into the house, he beckoned for Tara again. An upstairs door flew open and a tan skinned woman with plaited dark hair of a slightly younger age than Naz, ran down the steps. He lowered her onto the couch in the front room before he lit a candle with a snap of his two fingers around the wick. She had her hands on the woman's forehead and pulse in the span of ten seconds before Naz could even indicate what he needed from her.

"Get all the blankets that you can muster," she told him. "I'm going to get some bed warmers."

"I think it should be the other way around, " he smiled calmly at her.

"Yes, yes, that's fine." Tara scrambled and found every scrap of warm fabric that she could find. Then, she placed her hands on the woman's wrists. Closing her eyes, she reached inside herself and found the energy circulating through the woman's bloodstream. She attempted multiple times to pull it out until she realized that the energy that remained within the woman was being eaten by the cold parasite. Naz hurried in, juggling three hot bed warmers.

"She needs energy put into her," Tara told him, positioning the water bottles around the key energy areas of the woman's body, as she had learned. "Do you have any left?"

"Only a small bit."

"Anything will help."

Naz nodded. He held out his hands.

"First the blankets, so it will hold in the heat." They piled blanket after blanket all over her body, until she was but a mound of blankets. Naz pulled away the blanket from her face, so that just her nose, eyes, and cheeks were visible. Placing his hands on her cheeks, he reached inside himself and pushed the energy into her. He could see her facial muscles relax into sleep, breathing a bit more audibly, which made him less scared. When he had poured all that he could into her, he almost fell over. Tara caught him under his arm.

"Let me bring you to bed. We've done all that we can. If she makes it through the night, she will be fine." She walked him to the master suite on the other side of the house.

"I can take it from here, just help me sit on the bed." She lowered him down and pecked his cheek.

"You've done enough," she assured him. "Goodnight." And she closed the door behind her. Tara considered staying up to monitor the woman; however, time was the only cure. She needed to thaw and warm up. So Tara made sure the door was locked, the candles were extinguished, and the house was settled before she returned to her soft bed.

Meanwhile, Naz considered the circumstances around the strange ordeal. So many questions. What had happened to Jeb? Who was this woman? And why did this old man seem so familiar? He quickly dozed off before he could imagine any sort of hypotheses to the situation.

Across the first floor, Grace dreamt a dreamless sleep as her body attempted to repair after another close call with Dimin.

And outside, the dragons carried one of their own home.

TWENTY-ONE

Blue eyes stared into his when he opened them in the morning.

"Daddy, there's a girl on the sofa in Momma's parlor."

"I know, I put her there," Ignacio grumbled into his pillow, turning his head away from the baby blues.

"I thought it was all of Tara's washing so I started to fold it this morning, and then I got to the bottom and there was a person! She's pretty. Dirty, but pretty!"

He smiled. "You couldn't tell that the pile was moving up and down with her breathing?"

"No," she bounced. "Probably because I was moving up and down."

Tara walked in with a cup of coffee. "It's about midday, so I figured you might want to be up."

"Meh, I'll need another day to repair, but I'll do it quicker outside in the sun." He hadn't spent that much energy in a long time. Normally, he expended just enough during the day so he could sleep dreamlessly throughout the night. Some say that the dead visit you in your sleep. Every night he went to sleep hoping he could interrogate Esperanza in his reveries.

Every morning, he woke up having dreamed of winter and pianos, he would be in a sullen mood. Better to have not dreamt at all.

Reaching out for the cup of coffee, he uttered a thanks to Tara. Forever calm, forever his opposite. His younger sister was as scheduled as it came. He would never truly understand how deep her still waters ran, though he appreciated them.

He wondered back to the woman that he had brought with him. Her body was so cold, so frigid. How had she known Jeb? Where had Jeb been? Why was Jeb gone? So many questions that he must have answered.

He stood up, pulling his braces over his shoulders. He had fallen asleep in his clothes from exhaustion. Good thing, too, as he was awoken to an audience. His harem left the room as he threw the rest of the coffee back.

As he left his bedroom, his shadow danced across the hardwood floors. Naz entered the delicate sitting room intending to just "check on her," for appearance's sake. He did not want to get involved in whatever troubles she had brought upon herself. He expected to see the woman still sleeping in the same position he had left her the night before, just as he did when he put Marjorie to sleep. Instead, he found the woman sitting upright on the couch, nursing the entire pot of coffee. He proceeded to sit in front of her, wanting to pepper her with questions. But he was distracted by practicality—what did she need? What could he do? Which question should he even ask first?

As if she was reading his mind, she looked up and gave him a sad smile while readjusting the blankets onto herself. Apparently, Marjorie's folding job did not hold up to this woman's need for warmth.

"I don't even know what to say. I don't even know what happened, but thank you for helping me." She cut through the awkward silence with the ease of someone who had been trained to run a room. She would have put Esperanza to shame in her confidence alone.

"It was no trouble at all for a friend of Jeb," Ignacio choked on his friend's name.

"Jeb?"

"It means beloved friend."

"Yes, but who is Jeb?"

"My dragon that I found curled around you," he stated matter-of-factly. Realization hit her harder than a beam swinging from a ladder. Her eyelids could not pull apart any further.

"You mean SLEWJA? Slewja is YOUR dragon?!"

Coffee dribbled down her chin after nearly spitting it at her savior, and she quickly used the sleeve of her dirty dress to wipe it off. She could care less what she looked like. She needed to know more about this man and how he knew the most important male in her life.

"Tell me more," she said, refilling her coffee cup before placing the carafe on the small table in front of the couch.

He reached for it, noticing that the woman sat cross legged on the couch, blankets over her shoulders and lap. Her purple hands cupped the hot porcelain mug, holding it close to her chin, steam drifting upwards.

"Jebediah was my friend. He set off looking for my wife, who went east about a year, year and a half ago, looking for more roaming lands, or money from her father in order to purchase it. When she did not return, Jeb took it upon himself to search for her. It has been more than half a year since I have seen him. I received a letter confirming her death. Details are hazy, but something about the cold."

"Dimin," she exhaled, taking three gulps of coffee to try to push that man out of her system.

"The mint?"

"Di-MIN," she explained. "He sucks the life out of everything around him until the area is full of death, nonchalance, black vapidity. He brings with him cold and dankness. He came to my city, Hamber, in the east and he took it over in a matter of a year. He used his power to gradually infiltrate everyone's minds and bodies with enough cold that they could never see hope again. When I left, the death count was high, but the frozen mind count was higher. He needed people to still be in the city, catering to his sociopathic needs."

"You left?"

"I left," she said with a sad smile. "And my Slewja, your Jeb, saved me."

Her blank blue eyes stared out the window in front of her. Though sunny outside, she could only see the dim swirling snow and her friend's lungs ceasing to heave. Awake, but not in this world.

He sat on the table and lifted the pot, pouring the steaming, black liquid into his mug.

"Would you like some sugar?" Ignacio held the etched porcelain sugar bowl out to her with the tongs set inside of it. He held it within her field of vision.

She looked down at it, and tears began streaming out of her eyes. Just a few weeks before today, she had been dreaming with Eve in the kitchen about sugar. Poor Eve. Hopefully she was still alive, even if she wouldn't remember her friendship with Grace. Oh, her friends. Sao and Thalassa. She thought of her last view of Thal, as she flipped her off and ran into the assembly hall. The tears deluged her coffee, watering and salting it down until her tears turned the drink into ocean water. Her host gently pulled the mug away from her hands, which instantly flew to her face as she thought of Sao. His face's smile quickly converted to a stone faced acceptance as he returned to Rockdale. He would never remember all the good times that they had, their jokes, their giggles at night. He would never even know that he had loved her so much he was willing to forget everything about her in order to help her get away.

Maybe now he would be able to move on from her. Maybe he would meet some nice girl and she would fulfill his dreams. Maybe he and Thal would find each other in the mist somehow and move forward together.

She imagined her two friends, bonding over Dimin's evil nature. Thal would make sure that Sao got through it. She would carpenter a house for them and make sure that there was a room. And pretty soon, there would be little ones helping collect wood for building. Just as long as they kept the cards out of the house; she wished to Mother Maker that he would forget that vice.

Naz was at a loss. He pitied this person's grief; she had obviously been through the ringer. He put his coffee mug onto the table.

"Hey," he whispered, trying to get her attention. He reached out to her arm, shirking at how cold it was. The warmth of his touch got her attention; however, she did not want to use him. She had already used someone for warmth and all it did was leave both of them broken-hearted.

"Hey." He pulled her hands off her face. She was a broken, dirty mess of a creature without anyone in this world. And she had just put up one hell of a fight against some devil who wanted to end her. She needed someone to hold her, her eyes cried out for it. Grief had a way of excusing all behavior of the people who experienced it and those who wanted to help. Excuses could be made based on the madness of grief. But he also remembered how safe and not alone he needed to feel in the depths of his despair. Even if he was not completely distraught for losing his wife, he still grieved for the plans they had made and for his daughter's loss. Grief was never about just losing a person–it was a lamentation of the loss of the present and a stalemate of growth. He moved towards the end of the small table, and pulled her into him. Her fingers clung to the shirt on his shoulder, bunching up the crisply ironed cotton. Her neck curled up so her wet face rested just below his chin. He wrapped his arms around her back and held still, trying to be the best rock that she could find to anchor her existence to for a moment.

So he held her. Her hair smelled like smoke, and her body carried the scent of someone who had been camping out for days. For such a strong personality, her body seemed so delicate at that moment. He could not help but think that Jeb had called him because he was the only one he could trust with this person. And he was not going to let that dragon's final wishes be ignored.

He felt the woman slowly relax into him, sobs became the tapering off cry pattern of sniffle followed by gasp for air.

"Daddy, daddy!" Marjorie ran full speed into the room, dangling a frog by its leg. Grace pulled away, looking into her embracer's eyes.

"Sorry," she mumbled. He shook his head with a down turned mouth, silently communicating that there was no need to be sorry.

"Hey, you're awake!" The bouncy pigtailed girl happily observed. "What's your name? Why are you on the couch? Are you hurt? Do you have a voice? The lady in my book loses her voice when she is brought home by the prince." She gasped, "Are you a princess? I can totally make you a rose crown, or maybe weave some grass and a dragon scale for a crown. That might be more appropriate." The girl stared Grace into the eyes, never moving, and waiting for all her questions to be answered in that one moment, preferably quicker than she had spat them out.

"I'm Grace Eastbrook. I'm the furthest thing from a princess, but your dad" –she looked at him for confirmation, which he gave in the form of a nod– "has nonetheless rescued me." Looking between the two, Grace spotted the resemblances: dark inquisitive eyes, dark hair, though the girl's had a bit of a wave, tan skin tone though the pale spots behind the girl's ears betrayed her naturally pale coloring.

"What's your name?" Grace asked.

"I'm Marjorie, and this," she waved the poor creature hanging for its life, "is Freddie. He has been running away every day this past week, and I finally found him again. I worried about him so much."

The father looked at the girl with patience and love. "Maybe you should take Freddie out to the brook for some water, he looks a bit parched." Marjorie assented happily and ran outside. "Poor guy probably thought he got away." He stood up and refilled the woman's coffee. "You are most welcome to feel your feelings here. You are safe now, Grace." He added a sugar cube to her cup and began to head out the door.

"Wait, what can I call you?"

"I'm Ignacio," he said. "But all my friends call me Naz." He winked at her and walked out, leaving her with the faintest impression that he was a handsome prince in a past life.

TWENTY-TWO

All that coffee drinking led Grace to spending the second night half-awake in the house. She heard an odd chorus, not unlike a harmony of Slewja's final cry, and it weighed upon her heart. Turning to look out the front window, she could see black smoke with golden flecks in it winding up to the clouds.

Silhouetted against the smoke, a man walked towards the house, head hung heavy. What was his story? She watched him take slow, strong strides towards the house, with his hands in his pockets, shirtsleeves rolled up to his elbows. Grace imagined that Ignacio Fuentes knew every divet in the ground that he walked. His wavy dark hair mirrored the waves in the dark smoke. As he approached the front steps, she saw him heave a breath and brush his bare forearm across his face.

The door quietly latched, boots thudding onto the ground. As he stepped into the front foyer, Naz glanced over to the front sitting room and caught her eye. His mouth muscles merely spasmed in a movement of recognition. His cheeks, normally contoured by the sun and his stubble, were ruddy from crying.

"I would have invited you out had I known you were awake," Naz remarked guiltily.

"I've been in and out. The song woke me this time."

"You heard a song?" Naz asked incredulously.

"Whatever it was sounded just like music to me." She sighed. "Perhaps it's best that I didn't go. I gave him the ultimate good-bye." Tears welled up in Grace's eyes, obscuring some of the blue's brilliance. She used a blanket to dab at them.

"You?" He cocked his head in confusion.

She heaved a deep breath and stared at her culprit hands. "He saved me from Dimin. The first time. I had nowhere left to go. I had been injured by what I now know was some curse from Dimin's powers. I thought that I was at my end. And there he was, in a clearing, ready to scoop me up and fly me away. He brought me to safety and never left my side. When Dimin came back, we were flying." She started tearing up. "Slewja flew me away so fast, faster than he'd ever flown me before. I didn't see the wall in time. It rose out of nowhere."

"The wards on the borders," Ignacio realized in a whisper. "I moved the wards last week and reinforced them. He was flying home to safety and wouldn't have known that I moved them. I killed my best friend." He ran his hand through his hair and leaned against the door jamb.

Grace shook her head. "Dimin was throwing magic and cold and minions left and right. He must have thrown his magic ahead of us so it interacted with the wards. So I wouldn't self-flagellate tonight."

This clarification made Naz feel somewhat better that he had not caused the wall. But the pain stabbed at his heart when he considered that Jeb was just trying to get home to where he knew that they would be safe. Where he had grown up. Where his friends and family lived. He must have thought that Naz could keep him safe from whatever was chasing them from Below.

"Plus," Grace began. "I iced his heart to kill him, putting the nail in the coffin."

Naz furrowed his thick brows. "You froze his heart?"

"The wall appeared so fast that he couldn't bank. He smashed his belly against the icicle protrusions on the wall and they stabbed him like glass. I tried to use whatever power I had to heal him. When I could do nothing for him, he blew a ring of fire around us. And then I froze his heart to put him out of the pain that I feared Dimin would cause him."

She wiped her tear-streaked face on the puffed sleeve of the summer dress Tara had lent her. Though a bit big in the chest, it was nonetheless comfortable. Plus, it made a soft tissue. She offered the other sleeve to Naz who was also blubbering.

"I probably would have done the same," Naz admitted. "But how did you freeze it?"

"Dimin the Demon cursed me a while ago. Slewja saved me, but I carry some sort of coldness inside me. I normally have a problem staying warm, but it seems to have worsened since my last encounter with him." She waved her hand over the blankets to demonstrate the example of how she was still lying there.

"I should have never sent him out." Naz shook his head, wiping his face on his sleeve again. "I missed him so much. I kept waiting to hear something from him, or to see his wings flying towards here. I didn't expect that I'd hear a cry from him last. And now he's gone."

"Hey." Grace gently put her own guilt aside. "He'll have a home in your heart until you see him again."

Naz ruminated on her reassurance and nodded his head softly. "He was a wayfinder. He'll find his way home. He always did." He mustered up a small smile. "I guess I'm just torn up from the ceremony." He started walking away.

Grace lifted her head off the pillow, and called after him. "I'm glad that I didn't go to the ceremony. I'm not sure what happens at one, and I don't think that I would be able to say goodbye a second time. I'm sorry if you felt like you had to bear the grief of losing your friend alone. But maybe it's better that I have some strength so I can be a shoulder for you, at least for a little while." The vulnerability shone through his eyes.

"It's wild out here, Grace. The occurrences, the environment, the feelings. Every part of this setting is raw. I really meant it when I told you that you are safe to feel your feelings here. You'll just never grow used to how powerful they'll be."

"Then, I shall relish the feeling of life." She smiled at him with earnesty.

Ignacio regarded her for a moment. "You must be someone quite special for such a hero to sacrifice himself for."

"I wish he hadn't. Enough people have lost themselves all due to me."

"I see it more as Dimin has stolen enough people from this land, and you just happen to have been blessed with the ability to remember who they were before that occurred."

"But then how did you get rid of him?"

"Ah," he winked at her. "My handsome charms swept him off his feet and carried him to new lands. Good night." He trudged up the steps much lighter than he had entered the house.

Grace laid her head back down. She expected to hear Slewja's good night snort outside the window. What if he were still alive? Would she be here, or would she be on safer lands? She had no idea where Dimin was.

She began ruminating on all the what ifs. More than once, she caught herself saying "what if" and remembering how she would play the game with Thal. She attempted to imagine conversations with her friend, but tears only came when she discovered that she could not predict how her friend would have answered some hypotheticals.

And then remembering that Thal would not even remember her, she started wondering what had happened to Sao. Last she had seen him, he was running towards hell, challenging it to take him alive.

Would he remember her? Or would he fall to the sickness? Maybe it was best if he just forgot her, anyway. They had had their fun, but he wanted so much more than she could really give him. She did not have much of herself and she needed to retain that for her own living. Using him for heat had gotten her through this far. She would need to figure out a way to stay warm indefinitely. She could see that she could not tie herself to one person and rely on maintaining him for her own protection.

She circled back to her conversation with Naz. He carried the weight of the land and its inhabitants upon his shoulders. In that conversation, he did not seem so different from herself. Maybe Slewja brought them together because they both simply needed a friend.

When Grace finally fell asleep, she was awakened two hours later by Tara's footsteps moving around the house. With one look at the dark circles under Grace's eyes, she quickly offered her an herbal tea for the remainder of the day. Grace, relieved that she did not have to address the over-caffeinated situation to her kind hosts, settled down for another few days on the couch. Occasionally, Naz would pop in to see her, and change out the hot plates which he seemed to do at a rapid speed. On one trip back from using the toilet, Naz called to her from a room upstairs. Following his deep voice, her legs led her to his study. A bit unsturdy from lying on the couch the past few days, they carried her slowly to the source. She sat down on a chair across from the desk, next to the bookshelves that lined the wall.

"Your cold sickness. Is it contagious?" He did not mince words.

"No, but I do have a habit of attracting Dimin to my location, so his contagion could be attributed to me." He raised an eyebrow at her in confusion. "Wherever he goes, he spreads the cold sickness. I've seen it in towns before. First it starts out overall chilly, then it turns into winter, then he arrives on a storm. So since he seems hellbent on hunting me down, we have very little time before he finds me here and spreads out."

Naz did not seem perturbed by this at all. "The borders will hold him out."

Naz had a map in his study positioned on the wall over the cowhide loveseat. She stood up to look at it, examining the different towns moving from East to West. She named some cities, smiling as she recalled some of the exploits. Other cities her finger did not touch on, and she wondered if Dimin had overtaken them yet.

"And why does he keep hunting you down?"

"Because he is a maniac obsessed with me and I jilted him in front of the whole city," she said matter-of-factly, sizing up the large territory that the manor seemed to sit in the middle of, named "Titan's Creek." The land explained why he could hold such a manor, but not why he needed it. She continued her perusal of the map, eyeing the cities that were west of here. Not many, but some coastal towns before the sea separated the continent from the nearby. She wondered what life was like there.

"Have you ever been west of here?" Grace turned back to look at Naz.

Naz sat back in his chair, arms behind his head. "Once or twice, when I was a boy I went with my father to Elleboro. We had to go and see if we could expand our holdings."

"I don't see that city on this map."

"The map was made last year when the surveyors came most recently. I wanted to strengthen the borders so I needed to know where our boundaries are. Elleboro is part of our territory now, mainly due to those trips my father and I made together."

"Ah, you're an expansionist," she admired his work.

"Absolutely not," he scoffed. "Everything is for the dragons. They need the space."

"But you sent your wife out to find more lands for them to roam."

"SHE was an expansionist who CHOSE to go out searching to expand our empire. She wanted them to have a place that they could fly to at different times of the year, give the earth a chance to turn over from their constant grazing and lazing. I happened to agree with her on the latter account and she had a much clearer vision than I."

She studied the map. Her eyes landed on the coastal city of Lesea. She wondered about the bustling city. How much trade occurred there? Was it warm or was it cold being by so much water? Were women treated any better than out East? Would she want to leave once she reached it?

"What's Lesea like?"

"I'm not sure. I've only heard about it. Tara went there to study as a young girl, though. They have the oldest libraries on energy magic there."

"Energy magic? Tara has magic?"

"She is a healer. This family has been a holder of magic for eons. We use our magic to care for the dragons."

Dragons.

They had dragons. Multiple dragons.

Her heart skipped a beat and she yearned to see them. Their presence explained the large territory.

She had heard of places having magic, but she had only experienced Dimin's as of yet. She suffered on a daily basis through the cursed remnants of that night she ran away. Her father had always turned his nose up at those claiming to have magic. She learned later in life that he was absolutely jealous. For this one reason, the Eastbrook patriarch wanted his daughter to carry a child with his genes and magic. He was willing to pay whatever price for that to happen. She wondered if he paid for it with his life. Not that she cared, but she did love poetic justice.

"Thank you for caring for me," she told him. "I truly appreciate your kindness and your care. I will be out of your hair in no time." She stood to leave, the cold beginning to seep into her body again. She longed for the comfort of the quilts and the heat of the bed warmers. The apology boasted well-breeding, reminding him of the times he had courted girls in his youth.

"And then what?" He would not let her go without knowing where her mind was.

"I'll figure it out. I always do."

Naz had a feeling that no matter how resourceful this person was, she needed a better idea of her future than winging it.

"Why don't you stay for a while and we can come up with a plan for you to survive without freezing to death?"

"I've been handling it for this long. I can find a way to heal. Besides, I couldn't impede upon your generosity." She waved him away.

"I insist. I won't have helped you properly unless I've made sure you're better off than how you arrived. I won't have you leaving just to be put right back in the position that I found you."

"I have nothing to trade you for your hospitality." She knew that in this world nothing came free. She felt better laying out in advance what the costs of her giving into this plan and help would be. Naz thought for a moment. He could afford anything. He did not need another wife after having experienced how lonely and businesslike marriage could be.

"Maybe you just spend some time with my daughter for a bit? Give my sister a bit of a break. And she would be so happy to have someone new to tell all her stories to and just be girls with." When Grace made no response, he asked, "Can you play with dolls?"

She laughed in the doorway. "I should hope so! I had enough of them growing up!"

"Just play with dolls, do each other's hair. Do girly things. I don't know." He shrugged his shoulders as if he was completely unaware of how to father a girl. Little did he know that he knew quite well what he was doing as a parent to a child, through the communicating skills, calm logic, and never ending love that he outpoured to her daily.

"I'm not going to be her mother, Naz," she informed him directly. She had no desire to be roped into staying at a place as some stand in mother figure. Dimin was evil and so she had run from him. But marriage itself was restrictive, and she would refuse it. She knew she could fall into a trap of being a sucker for this man's amber eyes only to have her entire dreams for herself ruined. Furthermore, what advice could she give to the girl? She was not going to tell her to stay away from brothels. Her advice would be to use whatever Mother Maker had endowed you with in this world. She doubted that Naz would like his daughter to hear that advice. Though if you asked any self-sustaining woman living on her own in the world of man, she would tell you that this advice was good and true.

"I'm not asking you to be her mother." He clarified unconcernedly, with a hint of relief spreading through his body. "I'm asking you to be her friend."

"I can do that. Though I have a feeling, you didn't need to ask me to do it since I like her already. Which is a testament to you that you're doing just fine." She smiled, reassuringly, wiggling her eyebrows. Naz in an instant knew he was going to live to regret teaming those two up together.

TWENTY-THREE

After a day spent with Marjorie playing cards and doing puzzles in her blanket cocoon, Grace was ready for sleep. Marjorie got ready for bed, first. Tara had "left" a murder mystery on the chair next to the couch where Grace lay. She fell victim to its intrigue, sucking her in when she ventured a peek at it. She wondered if Eve had read it. If so, maybe Eve would get to read it for the first time again if she healed from the sickness. Hope cost her nothing. Tara came downstairs from putting Marjorie into her bed and had to clear her throat three times before Grace noticed her and guiltily looked up from the page.

"Are you at the duke discovering the armory yet?"

"Oh Maker, he just did!!"

Tara laughed and added, "That's only the beginning. I drew you a bath. I'm going to finish the last ten pages of it and I'll leave it out for you."

"I'm sorry." She handed over the book to Tara, memorizing the page number.

"Don't be. Books are fair game here if you leave them around. Why do you think Naz hoards all those in the study like he is an ogre protecting his treasure?"

"Because Marjorie does not need to be reading his penny smut?" Grace replied with a wicked grin on her face.

"If only he read penny smut, Grace. If only," she giggled. She walked away, leaving Grace to find the bathroom.

She could have fallen asleep in that bath, but the water eventually cooled. Clenching the sides of the tub, she drew a deep breath into her stomach and hoisted herself over the edge. After drying off with the soft cotton towel, she threw on the nightgown left for her. She used the towel to dry her hair before she braided it back. Attempting to squeeze the water from the tip of her braid, she heard footsteps in the hallway. Looking up, she saw Naz, hands in his belt loops, drawing circles on the ground with his boot toe. Grogginess had taken over her body once again. That stand against Dimin must have required way more of her magic than she had thought; her energy supply seemed to not be rebuilding quick enough for her to be on her way. These consequences of the magic reinforced her refusal to use the magic unless in dire circumstances.

"Thank you, for the bath, for everything. I don't quite know how to thank you." Grace's blue eyes held Naz frozen for a moment. Taking a few steps forward, her head started tingling before her legs went weak. Naz snapped out of his dive into her eyes, and reached out and caught her under her arms before she hit the floor.

"I'll take the couch tonight," Naz told her, "I'm moving you to my bed." He scooped her up, blankets falling to the ground and dragging the path he trod. As he touched her, he felt the coolness of her skin start to dissipate. He searched her face for some acknowledgment that he was not the only one experiencing the sensation.

"Oh! You're so warm," Grace said, she laid her head on his

shoulder, breathing into his neck. Her cold hands seemed to thaw as she placed them around his neck to hold on.

"You'll have an easier time of maintaining your body heat in my bed," he chuckled. He pulled open the crisp white sheets that he had changed that morning. He kicked himself that he had not put her into his bed last night, but he had not been thinking straight upon his arrival home from the dragon funeral of Jebediah.

"I don't know why I'm like this," she explained, running her hands through the bottom loose ends of her braid. "I feel so helpless." She curled her legs into herself. Naz took the opportunity and extra space to sit down at her feet.

"Hey," he pulled her hands off her hair and took her hands in his. "You are not helpless. You are anything but. How you staved off that force absolutely baffles me. I should have found you dead, but there you were, fending off this demonic entity and holding on for dear life. Your body needs to replenish its energy after consuming so much out there. Rest."

Sinking down into the mattress with a sigh, she curled into the fetal position. He tucked her in, pulling the quilt over her. After asking for more blankets four times, a joke slipped out of her mouth that he should just climb on top with his warmth. He blushed! She could not remember the last time that she had made a man blush with her jibes. Tucking the covers up to her chin, he bent over and kissed her cheek. Then, awareness washed over his face as he realized what he had just done. He ran his hand through his dark hair and through the stubble on his jawline.

"Uhhhh, sorry, force of habit. I'm so used to tucking Marjorie in."

"No worries," Grace yawned, settling in. "I liked it."

With that, she fell asleep almost as soon as he brought the candle out of the room. The room was toasty and safe. Lilts of voices outside the door lulled her to sleep.

☙

When he came out of his bedroom, Tara sat at the dining room table, papers spread around her, trying to use the three ledgers to tell the story of the past month at the ranch.

"I'm surprised you're not in there with her," Tara's attention remained on the ledgers as Naz shut the door behind him. His face contorted with confusion before he shook it off as he realized she was not going to clarify without prodding.

"And pray tell, why is that?"

"You are both around the same age and you are out here without any company, and with all her complaining about the cold and your being you-know-how, you know."

"I met the woman yesterday!"

"Romeo moved quicker getting over Rosalind and getting with Juliet, bro, that's all I'm saying."

"You do remember how that story ended, right?"

"Peace to all." Tara avoided the obvious answer to annoy her brother.

A year and a half had passed since he had last spoken with Espe. She had traveled out east, hoping to secure more land for the dragons to roam to. The message came a year ago that she had fallen sick with an unknown disease, flu related. In her sickness, she had written him a note. The handwriting appeared as if she felt fine, though. In fact, he had read the note more than two hundred times. She alluded to Jeb and to Marjorie, which seemed so odd, considering Esperanza never seemed to care what happened with her only child. Espe had not wanted to go, but she felt such guilt in her heart for how the dragons needed roaming space. The dragons were her family, too, she reminded her husband in bed the night before she left. She took this three week trip upon herself to scout it out, telling Naz that she would be back in time for his birthday.

Jebediah had left months ago to find her. Instead, he barely returned with a completely different woman. A beautiful woman. But different, nonetheless. Maybe Naz could help this woman in the way he could never help his wife.

Dawn shone like honey on Ignacio's tanned face through the windows. Lying on the couch, he made a mental note to tell Marjorie to grab some chicken feathers from the dragons' field so that they could stuff the cushions a bit more. No reason to let the house go to pot; his mother and his grandmother would have never stood for it. Titan's Creek Manor had been in the Fuentes family longer than the nearby town had existed. Family lore held that a hotel popped up on the outskirts of the manor when people started traveling far and wide to look at the majestic dragons. Pretty soon, traders began bringing in their wares to provide sustenance and necessities for the sightseers. When rumors of the training and quality of the dragons started to make the national Cosimo papers, the trading began. His family had always been the caretaker of the dragons; he personally ensured every rider would treat the dragon with respect and love. It was a lengthy process to acquire a Fuentes dragon.

Income from the dragons had allowed the family to invest in a diversity of new equipment, new innovations. They acquired more land. Now at over 640,000 acres, the Manor was much more of a ranch, though the luxury of the house retained its name of manor. And as caretakers, Tara and Ignacio trained Marjorie in how to take over when they were gone. She currently spent as much time around the dragons as she could, getting to know their signals, their behaviors. Dragons were docile unless provoked, and Marjorie cared even for the long legged spiders. She would be an excellent caretaker one day. She would need a partner for it; living on the manor alone would be lonely indeed.

He ran his hands over his face as he stared at the ceiling. What was it about Grace's defiant chin and sparkling eyes that made her seem up for any sort of mischief? She looked like a woman who stumbled into trouble on a regular basis. Her holster, wrapped around her waist when he found her, hung on one of the wooden pegs by the door, next to his and Tara's. At Marjorie's fourteenth year, she would receive one, too. That peg currently held his daughter's bonnet. She had tied the strings together and hung them over the hook, so the bonnet acted as a swing for the trimmings that she had collected from her forays yesterday. Curious, he stood up and walked to the pegs. Pinecones, feathers, scales, talons, a rabbit's tooth. What a day she had had out at the field.

Catching a whiff of his armpits, he decided that he needed to change his shirt. And he had to be out of the house early so he could meet with the banker. They had had the appointment for weeks and he wanted that piece of land that the old hotel had stood upon. Cracking the door open, he leaned his eye into the space. Grace still was asleep, or at least he thought Grace was in there. A huge bump centered on the bed. Mounds of blankets piled over it. Where had all of those come from? He realized then that he had awoken without any on him. Poor thing. Slowly opening the door, he tiptoed for the closet. Midway to his destination, he froze for a moment, checking for the rise and fall of her breaths. When he could not see it, he crept closer. Her hair was outside of a corner of the blanket. He peeled it back towards where the hair seemed to lead, and found her peaceful face. Holding his hand in front of her mouth and nose, he checked for life. She breathed calmly. As he moved his hand out from her respiratory path, he brushed a piece of hair off her chilly cheek.

He grabbed a shirt from his closet and creeped stealthily towards the hallway. Pausing to close the door behind him, he felt a tap on his shoulder and nearly jumped out of his skin. Tara stood already dressed with a shitass grin on her face.

"Sweet Mother Maker!"

"Going somewhere?"

"I need to go to the bank about that plot of land that I want." He pulled down his braces and started unbuttoning his shirt.

"You're going to want to bathe. You were sweaty all night; I figured you wouldn't mind if I took your blankets for Grace. Her body was physically shaking from the cold." Tara shook her body in demonstration.

"Damn. Again?" She nodded. "Well she seemed to be doing alright when I was in there a moment ago."

"Probably because your sweaty seconds were on her." He rolled his eyes at her sisterly jab.

"Well, just let her sleep while I'm gone, I'll be back around midday."

"What am I supposed to do with her?" she whispered back.

He threw his hands in the air with exasperation. He needed a break from all the decision-making of the past few days. "You're a healer! Heal her!"

"Damn your logic, sir," Tara retorted, snorting at him. If she turned into a dragon in front of him, he would not be surprised. Alas, that power had left their family. Once, their family had been dragons. But as the dragons evolved, they began specializing in roles to help their herd. Eventually, some of the dragons evolved into holding close to human forms. The Fuentes family hailed from these beasts, which explained why they maintained their magical powers now.

Ignacio shook his head at his younger sister, laughter caught in the back of his throat. He made his way to the bathing room, where he stripped off his clothes. Standing in the metal vat, he poured the buckets of water into the bottom so it covered about two feet deep, halfway up his calves. Placing his hands in the water, he looked out the window at the sun. He inhaled, exhaled and on the next inhale, he pulled the energy. The water began to bubble, warming from the energy that was surging through it.

Removing his hands from the boiling water, he reached for the cloth before cleaning himself off. He hadn't realized that he had several scratches from wrestling the dust devil earlier that week. Grabbing the lavender scented lye soap, he lathered up the cloth and rubbed it over his hairy chest. The suds made tiny bubbles between the follicles; they did the same on his stubble as he washed his face. With his eyes closed, he reached for the pitcher that sat at the corner of the counter next to the tub. Instead of the glass water vase, his hand found a smooth, hard object. He dropped his opposite hand to the water, washing the soap off of his face. Opening his amber eyes, he found that he was looking at a chain with a pendant of the Maker's Mark. A tiny emerald sat in the middle of the thorny rose, symbolizing that one's heart is more important than appearances. Grace must have left this chain here from the night before.

Thinking about Grace in her nightgown last night had his hand finding his cock. Leaning against the wall with his other hand holding the chain, he immediately hardened. Moving his hand along his length, he thought about how soft her skin was to touch. Kissing her had been a complete accident; he was anything but a liar. But was she lying when she had said she liked it? Picking up his speed, he imagined that he had laid her down with himself on top of her and kissed her soft lips. The way her soft thigh would feel as he pushed her nightgown to her hips. He had felt her firm breasts pressed against him as he had carried her to his bed. Would she gasp when he licked her dark circle? Or would she moan when he took her nipple between his teeth? Or would it be vice versa? His damp shower hands mimicked the wetness of her sex. He pictured slipping his cock into her tunnel and feeling the tightness squeeze around him. His hips rocked as he pictured her gasping and hanging onto his hips as his palm held her hips into his. Each time he would take her deeper and deeper before she would finally call out his name to the ceiling. And that was his undoing. Panting in the bathroom, he cleaned himself off again. That bankers' meeting would be a piece of cake now that he had gotten her out of his system.

When he left the bathroom, he almost smacked into Grace. She was groggy, eyes half open.

"Morning," she muttered, taking in the scenery. "I could get used to this wake up call."

"Hi," he said, blushing and pushing past her to his room. How odd of him, considering most men would have had some-thing to say in reply to her. She went into the bathroom. The bathwater still remained, with some floaters in it.

"Don't worry. I drained your come water so your daughter doesn't think it's leftover soap when she wakes up." She told him when she had returned from relieving herself.

Naz had finished changing in his room by then. His eyes bugged out of his head. How had he forgotten? Furthermore, how could such a lady as herself speak to him like that? Maybe she was not as much of a lady as he had started considering her to be. He kept needing to remind himself of the image of her as he had found her: in her hat, and torn dress, holster on her thigh, gun in her hand, tucked behind Jeb. Feisty ladies he could handle; ladies who did not give a fuck were a different breed.

He caught a glimpse of her thigh as she climbed into bed, pulling all the blankets up again; he could feel himself growing hard at his thoughts from the bathroom five minutes earlier. "It was phlegm," he told her.

"Yeah, from your cock," she retorted with laughter. He rolled his eyes at her; she raised her eyebrows at him.

"How are you feeling?" He changed the subject.

"I was able to sleep without shivering."

"It should get better soon. Tara will check in on you periodically. I'm leaving for the day. Marjorie is asleep, but I'm sure she'll be up and willing to have a playmate. We'll assess your recovery at the end of the day." He threw on his hat, brushing the tip and nodded goodbye to her.

The room was tastefully decorated. Her mother had the same wallpaper in her sitting room: navy blue with hand painted green vines in parallel. She would often stare at the vines as she drank her tea and listened to the gossip about who was off the table for marrying. Damn society women really should have been debating why wallpaper and not good ol' lead paint. She herself knew why, but they should probably have run the experiment themselves. She would have loved to have seen the results.

Espe had always told Ignacio what to do, how to command the house. In her absence, he had come into his own as a stronger decision maker in the family. He and Tara had found a good rhythm; most of the decisions were made by both he and Tara, now, after pooling both of their knowledge and ideas. Mutual respect. He had come to find safety and comfort in it. They would have to discuss what would become of Grace. But for now, the derelict hotel.

Striding up to the meadow, he called out to Agrippa. Damn that woman, he had forgotten his coffee. Perhaps the bankers would have some readily available, with a pastry. His stomach grumbled whenever he was nervous; right now was no different, even though he was confident in his strategy. Jumping on Agrippa's tail and running up his back, he sat on his father's old saddle. Whistling ahead, he held on to the pommels on the saddle. Looking at the house, he could see Grace watching him through his front bedroom window. He tipped his hat at her, before moving Agrippa to fly away; she nodded in return, hugging the quilt around her. He turned Agrippa towards the southwest, the image firmly cemented in his mind. Her eyes sparkled like jewels in the sunlight. As he set about considering how to avoid being blinded by their luster, he overlooked how they reflected a growing brightness inside of him.

TWENTY-FOUR

Blue had always been his favorite color. Bright blue skies that enveloped him over the land. Crisp blue brooks that promised cool respite. Baby blues that smiled with the sunshine of unending love.

And a new blue that taunted him with the sweet adventure of becoming lost in the unknown only to learn a fascinating new place.

Those blues met his browns as he entered the kitchen.

"Would you show me your lands?" The owner asked him as she daintily ate her chili at the table.

"It would be my pleasure, Grace. When would you like to go?"

She stood up, and brought her bowl to the sink. "Now," she declared as she smacked her lips at him playfully. "I haven't gotten colder, and I don't want to waste another day on the couch!"

He walked out the door and motioned with his head towards the outside. "Well, if you get cold, the dragons can light a fire under that ass of yours." She laughed at his spirited response.

She followed him to the front of the house and off the crisp white porch. Grace had not been outside in days. The sun shone strongly and reflected off the whiteness of her skin. Naz rolled up his shirt sleeves to his elbows and jammed his hands into his pockets. He walked as though he were going on a Sunday stroll, whistling a lively tune in G major that she could not place.

She scurried to catch up with his long steps. When he caught her out of breath, he slowed his pace. "Sorry, I'm not much of a tour guide, but I will happily show you the area." Perhaps he should have offered her his arm, though she very much seemed like the type of woman to ignore it.

"Just the dragon lands."

He leaned over to her and in the best magical storyteller voice that he could muster, he uttered, "All the lands are dragon lands."

And with that, they reached a high point overlooking grazing lands below. They had hiked up a large hill, not quite a mountain. Below, as far as she could see, for miles and miles, dragons lazed about in the sunshine. Some napped. Some flapped their wings. Different colors, different sizes, different textures. The dragons sprawled in a motley grouping of colors. She had never seen anything so beautiful in her life.

"I cannot believe that you have so many that want to be here. There must be hundreds."

"More like thousands." He smiled as her already large eyes grew bigger. "They like it here. They have plenty of room. The weather can always be made amenable. If they want to leave, they can leave. We're caretakers, not masters. Always remember rule number one: no one is ever truly the master of a dragon. But most of all, we have peace."

"What do you mean made amenable?"

"Don't worry about it," he tried to adjust for his mistake. Most people would have just let it go. Grace, he was learning, was not most people.

She cast him a sharp look and threw her hands on her hips. "I'll decide where my anxiety stops and starts, thank you very much. Now, what do you mean?"

"As descendants of the dragons and as their caretakers, my family has the ability to care for the weather surrounding these creatures. So we can adjust the environment accordingly." He changed the topic quickly, which did not go unnoticed by Grace. "Marjorie told me that she noticed when she was gathering feathers for the understuffed pillows that I apologize for, that the adult dragons were having trouble staying together. They should be getting ready to protect Newa and her egg during the hatching in the next twenty-four hours, so it looks like they might need to be helped along a little bit. Do you want to help me herd them?"

"Absolutely I do!" she exclaimed with excitement, letting the topic change go.

He grinned in response, "Just follow my lead." He nodded to her right, and an orange dragon with a toothy grin drunkenly stumbled to her.

"Hey there!" she greeted him. "I'm hoping you fly better than you walk, big guy."

"Grace meet Yokel. Yokel meet Grace." Naz introduced the two.

The dragon waved his head in swirls before bowing down. Grabbing his horns, she hoisted her legs upward then pulled the rest of her body behind, turning midair. She was on his head holding onto the horn. A bigger dragon with a more noble bearing approached Naz. With great agility, Naz climbed aboard the bare back of the dragon that he had called Agrippa. While the saddle functioned well, he preferred to ride with nothing between his body and that of the dragon. He then guided Agrippa closer to her and handed her what appeared to be a dragon horn with holes on either end.

Grace held it up to her eye and looked through it at Naz. "Ahoy, Captain Ahab!"

"Blow," he instructed her through his chuckling at her play. He demonstrated first by placing a second dragon horn into his mouth and exhaling. The instrument emitted a soft wind noise. Several sleeping dragons woke up and turned to him with half open eyes. Grace emulated the action through her horn and the dragons looked at her as her goofy orange flew by. Her prediction proved correct–his wings handled the air with a certain grace that his legs lacked on the land.

Slowly, the creatures began standing up to follow the two dragons with Naz at the front and Grace bringing up the rear. They stretched their wings out, miraculously not hitting any of the ones next to each other. They would adjust their height or distance from one another as if instinct to look out for one another and respect each other's autonomy. And so they soared over the green oasis in the middle of the desert, made possible only by the "amenable" weather.

A sparkling brook in the middle of the land called out to them. They landed at midday, hoping to slake their thirst. Naz jumped off his ride, expecting to be ready ahead of her so he could help her off her dragon. Even if she did not need help, his momma taught him to offer. She, however, slid off the rear way, giving the orange's posterior a pat as she landed on her feet and strode away. Taking his hat off his head, he reached into the brook and doused his face with water. He was so warm from the flight. He cupped his hands and pulled some water up to his mouth, the sweet coolness reminding him of Grace's touch. He wondered if her mouth would be as cool on his. One more sip, and as he wiped off his mouth with his forearm, cool water poured over his head, drenching him.

A melodious laugh came from behind him. And he stood up, whirling around to find Grace, doubled over with the hilarity of the prank she had just pulled. Moving stealthily he took advantage of her momentary weakness. As she was already crouched down, he bent over and picked her up, and tossed her into the brook. The surprised look on her face made him laugh so hard that she pulled him in with her. After wiping the tears of laughter from their eyes, they sat in the brook in peace.

Various dragons came by to drink from the brook. One

caressed Grace's hair, nuzzling her neck. She returned the affection by patting its nose, marveling at its friendliness. It snorted at Naz, starting to pull her out by biting the waist of her clothes. Naz quickly stood up, telling the dragon to move away, before he explained to Grace the dragon's desire to keep her as a jewel. They laid next to the brook, on their sides, just chatting about the different dragons that passed. And being quiet together. The sun smiled upon them, warming them and drying their clothes. Agrippa came by and he flew them back up to the manor house. Grace held onto Naz's waist, in no place but the air current. His warm back kept her front and cheek warm in the coolness of the higher altitude. His steady breathing echoed throughout his chest. He did not seem to mind that she held on tightly to him. Though she hardly knew him, his stable presence gave off an air of trustworthiness.

"Make no mistake, I am not ordering you to stay. You can do whatever you want. Say the word and I'll help you find a dragon to leave upon. But I want to help you. Jeb would want me to, too."

Grace looked straight into his brown eyes. Gold flecks radiated from the irises as rays from the sun.

"I want you to help me, please."

He nodded in response. They walked side-by-side into the house, their fingers brushing. Neither one of them put distance between them to stop the sensation from occurring. Naz wanted more, but he did not want to push this flitting butterfly away. With time, maybe she would warm enough to him.

Grace's fingers heated with the sensation of his nearness, like the spark of a flame. And she wondered to herself if she should consider fanning that fire.

That night, Grace dreamed of flying and dragons of fire. They screamed guttural sounds that she had never heard before. A banging on the bedroom door interrupted the flames that had approached where she stood watching, and she opened her eyes. Ignacio barged in, a wide smile on his face and excitement in the air.

"Newa's giving birth!" He chucked her boots from the corner at her where she sat up in bed. Shoving her bare feet into them, she threw back the covers haphazardly. Naz noticed that her nightgown had ridden all the way to the tops of her thighs, exposing the lace underwear that she wore.

She jumped out of bed and landed with both feet on the ground. She ran past him, shouting, "Come on!" as she grabbed his hand. He laughed loudly at her exuberance. She had speed, even in her boots. Having grown up riding dragons all his life, Naz was able to keep up with her. She pulled his panting and laughing self along with her. They reached the meadow, where at least fifty dragons had made a circle. Tara stood as a part of the circle next to a gray dragon that Grace did not recognize. Perched on Tara's hip, Marjorie stroked his wing softly absent-mindedly as she stared ahead at the middle of the circle where the bronze-hued Newa was sitting on an egg, barely visible beneath her body. Agrippa stood in front of her, staring into her eyes.

"He is the alpha of the group but he doesn't mate with just anyone," Naz explained as they approached the circle. "And this is the first dragon from the two of them."

"Why Newa?" Grace looked at the calm, docile female.

"Ah, that's a question only for Agrippa, and I doubt he'd give away what makes his heart so vulnerable to her. If other dragons knew the weakness, they would exploit it. But here, between the two of them, everyone can see that they are inseparable."

"How do you know this?" His knowledge extended much further than just "how to manage a ranch." Grace wanted to dive inside his mind and see what he saw, so different from the world that she knew.

"My dad told me that Jeb's parents were like that. He didn't see it all the time, but I remember that he would comment on their pairing every so often at the dinner table."

"And what happens if one of them dies?"

"Grief. Life goes on. Maybe they find another partner. They're not much different from you and me." Naz gave her a bittersweet smile–the two of them had known far enough grief for their combined seventy years on the continent.

The dragons began to make a huffing chant in their circle. Naz called for Marjorie, who hopped down from Tara's embrace and ran over to her father. He picked her up to hold her in his arms. Grace could hear his whispering to her as the girl stared ahead in fascination.

Grace had never grown up with dragons. City life held no room for them. She had overheard men talking about them in her father's study where she would sit on the stairs and listen to the stories of their travels and smell the delicious cigars whose smoke wound up to her hiding location. To these men, dragons were a commodity and second-class citizens of a country that had plenty of room for both humans and dragons. But Naz revered them, speaking of their traditions in awe and understanding. Descended from the dragons, indeed.

The four humans stood outside of the giant dragon circle. Newa and Agrippa moved backwards to join the perimeter. Grace could see the egg's shaking. She realized in her mesmerization that she stood next to Yokel, who tilted a wing downward blocking her from her access to the center of the circle so she could almost not see. Beside her, another dragon had done the same for Naz. Grace moved her body trying to better see around the wing.

With that, the fire erupted. Fifty dragons blew into the middle of the circle at the egg, lighting the black scaled shell into a sunrise orange. Like the egg was the center of the sun, and the lines of fire the rays radiating from it. She hid back behind Yokel's wing that could withstand the heat. She worried her hair would go up in flame if he moved his wing away from her. But, as wacky as that dragon was, he was steadfast when it mattered. Next to her, she saw Marjorie burying her head into Naz's neck, seeking shelter from the intensity of the situation. Naz had his hand on her hair, caressing her. His lips moved in quiet calming reassurances, but his brown eyes, more gold than normal, latched on to those of Grace. He smiled, his face alight with the excitement of the moment. The smile assuaged any fears or anxieties she had about the situation, and she settled into the comfort of the birth.

CRACK!

The sound echoed across the meadow. The heat stopped.

Silence.

Grace's heartbeat throbbed in her ears.

Agrippa nudged the wing away from Yokel, snorting at him and nodding his head. Yokel moved his wing away from Grace, and she made eye contact with the baby. Agrippa pushed her forward towards it. His fiery orange eyes blinked from her to the baby. Naz nodded at her, not saying a word, and Marjorie smiled at her dad. Why did everyone know what was occurring but her? But she was not one to turn down a new experience, and having just had the protection of one of the herd, she did not even consider that anything in the situation would harm her.

Though her feet were booted, the warmth of the land radiated upward, a wave of calm through her body, up to her chest where it cozily nestled. Each sure step increased her warmth. The baby rested on its back and stared at the sky, decorated with stars of all the dragons that had arrived before so it could be born there that day. She reached out for the maroon-purple baby, intending to stroke its bronze burnished scales; however her heart overtook her, urging her to pick it up. The smooth skin that had not yet acquired bumps brushed her arm. The horns down its back were like raised hills on a rolling prairie, not yet deadly but enough to mark its individuality. The eyelids lifted, revealing Agrippa's fiery eyes that quickly cooled to the bright blue of Grace's eyes. Grace's blues stared back at them.

Naz walked over and with one look, declared the dragon a girl. How he knew this, Grace had no idea. She chalked it up to his being a dragon master and mentally noted to ask him later. Having him near pulled her from the shared moment of holding the new life. Tears started dripping from her eyes. The tears washed out of her body as her heart thawed. A new dragon. May this new dragon have all the spirit of her old friend. How fitting that she should be holding a baby opening its eyes for the first time when not that long again she had held a dragon closing its eyes for the last time.

An immediate calm washed over her as she watched the dragon take its first breaths. Should she wrap it in something? She held it in her nightgown, sitting cross legged so it made a cradle. Agrippa walked forward and the dragons filled in the hole that his absence left in the circle. He strutted over to where Grace cradled the offspring. Bending over the baby's face, he licked its brow.

Her heart burst like a dam overflowing. The love that this father had for his daughter made her question if her father had ever felt this way. And giving him the benefit of the doubt, she forgave her own in her mind. Because how could one hold such a tiny package full of hope and wonder and not feel a sense of pride and accomplishment?

"You have a beautiful daughter. May she be headstrong, independent, and clever. May you worry more about the people that cross paths with her rather than whom she crosses paths with. May you cherish her, and when the time comes, let her fly." Tears streamed down her face. She held the dragonette up to Agrippa, whom she had deduced was her father. He nuzzled the babe back towards her. Not understanding, she looked at Tara and Naz, also lacking dry eyes.

"He wants you to name her," Naz supplied.

What a privilege she did not deserve. What an absolute honor.

"Honor." The name escaped from her mouth before she had a chance to protest. "We'll call her Honor, for she has honored all of us with her presence. Plus, it has been an absolute honor participating in this gorgeous ceremony of life with you." The tiny dragon coughed and a puff of smoke emitted from her mouth.

Agrippa nodded his head, and reached out his large claw. Grace placed the baby into his palm, and then she backed up to stand beside Tara and Naz. She put her head on Tara's shoulder.

"It seems the dragons have decided that it was time for you to heal," Tara wisely remarked, before she patted Grace's back and moved to the dragon family to inspect the new child. Grace and Naz continued standing side by side, staring at the dragon family of three. Both wanted to look at the other but neither wanted their eyes to ask questions that could not be answered.

Finally, Naz stuck his hand out to the side, hoping to catch onto Grace's fingers. He had been regretting not holding her hand earlier that day when he had the chance. So, he slipped his hand into hers as they watched the new family. His hand brought her all of the sensations from the afternoon. And in that moment, she decided that yes, she wanted to fan the fire. She squeezed it in an embrace. and Naz looked at her with surprised eyes. He did not want to move, lest he lose her from this shared instant, so significant in their timeline. Marjorie's snore from Naz's shoulder interrupted the moment.

"Let's get this little dragon to the house," Naz said in a bittersweet tone. Grace and Naz turned from the dragon gathering, back in the direction of the house. Tara caught up to their location, not far due to the slow pace from carrying Marjorie. Together, the three walked to the house, which seemed much further from the meadow now that the adrenaline rush was not fueling their sprint. Tara seemed depleted of energy from caring for Newa. Outside the front door, she kicked off her shoes. Despite the sweat covering her, she beelined for her bedroom upstairs, closing the door behind her without muttering a good night.

With his daughter in his arms, Naz trudged upstairs behind his sister. Grace heard the floor creaking overhead where she assumed Marjorie's room was. Grace had forgotten to take her boots off though she watched Tara do it. Grace walked into the bathroom and sat on the latrine. She pulled her slimy boots off her feet, now swollen from the heat. Shedding her nightgown down to her lacies, she proceeded to pump water into the vat. It was so cold that she wondered if she could get a bucket and warm it over a fire. Thinking everyone was upstairs, she stepped outside the bathroom, holding only the empty glass pitchers across her chest. She clinked them together, saying "Cheers, Boris! Cheers, Amos!" and proceeded to entertain herself with a conversation as if each arm's pitcher was the arm of a sad sack sitting at the bar.

She started a fire on the stove with the matches that she found and proceeded to put the pitchers on them. Waiting for them to boil, she carried on with her conversation.

"Well Boris, we've had quite a day, haven't we?"

"All's well under the sun, Amos, all's well."

"Maybe we should clink our glasses to the new baby that arrived, eh Boris?"

"Oh, I suppose one excuse is just as good as another, Amos," she said.

"Chug chug chug, boys."

Once the water boiled, she flung the discarded dish towel from the counter onto the handles. She blew out the flames and picked the handles up, using the dish towel so she would not burn. Turning to carry the pitchers to the bathroom, she nearly dropped them. Ignacio stood in the doorway, head cocked to the side and hand over his mouth containing his amused grin.

"You know, it's only water, so I can still see through those pitchers," he broke the silence.

"Oh, well then good you can hold these while I boil more." She held out the pitchers so she was standing in her underwear only, breasts bare to the world.

"Your nipples are cold," Naz pointed out.

"No shit, my entire body is cold ALL THE TIME. Have you not listened to anything I have told you? Now let me find a pot so I can boil more, especially if you're going to clean off." She started rustling through cabinets for a metal pot. When she found one, she went towards the bathroom to fill it up with the cold water. Naz had not moved. He grabbed her wrist as she passed.

"Just stop. Come with me." He put the pitchers on the kitchen table, before he removed the pot from her hands and placed it alongside it. The water might stain the wood, but plenty of other things had stained it already through Marjorie's toddlerhood. Berries and animal gristle and red meats and chickens. Oh, the chickens.

He took her hand and led her into the bathroom. He directed her to sit in the freezing water as he pumped more, telling her to trust him. She stared him down, watching his muscles pulse as he raised and pushed the lever. Still in her white lacies, she wished she had thought to take them off. Instead, there she sat. Perfectly soaked in her underwear and freezing. After he had sufficiently filled the tub, he stripped out of his clothes, save his underwear, and sat down. The water raised higher on both of them. Their feet tucked to the sides of the other person.

"You're right. This is so fucking cold." He raised one corner of his mouth in a half smile. "Can I trust you?"

"I'm pretty sure I just proved how trustworthy I am by shoving my thermal deficient body into a tub of freezing water where I have waited while a man I met a few days ago climbed into it with me. Meanwhile, my fingers are turning purple and I'm starting to wonder why I went along with this cockeyed scheme."

"Patience."

"Is a virtue that I have not. Let's go, Mr. Promises."

Snickering, he submerged his hands into the water. The warmth seemed to radiate out of his hands and the water bubbled immediately around them. In a matter of seconds, the warmth had spread to the water at her torso level. Incredulous, she moved her eyes from his closed eyes to his open hands. The temperature of the water rose, eventually becoming so warm she started to relax into it. When he finally took his hands out, he ran them over his face and also sank back.

Tilting her head to the side, she told him, "Your way was definitely easier than mine."

He smiled, tired after expending his energy store. He would have to pull from the sunny day tomorrow.

"I'm glad. And I'm glad you're here."

"Did you ever expect that you would be where you are today?" She studied the ceiling, expecting to find cracks in it that she could analyze. Instead, she found smooth plaster so she looked over at him. Ignacio was staring at the tiles on the floor, searching for cracks that he would need to fix; finding none, he looked at her.

"No, I never imagined that I would be in a bath with a beautiful woman, just shooting the shit at midnight while she took a bath. But I'm not hating it." He could not pull his face from hers, so full of life. He knew that if he let his eyes drift, his body would betray how much he wanted this woman.

"Well, I'd love to say that I never expected to be in a bathroom with a man, but I've definitely had those days."

"Ah, did you enjoy it?" He wasn't repulsed by her admission that she had lived through some unsheltered moments in her life. Instead, he was curious.

"Sometimes. Mostly I enjoyed the warmth that I could temporarily feel, like in this bath."

"Well, I'm happy to warm a bath for you whenever you want," he offered like it was no big deal.

"You don't have to use your energy on me," she said. His selflessness enveloped her so easily. She wondered if she ever did enough for him. She did not want to be a chore to him, Mother knew he had enough of those.

"The sun always shines in the morning," Naz shrugged. He was required to give so much of his energy to this house and his family that it felt strange to want to give it away so freely.

Grace grabbed his foot that was next to her and started rubbing it. The callouses on the pads could use an emery board, but she did not have any around. As she pressed her thumbs into the middle of his foot, his face winced.

"Should I stop?" She asked, her voice laced with concern. After all, she had not asked him if this was alright before she started.

"Good Granny, no," he moaned, sinking further into the bath. As she stroked his foot, rubbing out knots, his face began to slowly melt into relaxation. The lines on his forehead smoothed. Once his breathing had calmed, she moved on to the opposite foot.

"Fuck, I didn't expect that!" He jolted upwards with her push at the first knot in the new foot.

"It'll smooth down in a bit, just hold on," Grace reassured him.

She shifted lower into the bath, getting her shoulders under and resting his foot on the crack between her armpit and her shoulder. They sat quietly, neither needing to fill the space with words. But if either had words, those were left unsaid. Naz's eyes were closed, relishing the massage. He thought about everyone; rarely did someone ever care to think about him.

"Well, I think the water has about run out of warmth," Grace remarked while returning his foot to the water. His eyes opened and he started to rewarm the water; but Grace stopped him, telling him to conserve what he had. They stood up and he handed her a towel from the rack. Normally, quite the gentleman, he should have averted his eyes. But he could not stop looking at her soft rosy body, pruned from the bath. She noticed his hungry look. Rather than facing the thought of what that look could mean for the two of them, she peeled off her underwear and threw it at him. His spit audibly traveled down his throat in a gulp. His eyes went back to hers and she gave him a playful look, wrapping herself into the towel. This woman never bored him.

Shaking his head, he pulled another towel from the rack and wrapped it around his waist. He bent over, reaching around her calves with his hand to pull the plug from the basin. He restrained himself from running his hand up her calf, to her knee, to her thigh, to where he could feel the smoothest parts of her body. If he moved a step closer to her, he could breathe on her sensitive bits through the towel. In that moment, Grace looked down at him, her smile fading to an intense stare. Oh, but if he would only move his hand up her calf, she would do the rest!

Naz stood up and stepped out of the tub first, then held out his hand for her to hold onto as she stepped out. She made her way to the door. As Naz walked out of the bathroom though, he stumbled, catching his foot on an uneven threshold. Wrapped in her towel, she quickly moved to help him, not quite catching him, but deterring him from hurting himself anymore.

"I'm spent," he confessed. "I guess the day took more energy out of me than I thought. I'm sorry."

Looking him dead straight in the eyes, noticing they were dark and lacking the amber glow, she said, "You never need to apologize for everything you do, nor for being selfless enough to give up your powers for others. You especially need never apologize to me, okay?" He nodded. "Now, let's get you to bed."

With his arm around her shoulders, her face was next to his chest of curly dark hair. It tickled her nose as she guided him into the bedroom. His strength astounded her, but if she thought too much about it, she would go weak at her own knees. Depositing him on the bed, she left him to change his undergarments. She returned with their clothes from the bathroom floor. She threw them into a pile in the empty corner.

"They go in the basket," Naz instructed her.

"Great, you can put them there tomorrow," she ignored his passive aggressive instruction. Noticing his wet towel on the ground, she picked it up and she threw that item into another corner of the room with a smirk on her face. He sat only in his underwear on the bed, he could hear her swallow loudly as he saw her trying not to look at the outline of him. She helped him get into bed. He burrowed into it to get comfortable, almost immediately falling asleep. Not wanting to bother him anymore, she grabbed one of his button downs from the closet and threw it on to sleep in. She figured that she would not want to pester him with where she would sleep that night; he should not feel bad about sleeping in his own bed. She curled up into the wingback armchair in the corner with the three blankets that she took off the chest at the foot of the bed. Knowing that he could probably heat his bed up himself, she doubted that he needed any of the blankets that she pulled over his shoulders; but she wasn't cold-hearted enough to deny him any blankets.

Naz could hear her rustling around, but he was too tired to figure out what she needed. She could handle herself.

He drifted off to sleep only to be awakened in the middle of the night by a nightmare of Jebediah's screaming for him across a canyon that he could not cross. He stared at the ceiling, shaking it off, before he heard the chair vibrating on the floor. Looking to the corner, he could see Grace's body physically twitching with chills. Enough of this act. He knew from her speech and her bearing that she had been raised in the east, probably in a life not much different from that of his. If they had known each other out east, would their mothers have tried to set them up for marriage? He stood up, moving the covers off of him, or what was remaining after he had kicked them all off. His bedding was mainly decorative. But it wouldn't be that night. With moonlight bouncing off his pecs, he walked the three steps to the chair. The same moonlight danced across her skin, casting shadows under her eyes from her eyelashes. Her skin felt like ice as he brushed her hair out of her face. Upon scooping her and the blankets up, she once again melted into him as she had the other night when he had brought her home with him. Walking to his side of the bed, he placed her in the center of it. He crawled in beside her, careful to leave a bit of space between them. He could maintain his distance, but his warmth might help her sleep. He pulled the blankets over her and with the last of his energy for the night, he let the last of his heat escape his skin. He passed out, waiting for the sun to re-energize him.

Grace awoke the next morning to this golden skinned god next to her. Oh wait, that was Ignacio. The sun bounced over his short, thick black hair, highlighting the red undertones. She woke so warm, and she burrowed deeper into the bed away from the edge. As she did so, she came up next to the furnace of his body. She was about to move out of the way, when his arm flung over her waist, keeping her near him and the blankets tightly around him.

"Sleep, we're safe and warm. If I don't hear danger, you will, and the dragons will hear it first." The open shutters shone upon his face and he inhaled deeply, pulling in the solar rays. He used a little bit on the small of her back, where she oddly was so cold next to him. She melted into him, relaxing, and he could hear her quiet calm breaths. He had not felt this at peace in a long time. He lay in bed thinking of what he was going to do that day, meetings to be had, rides to be taken. He found himself remembering the exhilarating feel of riding on a dragon again. Long ago, he had felt that way when he was first learning to ride and caretake. Now, he was so used to riding that it was like breathing. Involuntary and necessary. Grace reminded him that he could actually have fun and connect with the creatures. How could a girl this used to the ways of the world be this trusting of him? He supposed that he had given her no reason to distrust him, nor would he. . But here she was, curled up in his arms, completely defenseless, about to be taken down by some internal cold, and she hadn't known him that long. He drifted off to sleep, pondering thoughts of this mysterious woman.

And that's how Marjorie found them. She carried in her arms the baby dragon, who had tears streaming down her cheeks. The baby had been crying for an hour before Marjorie told its parents that she had an idea. So then she burst into her father's room without knocking. Pulling back the covers off Grace, she tucked the dragon under her arm. The baby sighed and immediately quieted.

Grace awoke to the smell of burning. The sheet in front of her was on fire and a baby dragon was sleeping within it. Thinking quickly, she tried to pull the cold from her back. It was harder to get to the power than normal. Sitting up, she focused on the cold within her, and willed it through her hands which she put directly onto the fire. Smoke emitted from the dragon's nostrils. The poor thing was fire snoring, no wonder he liked her cold. She was cooling him off. Though at this point, she performed it poorly, as she felt sufficiently heated through. Flopping back down after that wakeup call, she realized that she had slept almost the full night through. The sun shone high in the sky.

"Good morning," she told Naz who had stirred with the commotion of the fire in the sheets. He yawned, putting his hands behind his head.

"Damn, I haven't slept like that in ages," he told her.

"Me either. We must have really needed it after this week," she surmised.

"Do I smell burning?"

"Marjorie must have brought Honor in while we were sleeping," she explained, motioning with her head to the dragon beside her.

"Oh no, what am I going to tell her?" He did not need Marjorie having a fit about her dead mother.

"Nothing. Why do you have to explain yourself to anyone? It's not as though I was naked or anything."

He could feel his morning wood hardening against his leg. "Sadly."

"As tempting as you are, Mr. Fuentes, I have not slept naked since before I was enchanted."

"I'll just have to catch you trying to heat your water for a bath, again, then."

Grace raised her eyebrow playfully. "Oh, like what you saw?"

"The puppet pitcher show was incredible and I'd like to see the sequel." He winked and turned back over. "I need another hour. Take that creature out with you."

TWENTY-FIVE

Pulling the blanket off the bed with her, Grace let it drag behind her as she cradled the sleeping baby. Honor was so trusting lying there in Grace's arms. Not to mention warm. Grace could feel the warmth with every exhale. She sat on the rocking chair on the front porch and covered the baby and her bare legs with the quilt. Gazing down into her arms, she wondered if Slewja had looked this peaceful this young. Had he been born here? Did he learn his gentlemanly ways from Ignacio?

How she missed her friend! This little one in her arms was no substitute for him. Slewja had always seen her as a person needing help, never a damsel in distress. Or so she liked to believe. She would never be able to ask him what compelled him to help her that fateful day. A tear slid down her cheek, and she stuck her tongue out to the side so she could catch it before it fell on Honor and wake her up. So, she sat rocking and remembering. Honor nuzzled her head into her chest over her heart; a deluge of cold tears fell on her warm face. Warmth washed over her to her toes in a way that it had not since before she had frozen Slewja's heart.

As she sat lost in her daydream, Marjorie came running up. Grace held her finger over her lips in the universal sign for "shh the baby is sleeping."

"Oh good, you got her to sleep. She was screaming like a banshee," Marjorie said in her best imitation of a whisper.

"I did! Whatever made you think to bring her into the bedroom?"

"You've been sleeping there, and she seemed to like you. I couldn't find Tara, so I thought maybe you could try something to get her to stop screaming. If you couldn't calm her, then you and Dad would figure out something else to do."

Marjorie had not given two thoughts to her dad being in bed with a woman that was not her mom. Everything had happened fast around there since Grace's arrival. She was excited to have this rambunctious woman there at the house with her. She wanted to know everything Grace thought and how she could survive out in the wild without a man.

Grace was not too sure if she should press Marjorie on her feelings. She opted with taking the easy way out and letting the situation unfold on its own. If the girl had a problem, she could say something about it.

"Why are you crying?" Marjorie brought the blanket that had trailed on the ground up to Grace's eyes.

"Hmm. I suppose, the last few hours have been cathartic."

"Ew, I hear those hurt! Are you okay?"

"Catharses are cleansing. They are processes of relief."

"Oh, they're not those things that go inside where you pee?"

Grace smiled gently. "No, Marjorie. Those are catheters." She looked into the wide, not yet world-weary eyes, and continued, "I have felt healing inside my soul since I experienced Honor's birth. Holding her reminds me of all the good and innocence of bringing a baby into this world, rather than the grief of taking a life from the world."

Marjorie studied Grace for a quiet moment, contemplating whether she would share her thoughts with this woman. But perhaps, as the woman had seen quite a lot, she might understand.

"My momma's life left this world." The girl's hand reached

out to rub the dragon's wing that had pulled over the sleeping face.

"How very alone you must have felt," Grace empathized.

"How do I make the hurt in my heart feel better?"

"You find the good moments. You save those every day so you have a great book of happy stories to share with her when you meet her again on the staircases." Marjorie nodded her head, internalizing Grace's advice. The light blue eyes stared back at the dark, sharing the moment of life that lay between them.

In the heat of the sun, Grace napped soundly. How she could still sleep after all of last night, she had no idea. It had been so long since she had felt safe enough to just relax, though. And here, even out in the open on the land, she knew that nothing was coming up to get her. If it had been a problem, Naz would not have let his own daughter go running amok around the place. Honor's stirring woke her. She had no idea what to feed baby dragons. Baby chickens? Standing up, she realized she was still in Naz's shirt that she had borrowed. In the daylight, the baby blue tones stood out. She bet that it would bring out the red undertones in his hair. The blanket hit the floor. Holding Honor, she grappled with the door, using her hip and her elbow in some weird fashion to prop it open enough to wedge her body through it. She threw her pair of jeans on with the shirt the quickest she had ever changed after tossing Honor on the bed. The ceiling floorboards creaked above her and she guessed that Naz was finally working. Or at least pacing while he thought about working.

Upstairs, Naz was pacing, as Grace had guessed, but only because he was thinking about her. Sleeping next to her had been exhilarating, calming, a giant paradox. Such a calm confident creature so full of life. She was always cold, but seemed to not be cold hearted at all, judging by the way that she helped him to bed or cuddled with the dragon. Running yet here she was, stopped. He looked out the window, and could see her walking with purpose, hair blowing around her towards the grounds where the baby had been born yesterday. Was she scared of nothing?

And what had she meant about forgetting? She kept talking in her sleep that night, mumbling about the sickness and forgetting. Was she saying "forget me" or "fuck me?" She had been cold all night. He needed to find Tara.

She was out back, foot on the edge of a wash basin, using a stick taller than she was to stir a big pot of hazy white liquid. Her movements were slow and she was sweating in the afternoon heat.

"Is one of the dragons hurt?"

"Not that I know of, unless that's a trick question and you're coming here to tell me that one actually is hurt. It's soap."

"Has Grace told you about this cold sickness?" he asked his younger yet wiser sister.

"Mhmm, I've pieced some things together about it." Tara's patience helped where Naz was concerned. He often lived inside of a plan or idea for a little while before he presented it. Pushing him too fast frustrated him.

"Do you think it'll get here?" Tara swirled more and gnawed on her lip in thought.

"The wards should hold at the boundaries, shouldn't they?"

"I was down for a week after I put those up. They should hold for another four years in theory."

"You seem doubtful."

"I would doubt the sea if I hadn't touched it once myself." Tara laughed at the truth of the statement from her ever practical older brother. "Do you think you can heal her?" Naz asked her directly.

"My energy comes from the land. The land doesn't beat cold. Only fire destroys ice. It's going to have to be your energy. But I can definitely be involved."

❦

Later on, Tara threw a book down on the dinner table, where they sat waiting for the cook to clear their dishes. "I've been reading about different instances of this occurring, but not in my medgical books, my magic medical books, if you will. I needed to look through the dragon books. The manual states that if you are cold-hearted enough to kill a dragon, then your heart becomes that cold. Through an act of penance to the dragons, the curse can be lifted."

Grace gasped. Naz looked at her. "I froze Slewja's heart. I didn't tell you, but today, I was holding Honor and I had this catharsis."

"Which means a healing experience," Marjorie joined in.

"These cold tears poured out of my eyes when Honor slept on my chest."

"Through an act of penance, the curse can be lifted," Tara reread, pointing to the spot in her book to keep its place. "Otherwise, you have to penetrate the heart with physical heat."

"But if the act of penance warmed me slightly, why am I not better?"

"You need to get your back taken care of." She looked at the book with a twinkle in her eye, pointing to a passage, and read, "It says here that you need to put her on the source within her body, so her back, and insert that heat internally, Naz."

"Mother Maker," Naz rolled his eyes at her. "There are children here." He motioned towards Marjorie who listened intently to the conversation in case she could think of something to help her new friend. He refused to look at Grace; but if he had, he would have seen her blush for the first time in a decade.

"But really, because that is magic living within her, you'll need to pull it out, or put your energy in somehow." Tara pushed the book closer to Ignacio, who read the pages before and after. He took a sip of his red wine, sitting back in his chair. Marjorie started talking about how she helped Grace with Honor that afternoon, wanting to share a story from her day. Naz zoned out, mulling over the new information in an attempt to recall anything his parents might have taught him about the dragons over the years that could apply to the situation. Grace feigned attention to Marjorie, as she already had lived the story that afternoon. Instead, she tried to concentrate on the wine bottle label so as not to dwell on the prospect of Naz's magic needing to invade her. Tara listened to Marjorie, hoping for a clue to something they had missed.

Naz interrupted the silence.

"I know who Dimin is."

The room silenced and six eyes stared at him.

"Remember when Paps hired that overseer when we were little? I think I was ten because I was in my own room and you weren't sleeping with me." The two had slept together as kids for a while, mainly because Naz was always getting hurt, and Tara could heal him overnight. "I remember crawling out of bed because I heard voices downstairs yelling. Paps threw the middle-aged guy out by the scruff of his neck and told him he was cursed. I thought he meant that the guy was bad luck. But maybe what he'd meant was that he'd brought a curse upon himself."

"Dimin worked here. And what's worse: Dimin murdered a dragon."

Twenty-six

The next morning, Naz sat at his big wooden desk, opening letters of correspondence. His reading glasses perched on his nose, the glass refracted a rainbow onto whatever paper he was reading so he had to keep turning his head to move the rainbow. His study was upstairs, in the back of the house in the room that caught the most morning light. He had thought that Esperanza might turn this room into her sitting room, it seemed the happiest. She, however, had thought it best to have her sitting room be the first room of the house that people saw upon their arrival to call. He secretly surmised that Espe could have her morning coffee there while watching out the window and ensuring that everything was occurring as it should be.

Ignacio was the furthest thing from a cuckold. He just believed that every person had their own personality and ways of handling the world. He gave Esperanza the freedom to be who she needed to be, which is why he did not stop her from going off into the world on her own. When their marriage was set, he had admired Esperanza for her knowledge of how to run an estate. She understood that children were the key to helping maintain a future and purpose for what one did in this life. She did not falter when he told her of his family's importance to the area, and agreed with his purpose in life. Everything was for the dragons. Except Esperanza demonstrated her understanding in a way that did not reflect any side of compassion, kindness, or empathy. Had Ignacio known that she lacked these three traits, he would never have acquiesced to the deal that their parents had finagled for them.

Esperanza worked hard to further the dragons' needs; however, Naz never saw her out there with them. Everything to Espe was a duty, and nothing was a feeling.

Which is why every morning he started his day with a cup of coffee and a reading of the last puzzle she left him. A letter, written in someone else's hand, as so many final words were.

> *Dear Naz,*
> *I was not able to find new roaming lands. I am*
> *so cold, so cold. Send Jeb to warm me up. Tell our child*
> *I thought of her.*
> *Espe*

For one, she never acknowledged that they shared Marjorie. Whereas he devoted himself to the girl's upbringing, Esperanza had relinquished any tie to her once she had been delivered and the umbilical cord was cut. As far as Esperanza was concerned, her family duty was performed. If he wanted a male heir, that would come in time and they would have to discuss it first.

Also, her admission of defeat perplexed him. Never once in her life had she ceded to doing wrong or failing in her actions. Esperanza would have said that someone else had intercepted her plans. Thirdly, she ended the note with "Espe." While this was his name for her, she never acknowledged it or embraced it. She always ignored him when he would try to call her Espe in intimate moments between just the two of them.

Every morning he would read this letter and ponder what he had missed in their marriage. Was she acknowledging that she cared in her final moments? Despite last night's revelation about the perpetrator of the cold sickness that had claimed his wife, none of the new information shed a light upon this note's mystery.

"Where did you get that letter?" A voice sharply cut into his rumination routine. Grace, freshly clothed in a brown cotton dress that barely fit Tara but seemed to fit her perfectly, strode forward, arm outstretched, ready to grab the paper. But Ignacio had not held onto this scrap of his past just to let some fragment of his future take it away whenever it was decided by Mother Maker that he was ready. He held it out of her reach, like a five year old would hold a rattle from a baby. In doing so, he realized that this letter bore some importance to Grace.

"What is this to you?" he asked, standing and holding the note outstretched over his head in his left hand while his right hand maintained a distance between him and the feral Grace.

"That's my handwriting. I wrote it for someone."

"You wrote it for Espe?"

"I wrote it for Esperanza. She mentioned that she was sometimes called Espe, so I added that at the end so the letter would sound believable. I wanted her loved ones to move on with their lives, and not be left wondering if it was actually true what had happened to her since she hadn't written the letter."

"You... WROTE it?" He waved the paper in front of her face.

"Yes I did, and I would like to know how you obtained it."

Naz scrutinized the woman's face, which was the picture of comfort in the truth.

When he continued staring at her, she offered, "Would you like me to write a copy of it to prove it?"

He did. He quickly stood offering his leather chair to her. Though in a simple dress, she sat as if in her corset and hoop skirt awaiting lemonade to be brought to her. Not once did her spine touch the back of the chair, and he longed to put his hand on the small of her back in encouragement. Ignacio understood her words, but could not wrap his head around the full picture. He needed to see that her declaration was true.

Reading glasses returned to his nose, with his left hand leaning on the large desk, he stood to her left so he could watch her write each word that he dictated. Perfectly poised, as if she were writing a bread and butter note, her hand scripted out the letter. Standing so close, he could smell fresh grass and feel the calm stillness she emanated despite being always on the go. When she finished, he snatched the writing and held the papers up next to each other. Copies.

"How?" He asked incredulously, seeming to address the papers more than her.

"When Dimin arrived, people started getting sick. As his power took over the city, some people took a while. Some people were done rapidly. No rhyme nor reason could predict who would make it. For some reason, I never became sick. I volunteered every day at the hospital once my father informed me of the engagement. I kept hoping that I would become sick. Esperanza went quickly." She watched his eyes water.

"You must have loved her quite a lot," she added quietly.

"No," he said, "that's the funny part. We saw eye-to-eye on the duties of this place but we never quite had the passion that I wanted. Maybe one day it would have grown. She was not a bad person, we just complemented each other rather than complimented."

"Dimin's disease killed just as many strong people as weak. She would not have felt much going so quickly. Mainly cold and exhaustion. I could barely hear her whisper to write the words."

"She didn't mention Marjorie at all, did she?" Naz interrupted the conversation as a new idea took over his head.

"Why would she not mention her?" Grace was taken aback by this accusation, and covered her tracks.

"Because she could have cared less about Marjorie aside from her being the future of this empire."

Grace looked behind her to make sure Marjorie was not around. "It'll break her if she knows. No daughter should ever think her mother does not think of her at all moments."

"So you wrote yourself a happy ending?"

"In time, Marjorie is going to idolize Esperanza through stories that she imagines of her own through those rose colored glasses of the past. I wrote history so that she was remembered by her mother."

Naz nodded his head. This woman before him continually surprised him in her dealings with life. She could be so calm and collected about working at a brothel. She could be so impassioned and emotional about a child's future. Did nothing faze her?

Maybe just Dimin.

TWENTY-SEVEN

Sitting in the town, recuperating from his wounds, Dimin remembered seeing those fiery eyes on the face of a young boy. Ignacio, his parents had called him, then. He must have grown up and developed his powers. That dragon hoarding family had no idea the power that they could be harnessing.

His mind flashed back to that day at the meadow. He was working with a female greenback. She would not heel to him. In fact, she kept circling him and blowing smoke out of her nose in circles around him, playing with him. He brought out the whip and cracked it in her direction. She cried out at him, in pain, backing away. He had not meant to hurt her, but the move had worked. He whipped again, and she backed away. She grew tired of the pattern, blood running down her legs. The black dragon came out of nowhere, standing between the female and Dimin. He blew small flames at Dimin to make him back up. As he moved, Dimin recalled from his first day's introduction that the dragons had a code not to hurt the humans.

This dragon would not make a fool of him. The male pushed him away; yet Dimin would not be put off. He pursued the female, who had almost bent to his will. Jumping in front of her again, the black dragon blew a ring of fire around them.

"Leave us alone, I've got this!" he called out to the crowd of hands that had begun to draw around him and offer out advice. He would not appear weak, not to the hands and not to the dragons. He would be obeyed. He pulled the gun out of his holster and fired a warning shot in the air. The yellow eyes of the black dragon stared at him with fury. He roared, flapping his wings, trying to intimidate Dimin. The other dragons started coming around, and soon a full out melee would occur. Dimin needed to stop it. He cocked the gun and took aim.

No sooner had the bullet pierced the dragon's heart than Dimin's own heart seized up. He fell to his knees on the ground clutching at his chest. The owner of the ranch, Fuentes, called him to the manor and dismissed him that day, as the cold overtook his body. Turned away from the dragon lands, he headed east, all the way to Hamber.

And back at Titan's Creek Manor, a handsome green-black baby boy dragon broke open his egg shell ready to make his mark on the world.

As Dimin journeyed, he took solace in the cold. It kept him one step from the grave at all times, yet he could pull the power for his own dastardly deeds.

The power multiplied within him, as he considered how to use it for his own gain. Growing in size like a rolling snowball, it encompassed his heart. With every lie he told, every life he condemned, the cold consumed him physically and mentally. The quest for power erased his memories of his former self. He forgot that he had once loved riding the gentle beasts as a child. He once laughed; now he yelled and grimaced. The internal fed on the external until he stood one step from Below. While dwelling in Hamber, he noticed the citizens' gradual respect for him before they started falling ill. He brought a plague of forgottenness and cold wherever he stayed too long. The more towns he assumed under his command, the stronger the weather. His plans to assume the continent of Cosimo rapidly fell to the wayside as Grace refused to conform, though.

He would not tolerate any creature, let alone a weak female, challenging his authority. Therefore, he set off to find her.

He had come so close to bringing her back with him. Once intent on bringing her home, he realized that if he did not do that, he would just put her down. He had known that the wards existed on the outside. He had tried re-entering the haven many times before that moment. The wall creation was an unplanned surprise for him. When the dragon boy sent him back east, Dimin's powers needed a bit of time to recharge. But the sickness took new souls, and he acquired a boost. Pretty soon, he would have enough power to challenge the wards.

Then, Grace and the dragons would be his to compel.

TWENTY-EIGHT

Wildflowers stood in a vase next to her bedside, her pistol cradling it. She reached her hand out of the covers, trying to retain the heat, for the note propped up against it.

Dragons, rawr.

Naz had such neat handwriting for a male. Throwing on a shirt from the closet and borrowed worn denim trousers, she tossed her sandy hair into a makeshift bun with a bandana so it was off her neck. Walking into the kitchen, she saw that it was still quite early. The coffee maker was cold so Tara must not even have been awake. Throwing some scoops of the ground beans in with the water, she brought the percolator to the back door. She put her boots on one-handed and grabbed her white hat to shade her face. She had started to gain some color since being this far west.

Striding out to the pasture, she expected to see Naz in the middle, checking up the creatures. She did not expect to see him tossing live chickens in the air for them to catch. Honor bounded over; she was growing exponentially day by day.

"Can you heat this please?" Grace asked her little friend. Eager dragon eyes blinked at her as she loped over and positioned herself below the canister. She blew small flames upwards until the coffee pot boiled. Unstringing the coffee mugs from her belt where she'd tied them for ease of carrying everything, she then filled them up. Though dragons often did not use their fire, Honor was testing her newfound capabilities at any opportunity.

"She'll cool down once she gains some more control with practice," Naz commented, surveying Honor's impressive accuracy.

"Figured you might want this," Grace said as she handed Naz a mug. She poured the coffee in it as if she were conducting tea service.

He thanked her, quite surprised that someone had done something for him for once. He was so used to taking care of every other creature on the Manor. "I've been thinking, and I have something that I want to show you."

"You know I love a good exploration," she told him, throwing back her coffee. She left the pitcher on the fence. They hiked through the woods, and up the big hill about a mile from the house to the derelict hotel.

"You bought it!?"

"I've been wanting to explore it, care to join?"

"You know me too well," she beamed. He pulled a hammer from his back pocket and prized the slats off the front door, allowing her to push it open as dust fell from the rafters. Spiders occupied their own rooms in the corners.

"Allow me to give you the grand tour," he said in a playful tone. "Here we have the sitting room, and the room you sit in before the sitting room. Here is the sun room. Here we have the kitchen, state of the art, flour dust on demand." They both coughed. "Out here is the morning room, with its own piano." The forte was cut in half with a beam peeking through it. You could see the snapped strings. Maybe Tara could heal it; once life breathed through it.

"Well, the common rooms look quite stylish, but have the bedrooms been updated?"

"I assure you ma'am, we have but the finest suites." He led the way up the stairs, warning her not to lean on the stair rail. As he was two feet from the top floor, his leg sank into the stair. "Well, ma'am, as you can see, we test everything out for our guests to make sure that their experiences here are top notch."

Grace put one arm below his armpit and another above as she helped to yank him out. He brushed the dirt off his pants, looking disheveled but nonplussed. They climbed the final two steps together before walking straight across to where the two large french doors open. "And here we have the dining room," he said.

"Oh, but I'm sure it's the presidential suite," she said. "All grand hotels have a presidential suite that everyone wants but no one can afford."

"Unless you're me." Naz whispered into her ear before whirling about.

"But there's no bed in here!"

"But the view is unmatched." He threw open the shutters and the windows and the view from the hill encompassed the land all around. The sun kissed all the green in the area in spots with clover, white little flowers. She used to remember all the different names and meanings of the flowers; that was in a different life. The bumblebees fluttered, the butterflies flitted. The river a bit away sparkled. So much life to be discovered. She wondered what was over the hill but a bit away, past the town.

"It's beautiful," she sighed, etching the scene upon her memory.

"It is," he replied, memorizing every nuance of her face at that moment. They explored the rest of the rooms, both more focused on avoiding what they didn't want to see than on decorating.

Returning down the stairs, he led the way once more. Except it was Grace who plummeted three stairs down into Ignacio's arms. She had never noticed how much taller he was than she. He had never noticed... well there was not much that he had not noticed about her. In that moment, as he stared into her bright blue eyes and she into his sunny brown, they saw themselves. He leaned his head downwards and she tilted her head upwards. Their lips met somewhere in the middle of time and space, where both ceased to exist beyond feeling. His strong lips sought out her soft lips that desired nothing more than to be massaged. Their tongues tangled up in knots, each trying to write a love letter to the other. Her hands remained on his arms that had caught her, feeling his biceps flexing beneath his shirt as he pressed her back closer into him. He took a step backwards, pressing his back into the wall. She took the opportunity to step forward, fitting her legs so his leg was between them. Moving his hands downward, he pressed her firm ass into him, scooping her closer. Walking her fingers up to his shoulders, she pulled his chest into hers. They finally pulled away for a breath and they rested their foreheads against each other.

"I've been wanting to do that since I saw you after dealing with Dimin."

"Oh yeah? Helpless girl in need of rescue?"

"The furthest thing from it. This woman who gave her all and was ready to die trying."

"You should have done a little mouth to mouth resuscitation. I would not have said no."

"You were not in the position to say anything, and I wanted you to say everything."

Tara peeked her head into Marjorie's bedroom where Grace sat on the floor playing with her. The younger girl had devised some new version of checkers after she had pitifully lost her first game. The rules constantly changed, and Grace was enjoying the adjustments that Marjorie would make to try to bail herself out of the underdog position. If she would just stick with the original rules, she actually would be winning this game. But she had to applaud the creativity. A girl should always be able to get herself out of a sticky situation.

"Grace, do you have a moment to come downstairs? The lawyer wants to see you before he leaves."

Standing up from the floor, Grace maneuvered around the board so as not to disturb it. Marjorie looked up at her searching for some sort of promise with her eyes.

"We're not done," Grace assured her. She padded down the pine stairs in her bare feet, noticing how smooth the wood still was though the house had been around for more than a century. Her light day dress, not a normal staple of her wardrobe, swished behind her. It was hot and she enjoyed hiking her skirts up as high as she could, especially when sitting on the cool floor while playing with Marjorie. She and Marjorie had a pact that lady-like performances were lost at the bedroom door.

He motioned for her to sit next to him. The lawyer adjusted his glasses and motioned for Grace to sit at the head of the cherry wood dining table. A pen and sheaf of papers awaited her. So still yet so powerful.

"Now, Ms. Eastbrook, was it?" She nodded, wary of what was about to happen. The last time she sat across from a lawyer, her father was working out terms for her imprisonment—er, engagement. "If you would please sign below every spot that Mr. Fuentes signed, we can be done with this in no time."

Confusion due to men's decision making was no foreign feeling to her.

"I'm sorry, what am I signing?"

"A deed for the old hotel and the thousand acres that surround it. Ignacio said that you would be thrilled to have it."

Oh, so now was to be no different than the time her father negotiated her future. "Oh did he now?" The anger started refluxing up her esophagus. That familiar feeling of claustrophobia caused by men–being contained by societal norms, clothes, anything that stifled one's freedom as a person to just be that were created by males as a way of subordinating the opposite gender.

"And where might the lord and the master of the manor be?" She pushed away from the table and made her way to the front door.

"Don't you want to live there, Grace?" Marjorie asked, peering between the banisters on the staircase where she sat looking in, her legs dangling in front of her in all her childhood innocence.

"No, I don't," she said firmly. "And your father would have known it was a waste of time to have the Mr. Lawyer in if he had bothered to talk to me about it first. If you'll excuse me."

After angrily shoving her feet into her boots, she stormed out the door, letting the screen slam behind her, a warning to all of a woman's wrath seeking its offender. The confrontations, the anger, the captivity. She was not their captive. She could leave any time that she wanted, so why was she still there? The wind blew her skirts and her hair. She needed to be in that wind, she didn't care which direction it was blowing. She breathed deeply as she headed with purpose towards the clearing. Honor still had not grown enough, but maybe Yokel would take her. She would give the dragons a choice, unlike the courtesy that others gave to her.

Honor skipped towards her when she saw her. What a trusting little soul. How could she leave her? In a few weeks, she should be grown enough to ride, Naz had said. Tara gave her a month; they had a bet standing that whoever lost would have to rewire the chicken coop.

"You stay here this time, okay, baby?" Grace patted her on the head, smoothing the wrinkles behind her eyes. Honor leaned into the touch.

"Where is he?" she seethed at Mr. Milton, the overseer, who was in the middle of the clearing with a few hands going over the herd. He tipped his hat and pointed out towards the brook. He knew better than to stand in the way of a fight. Off she stomped, fury boiling through her blood. "HEY, YOU! Were you too much of a coward to stay at the meeting that you set up for me to have without checking my diary?"

At the word coward, the hairs on Naz's neck stood on end. In all of his thirty seven years, he had never ever been called a coward. A careful planner? Yes. Cautious? Yes. Coward? Hell no.

"What in Maker's name has you so pissed off now?" He turned around from where he was tracking whether fallen scales were due to shedding or disease in order to meet the verbal onslaught.

"You were just signing lands over to me without asking me?"

"Most people would say thank you."

"Most people would have a choice if they wanted the lands and a fixer-upper or not!"

"You don't want a safe place to live?"

Grace had hit the point of frustration. She thought that Naz would understand. He seemed to want to so much, and when she explained herself, she thought that he would have made that connection. So she did the only thing she felt like doing. She yelled at the sky, threw her hands into the air, and turned to walk away.

Naz, still angry about being called a coward and having had no resolution to what he did wrong, followed her path.

"Why the fuck would you call me a coward? Look around. Here I am following you. I'm not the one who runs from people or things, unlike you. You run off every time something bothers you!"

Naz had reached her. She didn't turn around but kept walking. Now she just wanted to be done with the conversation.

"Okay, or ignore me. But you know that I am right."

She whipped around. "You think you know everything about me, but you don't. You think that you're saving me. You think that you're going to be the one who brings me the life that I secretly always wanted. But you're only condemning me to a life of misery."

"I'm keeping you from being alone! I'm giving you a permanent roof over your head!"

"I'm not lonely! In fact, right now, I want you to just leave me alone." Grace turned on her heel and proceeded to walk towards the trees that were at the edge of the meadow. She whirled around, to conclude her argument. "What's your problem with my being alone anyway? I think that you're just tired of being alone, yourself, and so you figure that I must have a problem with it, too!"

Maybe she could find some solace in the canopy covering the area by the brook. She prayed that he was maintaining his distance. She needed some solitude. Luckily, when she turned the corner, she could not see him in her peripheral vision. Good, maybe he had finally listened to her. She picked up a slender branch and proceeded to wave it around. When she was younger, she had often listened to the stories her mother would indoctrinate into her about knights rescuing princesses. While her mother focused heavily on the damsels in distress, Grace wondered what it would be like to be a knight and nobly quest through undiscovered lands. She sat down and put her feet into the brook. Drawing in the lush land next to it, she pondered her next move. She would need to leave and soon. She would keep heading west. How would she stay warm, though? Was that why she was here? Just to remain warm? She laid down on the ground next to the brook, washing the dirt from the stick lazily off in the water, drawing swirls in it. Eventually, she drifted off to sleep with her head on her left hand and her right arm out. The stick floated away.

She awoke to Naz uttering her name and shaking her shoulder as he sat beside her.

"Good, you're not dead," he joked.

Grace sat up, using her forefinger to rub the sleep out of her eyes. "Naz, I am the biggest lumbug this world has ever seen. I'm not going on anyone's terms but my own."

He truly believed that if she had not been killed by now, the situation was purely due to her refusal of it.

"I loved Esperanza, I truly did. When she offered to go east and look for roaming grounds, I jumped at the chance to be alone without her. I wanted the chance to figure out myself, who I was. Could I carry the decision making on my own? She ruled so much of this place, the decorations, how Marjorie was raised, the types of chickens we fed the dragons, daily meals, when I could see Tara, what my daily routine looked like. The woman had been bred to run a house. So amazing, that she forgot that I, too, was an adult and could make decisions. I suppose I did no better than what Esperanza would have done when I brought the lawyer here. And I apologize. I thought I was gifting you a future."

Grace was taken aback. Never had she been apologized to, never had she been given a second thought beyond how she could complete someone else's life. And here was a man who wanted nothing more than to do what was right by her. She lifted her hand to his cheek.

"I think sometimes people are so concerned with the future, that they forget the present is where it is built," she channeled her best Thal. A tear dropped from his eye. Her calloused thumb gently wiped it away. "Why are you crying?"

"Since you arrived, new mornings excite me. I don't dread the night times with you near. I want to talk to you about everything and nothing. I want to tear apart all the reminders of how weak I was and actually embrace who I am. You elate me. You know who you are and your strong convictions define you. You fear neither man nor animal. Your smile lights up any room and you treat everyone as if they are the richest person in the world. I have never seen you turn down someone who needs help, and even now, when you're pissed as hell at me, you listen to me. And fuck knows, I love you for it." He stopped abruptly, realizing what he had said. Grace's eyes grew wide. "Well, it's out there now. I love you. I don't want to cage you; I want to support you to teach yourself to fly. I want you to have everything you could possibly want in this world and the next. And Mother Maker knows that I may not be with you immediately in the next world, and we might not look the same as we do now, but I will be sure to find your essence through your laugh. Learning you has been my greatest adventure and I never want to stop."

She sat up and kissed him. She did not want to say those three words back to him only to have them hurt him later. She feared that she could be subconsciously using him, as she consciously did with Sao, which was the last thing in the world she wanted to do. No, she respected this person too much. Could she love someone, truly love someone, if she did not need him at all?

TWENTY-NINE

After dinner, Grace sprawled on the floor of Marjorie's room with dolls in her hands this time. He watched through the crack in the door as the two played.

"Oh Bonnie, please tell me you didn't forget the jam!"

Grace adopted a high-pitched, heavily affected voice that he recalled from his days of courting. "Well, Alice, I did. And if I'd brought it, I'd jam it up Caroline's backside after the things she said to me after service the other day."

"Oh you know you probably misheard her, she would never hurt a spider." Through the crack in the door, he saw Marjorie waddle another doll over. "Hi Bonnie, I'm Caroline. Did you bring the jam?"

"NO I DID NOT BRING THE JAM!"

Grace and Marjorie laughed from their places.

"Grace, when you were a lady, did you ever learn to make jam?"

Grace went on to explain that she was a terrible baker and a more horrendous artist, but she could play the piano and she could embroider. Both skills had helped her in the real wide world, and not just the society parlors of Hamber.

"I like to draw," she said. "Is that a lady's skill?"

"I think it's a skill needed in the world. We need people to imagine new things and draw them out. Portraits can be drawn to be used for wanted posters. You could maybe draw the new design for coins. Or maps!"

"Oh, I want to draw a map of our land!" Marjorie shouted running out the door, past her father who still stood there.

"I'm not informing her that you have one already." She got up onto her feet, brushing off the dirt from the floor on the knees of her jeans.

"Yeah, but I don't have one drawn with love by her."

"It's time for you to get ready for bed," he told his daughter as she returned with pencils and paper. "You can make a map in the morning. I'll let Tara know you're ready to hear a story." He walked into the room where she sulked with a frown on her face after having thrown the drawing instruments on to the ground. Smiling at her free expression of her emotions, he kissed her forehead. "Good night, Princess of Dragons."

Marjorie threw her arms around her dad's neck in a tight squeeze, which he returned. "Good night, King of Dragons!" She kissed his cheek. "Good night, Grace!" she called out the door to Grace who stood at the top of the stairs so she could give the two their private moment together.

"Good night, Marjorie! Sweet dreams!"

Naz walked past Grace on the stair, grabbing her hand and leading her downstairs and into his bedroom. Closing the door, he told her to get on the bed. Her heart beat wildly, wondering what he had planned.

"When she dropped off the lawyer in town, Tara visited with an elder healer today. He said that he had never seen this dragon curse before."

Her shoulders sank as she mouthed a silent and disappointed "oh."

"But." He held up a finger. "He had seen many curses that were localized in an area of the body before. Together, the two of them reasoned out a course of action."

"And?"

"Just as sugar and salt are opposites, magic goes up, you push it down. A curse is cold -"

"The healing needs to be hot." Grace finished his sentence. Tara's initial thoughts had been correct, of course. Though she lived on the ranch, she had been one of the brightest in her class. Dragon magic is rare indeed. Many healers attempted to persuade her to remain at the university. Her gift needed to go home, she would reply. She needed to go home. She liked home and felt one with the earth there.

"Okay, get ready to try this!" he said hopefully. Even though he had no idea what he was doing, he trusted Tara's instructions. And Grace trusted Naz to follow the plan, as well as keep her best intentions in mind. He had declared he loved her, after all.

Naz directed her to turn over so she laid on her stomach with her face into the mattress. She turned her head on its side so she could breathe which gave her a view out the side window. He adjusted so he could put his hands on her back. She needed not to think about how he was straddling her legs, so she could remain calm.

"I'm going to put my hands on your lower back, but I need to touch your skin."

"Okay," she choked out. She could feel heat without his touching her. He pushed her shirt up her back, revealing her lower back. He tried to ignore his hardness and the heat forming inside of him. Maybe he could use that bit to help them both.

"My magic pushes, so just try to push back into it." She nodded. His warm hands relaxed her. The pair's deep breathing matched in rhythm. With a final deep inhale, the surge of the power rushed through. She could feel it rushing through her.

Gasping for air to cool her insides, she finally choked out, "Naz, stop."

Immediately, he pulled his hands away.

"You're just spreading the cold as it melts. I feel it." Naz bit his lip in thought for a moment, scratching his head. "Okay, turn back onto the bed. I'm going to try pushing it out into something. Let's see if I can find something to put this evil shit into. It'll need to be of strong enough significance to keep the power at bay. So a marriage curse can be contained within an engagement ring." He searched around the room and placed his hands over his pockets. He pulled out Grace's gold Maker's Mark necklace that he had been meaning to return to her.

"Grace?" he questioned her, implying that she should look at what he found. He dangled the necklace in front of her eyes.

Where had he found that? Her mother had given it to her as a wedding present. "That'll do," she admitted.

The two analyzed the previous attempt together. They deduced that the power was going to push out her mouth, so Grace would put the necklace into her mouth.

This time, she was ready for the burning. As gentle as his hands were, Naz's power boasted strength and surety. Centuries of wisdom and care. And he pushed it all into her.

Grace gagged on the power. She squeezed her mouth tightly, covering it with her hand. She wanted to ensure that the power did not escape her mouth, exiting into the world. Enough evil lurked out there already. Sweat gathered at his brow, as he pushed.

"Doing okay?" He worried about her, her entire body, save her lower back, had turned beet red.

"If I need to stop, hit the headboard twice." Stuck without her voice, she could only flip him off. Naz smiled with satisfaction that she was still handling the process. The magic pushed up and up. It burned and froze in her chest, the two extremes battling within her. She wanted to pass out and release herself to the magic, but she would not let the evil win. The forces pushed up to her throat. Naz could see the path of the white cold as he forced it out of her body. Grace winced as it pushed out of her esophagus and into her mouth worse than that whiskey vomiting she had accomplished after drinking with Verdis. It was a reverse blowjob. Her other hand went to meet the first over her mouth as she lifted her head off the mattress.

The mark on her tongue grew colder as it sucked the curse away.

Her mouth was going to burst open.

She had just raised her hand to hit the headboard to stop Naz when all the sensations stopped. Releasing a breath of relief, her head flopped onto the bed. Naz's hands pulled off of her and he relaxed. She dragged the now black charm out of her mouth, carrying drool lines with it and handed it to him. She did not want it near her.

"You have a red mark on your back in the shape of the Mark directly above your underwear line." Naz caressed it gently. "If you want, I can go find the other two, and brand them onto you, so that you can have the Full Trinity on your back." Still straddling her legs, he sat back onto his calves and dangled the chain in front of him, wondering how such a small thing could have had such an impact on her life. It only had a tiny bit of rust on it now.

"No, I think it's fair to say that I'm in my Maker stage right now. I'm completely okay with that." She turned over to look at him. He moved to the right of her lying down and offered the necklace back to her. She refused it, pushing it towards him. "Just put it on the nightstand for now."

The two sat in silence, reeling from the event. The red of Grace's skin equalized.

Finally, Tara's medgical curiosity could not contain itself within her. "Did it work?"

"I'm a warm woman, thanks to Naz!" Grace exclaimed through the closed door laughing.

"Good! Good night, you two!"

"Thanks to you, I'm good," she said softer to Naz, when she turned to look at him. "Thank you, Naz, for saving me."

"Grace, I did not save you. I merely harnessed the energy that countered the one that had been put inside you alr—"

She sat up and shut him up by putting her mouth on his. He responded gently and tentatively.

"You don't need to thank me this way, Grace."

"Oh, Naz. The amount that I feel in my soul for you. You've given me back myself. I know I couldn't have done it alone, I don't have magic. And I don't need you. Now that you've pulled your hands away, I feel just the absence of you. And I want that feeling back. The feeling when you're a part of me." She looked into his amber eyes, more golden with the sun reflecting off them through the back window. The vulnerability in her bright blue eyes was asking for him to respond. He swallowed audibly.

"Use me all you want, Naz. Just don't pity fuck me." When he did not respond to her again, she nervously started, "It's okay, I under-"

"Shh..." He kissed her tenderly. "I'm planning what position I want you in when you call out for more of me."

Her eyes grew wide and her jaw dropped with incredulity. He made that clicking noise he made when he had reached a decision. With that, he put his arm over her back, wrapping her up in him. And his mouth devoured hers.

She threw her arms around him as he rolled them over so he was on top of her. Her skin, now warm to the touch, reminded him of her kindness. His stubble tickled her neck as he made his way down from her cheek, causing him to smile as she giggled. He beamed back at her. Maker, the things this girl did to him. He put his forehead on hers as he used his hand to slowly unbutton the first four buttons on the shirt. He pulled the fabric apart so the area between her breasts was exposed. He could see the heaving of her chest. With each spot that he uncovered, she mimicked him. He kissed her there in the middle, licking her playfully. As he undid more of her shirt, he reached her belly button. Her legs started writhing. Good, he wanted her good and ready for him. At the last button, he used his finger to slowly pull the shirt apart with a downward motion, ending with his hand on her mound. She gasped. He propped himself up on his right hand, still maintaining eye contact as he massaged her bud. Her face started flushing, the reds highlighting the blues in her eyes. She grabbed his face and kissed him hard, putting her tongue into his mouth as far as it would go, miming to him how far in she wanted him. He showed his understanding by slipping a finger inside of her. With the second finger, she leaned her head back. Her hips were rocking slowly.

"So it does work," he said.

"You've never done that before?"

"No, but I wondered what it would be like to try."

"Anything else you want to try?" she challenged him.

He lowered himself down between her legs and began licking. He soon had her moaning. "We're not done until you call out my name, you little whiskey in a teacup."

"Naz," she said between breaths, "When I told you I wanted you, I was pretty sure it was right then. I take it back. I want you in me now."

He stretched up to her, and she pulled his boxers down, slipping his hard cock out. She sat up to where he knelt. Sliding him back and forth on her clit, he put his head into her neck, marveling at the feeling of her on him. He needed to feel more of her. She wrapped a leg behind his bottom and he slid into her entrance. He started rocking into her quickly and her pace matched his. Wanting him deeper still, she held onto him and put her other leg around his waist. He held onto her hips, moving her into him as he moved into her. Her back arching caused him to lose a bit of balance and she fell backwards into the pillow. He went with her, becoming closer to her and moving quicker. He could feel her pulsating around him. Never had he felt so in harmony with someone. She could feel him hardening. Their breaths matched quicker and quicker. They could not get enough of each other. Until finally, she called out his name, and he came hard inside of her, with her clenching around him with every fiber of her being. He held her tight, panting. They both lay there wrapped up in one another. He moved off of her and she grabbed her shirt and headed to relieve herself. She noticed that the sun had fully descended beyond the horizon. Tara must have finished reading a story to Marjorie in the girl's bedroom upstairs. She went back into the room and Naz was still contemplating the charm on the necklace as he rested with his back against the headboard.

"I thought I would have burnt up with you in me," Grace admitted.

"I don't just burn things willy nilly." He laughed and wiped the sweat off his face with both of his hands. She supposed that was true, considering he had helped to make Marjorie. She climbed back into bed with him.

"I'm assuming even though I'm not freezing anymore, I can still sleep next to you?"

"I'd hoped I'd made that abundantly clear." Those doe eyes could have asked him for her own dragon ranch and he would have given it to her in that moment.

"Oh, abundantly," she said, looking down at his crotch. He winked at her and they maneuvered into the sleeping position that they had adopted as their own with his back to the window and her front to the closed door. She had moved her pistol to the side table next to her the night she started sleeping in there.

"How do you feel now that you're not shivering with cold?"

Grace sighed and sank deeper into his arms. "I finally feel like I am free to be me."

That night, a cold front blew in.

THIRTY

Standing at the open window the next morning, a blanket wrapped around her naked body, Grace attempted to determine which way was east; no clouds loomed in the distance.

"Please tell me that you feel the cold too and that yesterday wasn't a dream."

"If it was a dream, I'm going back to sleep to relive it."

A bittersweet smile spread across Grace's face. "Then, we have a problem. There's frost on the window ledge."

She ran her finger along it, the blanket dropping low enough on her back that the red mark was visible. Naz sat up and grabbed his jeans from the floor. He walked over to her and placed his warm hand on her lower back, covering the mark. She leaned her head on his shoulder. Heaviness filled their chests.

"I thought I was safe."

"I thought I could keep you safe," he murmured into hair before kissing it.

"It's not your job to care for me like your dragons." She turned and sadly kissed his cheek before searching for the rest of her clothes on the floor. She threw her shirt on, tucking it into her jeans before she grabbed the pistol from the side table. She tied her hair up in a bun with Naz's bandana, like a knight taking a princess's favor into battle.

"Grace," he said in a more stern tone than he had ever used with her, aside from when he was yelling at her about the hotel. He scrambled to change and keep up with her. She threw open the bedroom door, ignoring his calling for her.

"It's no coincidence that Dimin's magic was pulled out of me yesterday and the cold front blows in today."

Tara blinked twice, and set down her coffee. "Probably not. But it could also be. Who knows." Grace thought she caught a scent of worry in the air, but Tara was waiting for Naz, who tripped and fell onto the floor as he was putting his boots on in a hurry.

His sister was worried. She would have normally had Marjorie up by now, but if she was sleeping, it meant they needed to talk.

"Round up the crew," he told her, pouring some coffee. "Give me an hour, and I'll have a plan."

Without saying another word, he heaved a deep breath and trudged to the study. Yesterday seemed millions of miles away. To have happiness and a sense of no care in the world aside from what he wanted in that moment. And now he was at a precipice of possibly losing everything - everything he had ever worked for, and everything he could possibly have–past, present, and future.

The women leaned against opposite ends of the counter towards one another and drank their coffee. "I'm surprised you're letting a man go off and plan your future right now," Tara surmised softly.

"I'd say the same thing to you, but I'm pretty sure that person in question is a planner whose life has been built upon taking care of others. That person," she was careful not to use gender pronouns in this instance, "has the most knowledge of the resources of this manor and what is at stake. We both know that that person will have the most to contribute if they have time to think about a course of action."

"But really, I said I'd give him an hour to think," she said, raising her eyes from the swirling black juice inside of the mug to Tara's brown eyes, that looked like fertile meadow dirt after a rain. "I never said that I would go along with whatever he thought of."

Tara clinked her mug with that of Grace in silent cheers. Tara had no ill will towards this Grace. Did she stir things up outside of the calmness they once had been? Absolutely. But maybe Titan's Creek Manor needed to be agitated a bit to change.

"I'm not one to pry, nor judge, as you can tell," Grace started. "But you're a healer, you can go anywhere. Why stay here?"

"I was away from here, in Lesea, for years. After the hustle and bustle of the city, I just decided that I don't like people very much. Just leave me alone. I would rather be here with the dragons and my niece. Sometimes my brother, when his sunshine isn't squashing my grump. I'm going to wake Marjorie or she'll never sleep tonight."

"What should we tell her?"

"Oh you know, that you're not a defined item, you're not sure where things are yet, you want to test the waters but you like where they're going..."

"TARA! That's not what I meant, and you know it."

"Well yeah, but I had to get one in, after I had to explain to her why you were shouting for her father in the middle of the night when you were in the same room as him."

On that note, she walked out of the room and up the stairs without looking back. All Grace could do was smile into her coffee.

Once the whole mixed gendered crew was gathered outside the house, their arms crossed to stave off the chill. Grace and Tara hurriedly passed around coffee that Naz kept heating in large pitchers on the front porch. Marjorie helped bring mugs out. Grace understood this as hospitality and taking care of their own. Each time she passed out a mug full of coffee, she would give the crew member a once over. She would call Tara over to help tend to that person. If they didn't do this on a daily basis, they really should start. Her mother, cruel to her as she was, would never have let the staff feel as if they went anywhere else that they would get better treatment.

Once everyone had their coffee, the women stood side-by-side on the porch with Naz. She caught Marjorie watching from the front window in the bedroom in her peripheral vision and waved at her. Naz saw but made no move to chastise either of them. He started talking and she tuned him out.

"Which one of these guys is the best in the stable?"

"My dragon doesn't fly that route." Tara winked, looking just like Naz as she did so, and Grace caught her eyeing up a couple of the female dragon hands.

"Alright, which one of these hands is the best in the stable?"

"Who's saying it's just one?" Tara whispered back.

"Alright, spice, come out to play!"

"Grace, I'm an introvert, not dead." Dragon relative indeed.

Grace tuned back in to listen to Naz's address to his employees.

"...This storm has traveled across the continent. It goes no further. Dimin Greystock was a man who could not handle the majesty of the dragons and what it meant to caretake. Our gift in life is to serve the dragons, Granny Good's finest spin on Mother Maker's creations. You are going to bring the dragons to safety." He made the clicking noise in his mouth to punctuate his speech.

Grace had no idea how this was going to end. If she went down, so be it. She was tired of running and refused to live the rest of her life on the lam because some crazed, cold devil was pissed off that she had jilted him at the altar. He was going to have to get over it, and get over it today. Fear didn't cross her mind. Anger, yes, the feeling of being fucking done, yes.

"The dragons need you," she told him.

"Wait wait wait," Naz stopped her. "We're doing this together, and right now, the dragons are fine without me."

"I won't see anyone hurt because of me."

"Have you ever stopped to think that you didn't cause this?"

Bewildered, she raced through her memories of what could have been changed.

"If your town had stood up to him, you wouldn't be in this position. He's coming after you because you are his sign of weakness. You are the thing that he couldn't control, and he is not okay with that. To dominate you, *that* would be the accomplishment."

Grace remained silent, looking in his steadfast eyes. Naz, ever the practical, logical thinker, had made a point. He looked back at her, hoping that she could see sense in his words. Could she do this on her own? Sure, but he wasn't willing to pay that cost. He looked around at the ranch, quickly judging its advantages.

"We'll hold him off at the hotel," he announced to everyone.

"Great! It'll be away from everyone." He turned her to look at the hotel and pointed upwards.

"More like, it's on a hill so we have one advantage."

"Who the fuck are you?" This newfound fount of knowledge poured out of Naz. And damn it was sexy.

"My wife's been dead. I'm here with two women, now three. I lock myself away and read a lot. It's a survival skill."

"I'm going to try not to picture you in your reading glasses, otherwise I might jump you," she joked, in a half truth. She let him turn back to his hands, who were grinning at their repartee.

"I'm going to send Tara and Marjorie out with Newa and the other dragons. We'll ask Agrippa and Honor to stay with us, but I want them to have the choice to leave. They can communicate with the others easily. And, all of us are going to stock that hotel with enough guns and firepower to let this asshole know that he's done throwing his tantrum."

One by one, the hands shook her hand or tipped their hats at her before jumping onto the back of a dragon. They would fly the ammo and supplies that they could up the hill to the hotel. Then, they would fly away to various undisclosed locations that only Marjorie knew. She had copied the map from Naz's study. Now as each person told her how many dragons they were leading on which dragon, she marked their final destinations down. The paper was hidden in a dark box, so only she could mark it. When all the hands had flown away, the only people remaining at the ranch were Marjorie, Tara, Ignacio, and Grace.

"Go get your bag, Marjorie," Tara gently said to her, after she had rolled up the map and tucked it into an oilskin.

"But Grace—"

"Go on, Marjorie," Grace said. The girl moved slowly inside and up the stairs, the realization of what was about to happen sinking in.

Tara was tying the bags onto Newa, who would be transporting both her and Marjorie towards the southeast. The three of them would await Honor and Agrippa's signal for what the next move would be.

"So, I'll see you tomorrow morning?"

Naz nodded, while looking at Grace. Tara pecked Naz's cheek, and gave him a big hug.

"Good luck." They had decided to avoid telling Marjorie that Naz actually was staying. The girl would never leave.

She moved towards Grace and gave her a hug. "Grace, I don't have the words. But I wish you get what you want in life. You deserve it."

Thal would have had something insightful and profound to leave her with. The image of her friend's recent demise appeared at the front of her mind, sending shivers down her spine. Some cold and evil could never be expelled from her, despite Naz's skills.

Marjorie dragged her back on the ground as she pouted towards Grace. Giving her a hug, she lamented, "I want to help you."

"You're in charge of keeping the dragons safe. Dimin will never expect that you are the most powerful woman in the territory, because knowledge, Marj, is power. Help me by ensuring that my feats aren't for naught." She pinged the girl's nose with her forefinger, and shined a smile at her. "Besides, you need to make sure that your dad doesn't do anything stupid tomorrow."

"Stupid, like what?"

"Like forgetting what I'm doing this for."

"I won't let him be stupid," she promised, giving her another hug. Grace fought back tears at the thought of this brave soul, perhaps on her own, with the secrets of an entire herd of dragons rolled up in an oilskin in her sleeve.

Agrippa and Honor nuzzled Newa, with her mate taking an extra moment to huff something only the two of them understood. Newa moved back towards the humans. Naz helped to boost Marjorie onto Newa, in front of Tara so Tara's arms held around her as she reached for the pommel.

"I love you both," he said to them. With that parting, Tara patted Newa to let him know to take off. The women, the perfect pairing of Mother Maker and Daughter Dreamer, departed the scene only to land who knows where.

Naz and Grace stood alone. Tears dropped down Naz's face as he thought of his daughter and how much he would miss her. He would sacrifice himself again and again for her.

"This ends here, Grace."

And though Naz meant her running and the Dimin situation, Grace couldn't help but sadly think of their entire circumstance.

THIRTY-ONE

She walked into the study which was covered in carved wood everywhere. Baffling, considering how much Ignacio could control fire. And heat. And the heat in her. Which she had not dreamed of having for a long time.

Sitting in the dragon leather chair by the fire, he focused on whittling away at a piece of wood that she had seen him pick up by the brook when they were out there. Her eyes gazed upon this person, so clearly intent upon helping her despite the ominous scourge that came for her, and by default, his entire world.

"Toy for Marjorie?"

"It was a doll, but now I'm just keeping myself busy. Trying to calm my mind, see a bit more clearly, maybe clear this tightening in my chest." She went over to the chair and knelt before him. She tenderly placed her hands upon his knees. He looked at her agitated face without moving the position of his head.

"Naz, I'm going to go up there alone." Before he could protest, she put her finger over his lips. His eyes glazed over. "My plight is not worth your family's legacy."

Her hand dropped to his wrist, where she rubbed the skin between his watch and his wrist.

"And where does that leave me if you leave me?" his voice choked, and he took his reading glasses off, under the ruse of cleaning them on his shirt, as he cleared his throat.

She softly told him, gaze remaining on his dark haired sunkissed wrist, "Same place as it did before, Naz. Peacefully caring for your daughter and the dragons. Tara obviously can take care of herself." They both chuckled. And still the fire crackled like the suckling pig whose last wish was it shouldn't be the best bacon on Trinity's Nigh.

She continued on, swallowing with the hard part that she could barely believe she was about to tell him. "You can come and get me in a few days. Let Honor cremate my body. Scatter my ashes by that brook. And if you don't know the spot, I'll haunt you. I've had a good run, but it's time for this to end." She raised her eyes to meet his, and seeing the tears falling from his dark eyes caused her own to drop.

He had thought his heart had been broken by watching Marjorie's face as she learned of her mother's death; however, in this moment, he was learning that heartbreak really was a heart wrench, twisting it so it extended from your esophagus to your tear ducts. "You haunt me already. This house has been infused with your presence. My brain roils with your essence. How can you be so nonchalant about this situation?"

"Because doing this is the only way that I can protect you. And I love you, Ignacio." The tears fell at a faster pace now. "I cannot bear the thought of my having done anything to hurt you. I want my freedom, and this is the price that I pay for it. You don't pay for my independence. I love the way that your practicality is nodding along with how this is the right plan. I love the way you wake up with the sun and your smile shines brighter than the sun outside the window. Your loyalty and sense of duty inspire me and make me want to reexamine every life choice that I ever made. Daughter Dreamer knows, I wish that you could just run away with me, but you can't. You don't deserve the pain that comes with my personal territory. We would always be running, and that itself, as you put it, drains one's life. I'm going to stop running and you're going to let me."

He nodded his head slowly, and the two sat quietly together, her head on his knee, his hand on her hair, staring at the fire. After half an hour or so, he heard her snore so he shook her shoulder to wake her. She stood up and he stood afterwards, putting his whittling into his pocket. Their hands found one another and they walked downstairs together.

Curled up in each other's arms, they held on with desperation. Neither wanted to move lest they break the quiet peaceful spell that had befallen the two of them. If one moved an inch, the other might fall apart. So they held each other together all night, like wood glue holding a beam infested with wood ants that was in the precarious position of being about to crack in half bringing the whole house tumbling down with it.

The silent house had no creaks. Only crickets in the field could be heard. Occasionally, Honor would let out a snort as she changed sleeping positions. They both slept a dreamless sleep.

In the morning, Grace awoke in the dark to a door slamming. Naz's spot was empty. No note beside the bed. His boots and clothes were gone. She got out of bed and went towards the front door. The holster and pistol were gone. He was gone. Like Sao was gone. And Thal was gone. And Sadie. And Slewja. Slewja was gone. She had loved her friend dearly and wished that he was here with her today. But he had helped her to arrive at this point. She took a steadying breath and wiped the tears from the corners of her eyes where they had pooled. No more tears would be shed. She would see him soon.

She reentered the bedroom, dressing herself in the dark. She already missed Naz and his sturdy, thoughtful presence. Shoving her feet into her boots, and checking to make sure her pistol was loaded before she took one last look around the room, memorizing the corners and the smell. This room. This bed had been her happily ever after.

Honor waited for her in the meadow, ready to escort Grace to her last stand. She was so hopeful, big eyes wide on her. How much she had grown in the past few days! Though nowhere near as big as Slewja, she would be there one day. She could fly but Grace was unsure if she could bear her weight. So, they walked the mile up the big hill together.

Grace breathed in the wind, hoping for a fragment of Slewja's strength. She would be seeing him soon enough. How she missed the feel of riding on his back with the wind blowing! Maybe she would be in that gauzy gown from last decade that felt so delicious but always caused stares. Hair wild behind her, her curls would never become ratty as the two flew the skies in perpetuity. If Daughter Dreamer took mercy, maybe eventually she would see Naz again and he would like to laugh alongside her as they flew side by side. He had a free side to him that needed to escape from the Manor sometimes. He had finally started to show it to her these past few days. She wanted to have forever to learn all the ways to make him laugh. And maybe he would have enough adventures that he would want to share with her when he saw her again. Though she planned to watch and laugh alongside him. Even if he did not know she was there. A lump grew in her throat as her eyes blurred again.

Shaking her head to clear them, she motioned for Honor to circle the hotel. It had been stockpiled with enough ammunition to last her the three days. Nothing she had on her could repay Naz. He still had her Maker's necklace that he could always melt down for coins.

"Alright girl, you know the plan," she told Honor, who blew a fiery circle around the perimeter of the hill. One last final blessing from the dragons. Honor gave her a nuzzle. She did not seem to think it was goodbye, bless her youthful heart. Honor flew out of the path.

And with her departure, Grace was truly alone. Isn't that what she had always wanted?

She slowly approached the door, relishing the last bits of the outdoors. She remembered how Naz had first opened it for her as they toured it together. The ghosts of their laughter taunted her broken heart. She took a last look at the sky, which was still dark overhead. Maybe she would see one more sunrise. She heaved a deep breath, exhaled and pushed open the double doors. Naz stood in the entry, rifles strapped over his back, ammunition packed across his chest, holsters at the ready, grin on his face.

"I made coffee," he said.

She ran and leaped into his arms, knocking him backwards as she smothered him with kisses. He broke their fall with his arm behind them.

"As if I would ever leave you," he whispered in her ear as he wrapped both arms around her and squeezed her in return. "We're on this adventure together."

"When do you think he'll get here? How do you know he'll come here?"

"Because that bastard is out for blood, Grace. You humiliated him. You escaped from him. He could not tame you, my whiskey in a teacup. So he intends to put you down, like he did that wild dragon all those years ago."

"Well, if he succeeds, it just means that I was no more special than anyone else that he killed."

"If he kills you, I will blot out the sun." Grace was not going to argue with him about his need for the sun. She had never seen Naz completely furious. She wondered if she ever would.

As dawn began to rise, the two scouted out the different vantage points. The crew had stocked the entire place with ammunition and guns in various locations. An archaic gunpowder keg that looked to be a liability lurked upstairs in the dining room, or was it the presidential suite?

Naz motioned with his hands around the room as he talked through some of the organizational tactics. "It's easier to get the keg down, than to get it up if you need it. Plus lots of strategic advantages for keeping it up high."

"I don't doubt your intellect and thoughtfulness."

"I'm explaining the rationale for the planning," Naz supplied.

"The plan is to end this rot of a being."

"Grace. How are we doing this?"

The two walked the house together in extreme seriousness, looking at the hotel from a place of vantage points. The dining room's view of the surrounding areas would be good for looking out. After dueling a tree in the dark, they decided that because Grace was the better shot, she would be downstairs. Naz could better strategize from higher up.

Recognizing his skills was not a detriment to either's ego. Saying that he was a better strategist, and she was a better shootist did not denote any weakness. It was an asset to the team to see these strengths for what they were and to utilize them to their potential. Their equality came from seeing eye to eye and acknowledging and appreciating the capabilities that they both carried.

Rifles were laid around the top floor. Pistols, donated by the crew, scattered across the floors in various points in case they were needed. One automatic sat next to the stairs, in case cover needed to be created.

She noticed a pile of clean scraps of fabric folded in the kitchen, which had been rid of dust. A bottle of whiskey sat with some antiseptic and fresh soap. Two pots of water sat on the stove ready to be boiled. She doubted that they would have time to piece themselves together, but then again, she had no idea of the onslaught. Because she had not seen Dimin's entrance at the wedding, she did not know what he would bring with him. She did not know when his magic would wear out. So many unknowns.

"We should get into position," Naz said as the snow started sprinkling on the ground.

They kissed like it was their last, with Grace's arms around his neck and Naz's arms around her waist. Neither wanted the moment to cease. But it did. Their foreheads touched and they breathed in deeply together.

"I love you," was all they needed to say. They had said it all already. Grace watched as Naz walked up the stairs to take the upper position. After a few moments of silence, she impatiently called up to him.

"Naz? What do you see?"

"SNOW! INCOMING!" With that, snow blasted through the windows, the doors, the crevices. High pitched howling pierced their eardrums. Grace crouched below the window, her shoulders and hat catching the snow that entered. She peeked out the window but couldn't see anything through the white. Something sharp sliced her right cheek, and she crouched back down.

"This shit hurts!" she shouted up to Ignacio on the floor above her. She could hear him stomping around.

"I know! Gimme a second!" He focused some of his energy out into the storm, in the direct field of vision, hoping it would push out the storm in a concave effect. Holding the storm at bay, Grace could now see about twenty feet in front of her. She fired off a few rounds just to scare whatever it was.

"You're only letting him know that you're still alive!"

"I'm pretty sure he knows that or he would've stopped!" She was pissed at this villainous creature who continued tormenting her. She held both pistols out the window and alternated shots out. Right shot, cock while left shot, right left right left. "Ughh-hh!" She was starting to become frustrated.

"Patience, Grace!

"I'm not just going to sit here and wait to die!"

She went to the kitchen and grabbed some bandages. A barrel of gunpowder was next to the back door. She made some quick packages of gunpowder and brought them up front with her. Peeking out the back window, Honor was on guard next to the maroon-purple Agrippa, who must have returned. She smiled, steeling herself for the next barrage.

"Agrippa's back!" she called up the stairs as she walked into the morning room and sat by the derelict piano. Some blue sprites had made their way in and were bending back the boards from the window.

"You little shits," she said, grabbing the pistol off the side of the piano and expertly shooting them down, before settling her fingers on the keys to play. She noticed another two blue flames creeping through the keyhole of the front door. Those sprites met their doom the moment they hit the floor. She jogged up the stairs, shooting two more in the back sunroom.

"Do you see these shits?" she asked Naz as she entered the room he was occupying.

"Yeah, they're creeping around here," he nodded with his head, still holding back the blizzard. A few darted along the floor boards. One had jumped onto Naz's hat that was on the ruined sofa and was freezer-burning a hole through the top.

"They're an annoying waste of ammo."

"I believe that that is the point."

"What if we just let it go? Let them all come up here and tear this place apart? I think you should let go. You need your strength and his plan is becoming clear. He means to hole us up. Let the blizzard and these little shits come in."

"What if he doesn't know that you're up here?" Naz said his thoughts aloud. "What if he just knows you're somewhere on this land and he's doing a sweep for you?"

"I guess I better let him know to come and get me." She ran downstairs and grabbed the makeshift bombs. Tossing one out the window, Naz shot it.

"Nice," she told him.

"I said you were the better shot, not that I'm a shit shot," he said. "You, on the other hand, throw like a..."

"DO NOT FINISH THAT SENTENCE, IGNACIO."

With fury, she threw the next bag as far as she could. In one swift move, she pulled the gun out of his holster and shot at the bag. Orange fire backlit the snow. Black explosive mixed with white snow on the ground. She threw out another and he hit it. She threw out the last three in a row and he hit all three, scattering the snow. The explosives did nothing.

"I'll go get more, maybe the dimwit hasn't figured it out yet, " she said. She went to go downstairs, but Naz caught her arm.

"Hold on a second. I can see something."

"Grace!" a familiar voice called out through the blizzard.

"Grace!" another familiar voice echoed it. Her eyes grew wide.

The snow stopped falling. The ice sprites continued their deconstruction of the house. She made sure to step on three of them as she made her way to the window.

"It can't be..." she started, then turned to run, taking the stairs two at a time. Grace flung open the front doors, searching through light fluttering of snow.

"Grace, close the doors! There's an army of them!" Naz shouted down to her. Listening to Naz, she slammed them shut. She heard his boots running down the stairs to her. She rushed to the bay window in the sitting room. Looking out she saw the people, all aglow with an eerie moonlight. Naz came and stood next to her. In the front of the pack, Sao and Thalassa floated over the ground. Even Thal's beautiful brown skin had a weird surging glow beneath it. All of her hopes that they had moved on to happier lives were for naught. All of the stories that she had written to console herself during her grief disintegrated in that moment.

"Well, Naz, a bit awkward, but meet my ex, Sao."

"Oh? Should I be worried?"

"Hardly. He never worried if I finished."

And she put her gun underneath the diagonal beam in the sitting room window. Thal and Sao never floated in life, she told herself, putting herself into the clinical survival mode. She aimed for a clean headshot and pulled the trigger.

"Oh, and this is my best friend, Thalassa. She was a carpenter. She would have been great at fixing this place up." She shot her friend in the head, downing her.

"Mother mucker," she said, hating this creature that was coming for her. He thought he could use the two people that had mattered most to her against her. Little did he know two things: one, they had already left her; and two, they did not leave her alone.

Naz picked up the rifle and took out the line of the rest of the floating people. She picked up the pistol next to her and felled the next row of six that came over the top of the hill. She quickly reloaded the pistols and awaited the next row of souls. But they did not come. All that was left was quiet. The tears that had formed in her ducts did not fall. When she brushed them away, all that fell were tiny pieces of ice.

"I guess he knows you're here, now."

As if in response, a voice rang out over the hill.

"Grace, darling! I've come to return you to our loving abode!" The offending creature shouted in the distance. She saw him come forward, floating on some giant ice sprite situation.

"What the fuck is that monster?" Naz asked. Grace shook her head. She did not know but she could imagine that it would hurt to be torn limb from limb by it.

Dimin had grown icier, frosted since the last time she had seen him at the wedding. He had always given her the weird feelings in her gut since she first met him. At the wedding, he had looked like a man on a mission. Now he looked possessed and maniacal. Frost painted his goatee and tipped his hair, once close shaven but now long and unkempt. His face, greyer than typical, hollowed under his cheek bones. The red rimmed eyes contrasted with the blacks of his irises. How quickly evil consumed oneself. His gaunt figure hunched over the giant creature, easily the size of Agrippa and twice the size of Honor. How had he even gotten onto that thing? He reminded her of the frosted ash that covered the ground.

"Ah, I had heard that you took a lover in my absence," Dimin tsked at her. With a movement of his hand, the other hand holding on to the pommel or protrusion from the creature's back, he sent those minions from her memory at them. They flew through the open windows, avoiding the beams, and headed not towards her but towards Naz.

"Naz! Fall!"

Without hesitation, from his standing position, he planted his stomach to the floor and covered his head. She crouched down under the bay window. The minions swarmed above them, flying overhead, towards the backdoor, where they were met by a stream of fire from Honor and Agrippa. The two dragons had received their instructions. Do not engage with the criminal. Agrippa was there to carry news back of what had happened to Newa with Tara and Marjorie, so they could reform the herd that they had scattered. Honor was there, because she loyally would not move from Grace's side.

Agrippa. Naz crawled on his arms and stomach for the back door, and threw it open. "Agrippa!"

The dragon sent a stream of fire across the house, frying every minion as it came through to the point of origin at Dimin. Dimin stopped, his hand burnt. As Naz caught his breath, he looked at Grace, both of them now on their stomachs on the floor. He started crawling back to see her. But though the stream of fire was concentrated, it caught onto a piece of wood hanging from the ceiling. It quickly spread to the upstairs floorboards..

"Naz! The gunpowder!" Grace jumped up, running for the stairs. Her foot fell into one, as Naz had fallen the first time they had been there. He jumped up running for the stairs to help her, but a beam fell onto his shoulder, knocking him down. Adrenaline surged through her. She yanked her foot out and went to help Naz. He had rallied though and saw her movements.

"The powder!" She took the stairs two by two, and he caught up to her. The upstairs had quickly become a hot plate. They targeted the gunpowder. No words passed between them as they lifted it. The ice sprites had pulled whatever cover had remained on the window. Nodding at each other, they knew the target.

All Dimin saw was a giant flaming keg flying at his ride. He only had time to fall off its back before the blast took it out. Still, the blast made him fly.

"Where did he go?" Naz coughed. The flames were starting to climb higher.

"I don't know, go check the other side of the hotel."

"Grace, you can either die inside with your paramour, or you can come out and die with your dragons."

"This fucking guy," she gasped. Heading towards the stairs, she saw him out back. "Naz, we have to get rid of the ammo or it'll blow up and hurt us or the dragons." They darted from room to room collecting the stockpiled ammo and tossing it out the window. They threw the rifles down the stairs. The floorboards started creaking as they ran around. Pausing in the center of the dining room, they looked out and Dimin was aiming a rifle at Agrippa who stood in front of Honor. He blew fire at Dimin, but with his remaining hand, Dimin sent out a blast of cold, slowing its progress so he could move out of the way.

"What do we do?" The floorboards gave way and they fell to the ground amidst flames. Naz stumbled to the kitchen grabbing the pots of water and tossing them onto the small part.

"Naz, this place is falling down, we have to get out of here." She pulled herself off the ground and grabbed her pistol and a rifle. They ran out the front door, coughing and finding cover behind the lifeless forms of Sao and Thal.

"Well, you wanted this to go faster," he joked at her. She nudged him in the ribs playfully, shaking her head. She opened the pistol chamber to see how many rounds she had left. One.

"How many bullets do you have left?"

"Oh, definitely zero. I definitely do not have a firearm, and that burning house is definitely the only thing between us and crazy."

The burning house. Realization struck her.

"We have to burn his heart. Can a bullet do that? Or can we somehow impale him on this house?"

"I've got a better idea." He whipped out the doll he had been whittling for Marjorie the night before. "Give me the rifle," he said. She handed it over, and Naz put it next to him. He began to whittle away at the toy.

"You've gotta be fucking kidding me," she told him. "Your dragon has a gun aimed at him right now."

In two minutes, he had cut and roughly hewn the wooden bullet. He loaded it into the rifle.

"I'm good with wood," he smiled at her. With that, the house crumbled down. They wasted no time as the surprise of it made Dimin turn his body looking for the two of them.

They shot the rifle together towards Dimin's heart. As it released from the barrel, Naz sent his power forward, igniting the bullet. As it accelerated, it became a fireball. All this occurred within the space of a split second. The bullet hit Dimin's chest, burning a hole and melting his heart. He seemed to be knocked out. Agrippa took the opportunity to fly off with Honor in his claws. Naz and Grace took deep breaths. Ash fluttered around.

"How long do you think we have?" Naz asked her, rubbing his shoulder from where the beam had hit it. She shook her head, hands on her thighs, bent over catching her breath. Her left ankle that had plunged a hole into the stairs was hurting her.

"Ah, there you are, my woman." A voice from the ground interrupted their nursing their wounds as they ducked back behind what used to be the wall separating the room with the piano and the kitchen. The piano crashed to the ground with a disharmonious thud. Whatever bullets remained on the first floor began shooting off with the heat.

"Maker MuckerFucker, we are not in a position for this." They covered each other's heads with their arms.

"Naz, it's just going to have to work." She ran for her pistol a few yards away. In her slowness due to her limping leg, Dimin, who was sitting on the ground, put out his unburnt hand. She ran back to Naz, who was watching with a smirk on his face.

"He can't push anything out, because he doesn't have any of

the curse left in him," he reported back, nodding his head in the direction to have her look. "He's a mess."

"We're not much better." She waved her hands over themselves to demonstrate to him. They had burn marks on their body. Naz's shoulder was bloody and his shirt was all but falling off from the fire. She had various holes in hers, and her pants were torn up to her knees. Scrapes, bruises, splinters, all polka dotted their bodies. Blood oozed out of a few slashes on their arms. Naz's energy dwindled.

"Mother Maker, help us," he said to the sky after assessing the situation.

"That's it!" Grace pulled the necklace off of her neck and handed it to Naz. "Quick! Melt this down." Under the cover of the kitchen stove, he melted it over the fire on the wall. "Make a bullet for my gun." With his hands he molded it into a small enough bullet. Naz attempted to load it into the gun. His hands had become so shaky he could not, though, and he knew what was about to happen next. Grace loaded it into the barrel and cocked the pistol. She steadied her breath, looking at Naz, memorizing his face so she could find him again.

"Remember when I told you where to scatter my ashes or I will haunt you? The joke is on you. I'm going to haunt you anyways." She smiled and leaned in for a kiss. And kiss her he did. His lips spoke with all of his heart, all of the memories that they had made, and begged with all his desire for her to come back. It filled her with warmth and sunlight and happiness. As he opened his eyes, and removed his lips, hers were still closed, and she had a peaceful smile on her face, as if she were imprinting this kiss on her very soul.

When she was ready, she turned from him, so she did not have to see his face as she walked away. If she had, she would have seen a face full of pride, misery, anguish, and love. A face that had resigned himself to following her into the next life. That look would have made her stay, which she could not do. In this war of independence, her life had come down to this watershed battle. She would persevere, in this life or the next.

⚜

Out she limped from the safe haven that she had been utilizing with Naz. Walking into a room full of women vying for the attention and money of a small sect of society seemed much more daunting of a task. She could not quite place her finger on why she could remain so calm in the face of death and this creature that perpetually frightened her with the terror of living under his thumb in society.

Weakened, the two foes stumbled towards one another.

"If I can't have you, then no one will." Dimin crawled toward her.

"You can't have me AND no one will."

She brought the gun with her. She had nothing left. The hole from the fiery wooden bullet stood out through his chest. Her future was as small as the probability of putting the bullet through him. She wondered which staircase that Sao was on and hoped he was happy and safe. She thanked him silently for whatever shit he put up with from her. She really meant him no ill will.

She raised the gun, pointing it at his head, standing twenty meters away. Back straight, she bore the same composure as she had when she was presented at the debutante ball all those years ago. Arm straight ahead of her in line with her eyesight.

"I am so fucking done with your patriarchal bullshit. You never lost me because you never had me. You never will."

He put his hands up in mock surrender.

"All I wanted was to be fucking left alone. To be free to live as I wanted. And all that dragon that you killed wanted was to be fucking left alone. To be free to live as he wanted. Look what you got for your trouble. So, what did we learn here, huh, Dimin?"

He shook his head bewildered.

"LEAVE PEOPLE THE FUCK ALONE!"

"Please. Show me mercy. My powers are gone. I have nothing left. Please, I appeal to you as the fairer, more compassionate sex."

"Thinking I'm just a pretty girl in a gown was the deadliest mistake you ever made. Grossly underestimated my value." He pulled out his gun at the last second, as she shot. The shots rang through the air. And then, two gasps followed by silence fell over the hotel.

THIRTY-TWO

In all her teachings, Mother Maker taught that the evil would reap their dastardly rewards. She never mentioned the cost to the kind. Grace's body hit the ground just before the devil's. She more crumpled than fell, remaining motionless in the snow-dusted dirt where tiny grass buds peeked through. Naz's vision blurred over as he ran to the duelers. Twenty feet out meant little to no chance of either of them living. Picking up Dimin's firearm, he fired rapid shots into the guy's slumped body on the ground. It jumped with each bullet that entered it.

"You Mothermucking selfish brute of a man."

He cursed at the body with each bullet.

"Blast you for never knowing love beyond your own ego."

Shot.

"Fuck your entire empire back to oblivion, where your lack of empathy can go too, you sociopath."

Shot.

"I hope the wild polmen feast on your balls."

Shot.

"May your soul know neither love nor peace. Damn you to a worse agony than the pain you've left me in."

Shot.

The tears filled his eyes. Now he had lost both the woman he had married and the woman he had loved. He knelt to the ground, unable to see anything around him through his blurry tears. The sun had come out from behind the clouds, and he could feel its kisses growing stronger. It was as though Grace were smiling down upon him.

"Naz, stop." A hand pulled the gun out of his hand. "I really appreciate that you took the kill shot when you could have checked me for signs of life. In that amount of time, I have now died and I'm haunting you."

She smiled.

He looked at the ground for a body but didn't see one.

"I'm kidding, I'm here." In one swift motion, he turned and wrapped his arms around Grace's waist, lifting her off the ground in his embrace. He never wanted to let her go. What if this was a dream? What if they had made it to the fourth staircase and were allowed to hold each other once more? He set her down and looked her over, hands patting everywhere looking for blood.

"But how?"

"He missed?" And lodged in the beam above the doorway was a bullet the size of Naz's thumb.

"But you fell?"

"Yeah, to the side, right before I fired my shot so it would miss my head when I went down."

"But how do you know where he was going to shoot you?"

"Oh like that asshole wouldn't have gone for the head or the heart? He had a weird angle from the ground so I just went to the side."

She brushed the dust off the bottom of her jeans, finding blood on her hands. They both looked confused. Naz turned her around and around looking her over as Grace patted herself down.

"Naz! It's my monthly!" Torn between happiness at choices and disgust at this plague returning and future choices she would have to manage, she started laughing. Because sometimes, all you can do is laugh. "We removed whatever Dimin had done to my back, and it must have done something to my insides. I'm not hurt. I'm just back to normal."

"Is that a good thing?" he looked relieved and supportive, but confused.

She shrugged. "It's a thing."

They looked around and surveyed the damage. Everything was blasted. Ash rained down over their heads. Trees in the distance had gunshots around them. Naz whistled and Agrippa came flying overhead. Honor was furious behind him, smoke coming out of her snout as she huffed to keep up with her father. Grace was just about to consider what to do with Dimin's body or those of everyone else, but Agrippa solved that problem right away. With a steady stream, he burned that body to ash.

Honor landed next to Grace and looked at her with a searching eye.

Grace looked at her friends who had now saved her twice. "Honor, would you burn these bodies, too?"

She nuzzled Grace before walking over and igniting a pyre.

"Let's let them burn. I don't want to breathe anyone in," Grace told Naz. She and Naz climbed aboard Agrippa's back. Flying away, Grace held onto Naz. She was ready to leave this mess far behind her. Just burn it all down. From the ashes let good come.

"I'm sorry we burnt your hotel down," she murmured into his back.

"Historical monuments are easy to come by," he reassured her sarcastically. "As far as I'm concerned, today's events deserve their own monument there." She hugged his waist tightly, still stunned by the day's events.

꧁ꕥ꧂

She was free.

He was gone.

She was free.

She did not have to run anymore.

She was free.

She had persevered.

Agrippa flew and as they made the quick journey to the house, an ache reverberated throughout her chest, a yearning to yell at the dragon to stay in the air and keep flying.

The cold in the air had dissipated. The sun was emerging from behind the clouds. As soon as Agrippa landed and they had dismounted, he set off to find the rest of the herd. It was a testament to Naz that they wanted to return to his lands, that they were a haven. Honor positioned herself in front of the house, drinking water that had come from the melted snow out of the gutter. The pair entered the house. Grace flung her boots off her feet at the wall, and Naz rearranged them next to his under the seat in the entryway.

They both just stood there looking at each other. Naz finally made the first move. He walked over to the sitting room and flopped onto the couch, messing back his hair. Grace could not figure out if she wanted to sit, if she wanted to cry, if she wanted to run around. What should she do with this newfound freedom, this weight off her shoulders?

She grabbed her white dress with the blue floral print on it. She noticed that Marjorie had been practicing her sewing on it–a rudimentary G was sketched on the puffy sleeve with a few stitches already in it. Making sure that no needles stuck her, she changed out of her shoddy clothes, grabbed a rag, and threw on the dress. Dresses had never bothered her, but the restrictive undergarments, which she did not wear today, had. The weather was still slightly chilly, though. Reminders of the day. Plodding downstairs, she made her way to the liquor cabinet that rested by the dining area.

"One of my friends and I swear by whiskey on special occasions."

"Is this one of your friends that I had the nightmarish pleasure of meeting today?" His eyebrow raised, questioning if she wanted to discuss it further.

"No," her voice cracked with her shudder. "I'm going to bury that image under some shots."

After a few glasses, they leaned on each other on the couch as they looked out the window, watching the environment get itself back together. Gradually the both fell asleep. When Grace woke, it was dark outside. She could barely make out the outline of Honor sleeping in the front yard. Naz slept soundly next to her, arms crossed over his chest. How the hell had they survived that ordeal? He looked so at peace, a contrast to his earlier looks of dread and determination. His smile lines around his eyes were starting to become more defined, or maybe she just knew where to look for them now. His stubble had become more beard-like over the past couple days in their hurry to take care of other priorities, and frankly, she quite liked it. She would have to suggest that he keep it. Placing her hand on his cheek, she rubbed it. This man had shouldered too much of the world for too long.

With the touch of her hand, his eyes blinked open. He looked around, surveying their situation as well. The others would return the next day, for they would all be anxious to reunite. Grace peered into his face with an analytical look. Was she memorizing his face? How could she see him in the dark?

He moved his hand to tuck her stray hairs behind her ears. "I was so afraid that you had gone. That despite defeating Dimin, you still lost your life and your dreams. That you had to die to be free. But here you are. What are you going to do next?"

"For once, I'm going to not think about what is next in my life." She grabbed Naz's arms and tucked herself in their warmth, before rapidly falling asleep.

THIRTY-THREE

The chill had left the air. Though in the middle of the night, Grace woke to nightmares of the events from the previous day. She found herself tucked tightly into Naz's arms in his bed. He must have carried her in after she fell asleep. Where did the man find the energy?

She ducked her head below the sheets, licking his legs.

"Mmm, yes, please," he said, his eyes peeking down at her. She took him in her mouth, wringing the moans from him as she twirled her tongue around him. He came quickly, thrusting into her mouth and gushing into her throat. Swallowing, she ran her finger along the sides of her lips, making sure he was clean off of her. Moving upwards on his body, she surfaced from the blankets for air before laying her head on his strong arm so her back was against his chest.

He wanted this moment to never end.

Drowsily, he whispered into her ear, "Marry me. Don't marry me. Just stay with me. I want to be with you. You can have a home here." She stilled in his arms, contemplating life. Tempting as it was, the image dropped into her stomach like a stone.

"A home isn't a structure to me. It's wherever I am the most comfortable."

"Are you not comfortable here?"

"Oh, right now?" She squirmed closer to him, kissing his forearm. "I am more comfortable than I have ever been in my life."

And she was. His arm, wrought with a calm sturdiness, grounded her in spite of the day's last events. The room's darkness seemed to be illuminated with their skin. She was actually glowing with warmth. But her spirit restlessly galloped around her diaphragm. She needed to let it out or she would be unable to breathe. Could she see herself tending the dragons every day? Maybe. She loved Ignacio, truly. She could see waking up with him everyday.

But she had finally guaranteed her freedom. The world held so much potential for her and she wanted to explore every nook and cranny of it. Were other dragons out there? What languages had she not yet heard? She had no desire currently to go east, but maybe one day, she would see her homeland when it thawed. She turned her head so her chin rested on her hand on his hairy chest.

"Come with me," she blurted out, eyes brimming with hope. "You've lived here all your life. Don't you want to see more?"

And he did, but there was so much to take care of here. And Marjorie.

"I won't leave Marjorie. Look at how your parental relationship affects you every day."

He was not wrong. She could care less if her parents remained dwelling in Hamber, or if they had made it to the bottom staircase.

"I mean, I'd like to think that it has made me an upstanding member of society. Apparently, good enough for you to want to marry," she giggled. He lifted her left hand, sizing up her fingers. "A lovely cut of tar, so that it doesn't glisten to distract Honor when you ride her."

"Tar!? You want the world to know I'm worth tar to you?! How will I ever turn that into money if you decide to leave me after befouling me? No one will want me with my cherry popped."

"Yeah, I'd believe that if you didn't just do that thing with your tongue."

She flicked it at him in response, licking the tip of his nose. "You could have more of that if you came with me."

He rolled over and poked his hardness at her entrance. That dragon blood was always boiling.

"You could have more of this if you stayed here." A sound escaped her mouth. He was trying his damnedest to convince her, and it was almost working. "And this." He leaned in to kiss her neck. She gasped. "And little" –he slid his cock into her very slowly– "by little, we could find new adventures to have here. And when Marjorie is older, we can escape together." He slid home. Her hips rocked wanting him to move. "Just a little wait."

She pulled his head into her face and kissed him til her breath ran out. "I don't want to wait. I want you now."

"Now?" He pulled out of her.

"Now." She moaned as he thrust into her. Her eyes looked into his, marveling at their presence. In the heat of the moment, they still seemed completely still. He looked back into hers, struck by the exuberance that seemed to emit.

And thus with their bodies, they argued. They negotiated in different positions. With his body, he pleaded with her to stay. Every touch was a question. Every kiss, a reminder of what they had. Every thrust a promise for the future. She answered with appreciation for his heart, thanks, and love throughout the heat of the day. When they seemed to have arrived at a conclusion, the other would rebut. Nothing was solved. By morning, both were exhausted and they finally slept.

Grace woke first, wrapped herself in a blanket, and padded to the kitchen to turn on the coffee. Was Naz worth losing every dream she had ever had for herself? Was there no way she could have the freedom that she needed and Ignacio, the man she wanted? Once prepped, she sat down in the Adirondack. Cupping the mug between both hands, she breathed in the hot brain soup. Did she satisfy the twenty year old dreamer in her, or placate the thirty year old adventurer? Watching the afternoon sun, she contemplated its path across the sky. Did the sun never bore of rising and falling daily? Did the moon ever want a turn to stay out longer? Could the two ever be visible in the sky together? Surely sometimes.

Finishing her cup, she went into the bedroom.

"Please," he said, taking in her form. "Please, stay." His eyes pierced her heart in ways that Dimin would never have felt. She stepped towards the bed, placing her hand on his cheek, and forehead to his. She closed her eyes to better breathe in his smell: cozy indoors on Trinity's Nigh. He placed his hands on her hips through the blanket wrappings. "You have the freedom to do whatever you want. Please choose to stay with me."

But she would be exercising her first time of being free at ending her time of being free. She would never be free of the land's traditions and needs. Curling up into his arms, she laid looking out the window, pondering her choice between the two lives. Naz must have fallen back to sleep, content with her in his arms.

She maneuvered out of his arms quietly. His wounds were looking much better, and after the day's performance, she knew he just needed rest. She picked up her leathers, watching him as she put each leg in. Placing her hand on the doorknob, she looked back at his peaceful figure. She looked at the spot she had laid in on the bed, fit so perfectly into the crook of his arm.

"Dream of my love for you," she murmured. "For your dreams are galaxies more than I could ever be." She blew him a kiss, and with a mournful smile, gracefully slipped out the door.

Honor met her out front, evaporating the salty wet off her cheeks with her warm breath. She rubbed her neck, and the dragon followed along. As the two walked through the meadow, she remembered another time, seemingly so long ago, when she had been crawling out only to be rescued by her friend. She missed his presence, and hoped that the Maker would be taking care of him as he had taken care of her.

From the window, Naz could see her erect silhouette on the orange rainbow canvas of sky. Forever proud, forever sure of herself. He had exhausted all his possible methods of keeping her. The bird must sing, the dragon must fly. He knew that Honor would follow her. He could not cage that dragon anymore than he could keep Grace. He stood, the melancholy of his soul meshing with the sunset. His chest burned. Tomorrow, life was meant to return to how it had always been. He would go look after the dragons, pretending that their family house guest had departed. Marjorie would find some shenanigans, perhaps recounting to him all the fun that she had without him, never to know of the terror that he had faced. Tara would shove her soul down into a corner of herself as their mother used to do.

As for Grace, she would triumph. But oh, what he would give to see her unbridled smile. Her personality seemed inquisitive, but what did that mean for the wide open world? The world beyond the borders of Cosimo.

A single tear fell out of his eye. He caught it on his tongue, licking out the corner of his mouth. It would be the last tear that he shed over Grace Eastbrook's departure.

Movement at the end of the gravel road focused Grace on the present. Shifting her head so the brim of her hat blocked out the red-orange sun, she looked ahead. A man in motley pants strode next to an orange dragon dragging a cart at its back.

"I should have known that you were involved. Last night, this dragon came into town flapping about some commotion." Verdis smiled at her.

"Yokel?" The dragon nodded its head at her like its neck was deprived of tendons. "What did you do?"

"He came in tearing up the town, knocking over barrels,

upsetting carts. He tried to make off with a baby carriage, but some woman smacked his nose. Anything to get someone's attention, save blowing a stream of fire down the middle of the street. When I approached him, he motioned that he wanted someone to follow. I wasn't about to leave my cart for ransacking or get on this lollipop, so I told him that I would walk with him. No one else seemed to want to join us, though."

He eyed her scrapes and bruises before pointing at her face. "Who gave you that black eye?"

"Man fucked with the wrong woman."

"I'd hate to see what he looks like now."

"Oh, you can't. This little one burnt all the evidence." Honor happily bit at the air, trying to catch a butterfly that fluttered in her vicinity.

"Hellion."

"Little old me?" she said mockingly with a raised eyebrow. "You say that like I'm important or something."

"It seems that our plan worked to divide and conquer."

"You bought me some time, for sure. But your problems are bound to catch up to you no matter how fast you try to run from them."

"As you're running now?" He looked at the manor at the end of the dirt road from where Grace had traveled.

Smiling at him, she took a deep breath. "I couldn't stay. Loneliness won't kill me, but confinement will. Even if I'm confined with him."

He put his hand on her shoulder in camaraderie. "And that, my friend, is why we drink with the sinners, dream with the lovers, and fly with the dragons." He patted her shoulder twice. "Come on. Let me buy you a drink. I know this great little saloon where there's an old piano that hasn't been played in awhile." He looked at Yokel. "Whaddya say? Are you coming with me or will the master come after me with a rifle?"

"The *caretaker* gives the dragons free reign. He'll only ask that you care for the dragon as the dragon will for you." With that blessing, Verdis clumsily mounted the dragon.

Grace turned her attention to Honor, internally debating if she would crush the dragon, despite her having grown in size since the previous day. Oh, the mystery and majesty of dragons! Honor sidled up to her, lowering her haunches to the ground. Grace placed her leg over the creature's back, holding onto the two protruding scales as she once had with her Slewja. Though smaller than a full size dragon, she carried Grace's lithe body with ease. Her time in the open air with her father had developed her sense of self well.

"Wait, Verdis, what about your cart?"

"Sometimes, you just need to leave it all behind and start again. That's where the true adventure of life lies."

And as the moon smiled overhead, the two friends rode off into the sunset.

EPILOGUE

In the lush meadow, the woman stared up at the sky as her head rested on the leathery tail of her friend. She breathed in the fresh sea breeze deeply, running her hand over the soft grass that her back laid upon. She had earned her moments of no worries and relaxation. Her once pale cheeks welcomed the golden sun upon them, and the kiss of the breeze to soothe its burn. The crashing of the waves could be heard just below the cliff at the beach.

She would never run again.

The dragon's head elevated; she could feel the stretch down to its tail. It would let her know if she needed to worry, though there was not much she could not face, not much that would make her weak in her knees.

And that "not much" was about to walk across the meadow. The dragon shifted around, making many movements until the woman's sandy brown haired head fell onto the ground. Swearing under her breath, she squinted and rubbed the back of her skull. A shadow shifted in front of the sun. No, it was not a cloud. She opened her eyes to the handsome man with dark hair and calm dark eyes staring down at her with a wide grin over his face.

In another life, guilt would have washed over her countenance. Instead, she looked back at the person who saw her exactly as she was and all that she could be. Why should she feel guilty for being true to herself?

With that, a second sunny face clamored into her line of vision. The girl held a curled up piece of parchment in one hand and her skirts up in the other.

"We found you! Oh please can we come with you?"

"How did you find me?"

"Just went as west as you thought you could go, which was Lesea. We're here to inform you that you can go further. Plus, Agrippa has a knack for finding his offspring."

The girl giggled, exclaiming, "We have another map! For the rest of the world!"

"Funny thing," he said, sitting on the ground next to her. She sat up so she could look into those eyes that she missed so much the past month. He put his hand on her cheek, and she nestled into his touch, still warmer than she was at that moment. "I never wanted to go anywhere until I met you. And now I want to go everywhere with you, my adventure-loving, trouble-making, no-shit-taking whiskey in a teacup."

"And I wanted nothing more than to be left alone. But now I want more than anything to venture with you, my loyal-to-the-end, plan-devising, lonesome sunshine."

She closed her eyes, and threw her arms around his neck as she kissed the man who saw her for who she was. And he kissed back this woman who appreciated him for his true nature.

"But what of the manor and the dragons?"

"Tara will mind the land. And we" –he beamed at her– "we will fly like dragons." And the two sat there, arms around each other on the cliff, the girl reading the map beside them, flanked on either side by their dragon friends, embracing the glorious present as they looked upon the wide-open sea.

The End.

PLAYLIST

Prologue *In the Dark of the Night* by PelleK

Ch. 1 *Sexy Sadie* by The Beatles

Ch. 2 *Walking on Broken Glass* by Annie Lennox

Ch. 3 *Piano Man* by Billy Joel

Ch. 4 *Stay With Me* by Faces

Ch. 5 *Goodbye Earl* by The Chicks

Ch. 6 *Folsom Prison Blues* by Johnny Cash

Ch. 7 *American Girl* by Tom Petty and the Heartbreakers

Ch. 8 *You're No Good* by Linda Ronstadt

Ch. 9 *My Maria* by B.W. Stevenson

Ch. 10 *Atlantic City* by The Band

Ch. 11 *Best Friend* (feat. Doja Cat) by Saweetie

Ch. 12 *Leaving Las Vegas* by Sheryl Crow

Ch. 13 *Wildflowers* by Dolly Parton, Linda Ronstadt, Emmylou Harris

Ch. 14 *Freedom* by Wham!

Ch. 15 *Got My Mind Set On You* by Geroge Harrison

Ch. 16 *I Love You Always Forever* by Donna Lewis

Ch. 17 *Dancing in the Moonlight* by King Harvest

Ch. 18 *You Won't Be Mine* by Matchbox Twenty

Ch. 19 *Colder Weather* by Zac Brown Band

Ch. 20 *Remember Me* (Lullaby) by Gael Garcia Bernal and Gabriella Flores

Ch. 21 *Song of Long Ago* by Carole King

Ch. 22 *Don't Rock the Jukebox* by Alan Jackson

Ch. 23 *All I Can Do* by Dolly Parton

Ch. 24 *Standing Outside the Fire* by Garth Brooks

Ch. 25 *A Song for You* by Amy Winehouse

Ch. 26 *It Had to be You* by Harry Connick, Jr.

Ch. 27 *You're So Vain* by Carly Simon

Ch. 28 *Sugar Shack* by Jimmy Gilmer & the Fireballs

Ch. 29 *Piece of My Heart* by Janis Joplin

Ch. 30 *Hey Tomorrow* by Jim Croce

Ch. 31 *Theme* from Lonesome Dove

Ch. 32 *Never Going Back Again* by Fleetwood Mac

Ch. 33 *I Will Always Love You* by Whitney Houston

Epilogue *End of the Line* by Traveling Wilburys

Acknowledgments

It's funny: I have written this entire novel, and this chapter is proving the hardest to write. Because words will never quite capture the feelings of love and gratitude that I have for these people.

Rob, our story is too precious to me for words. You will remain in my heart long after languages cease. This book would not have been written had you not said, "Do it and we'll figure it out." You're my all.

Daph, you little light, you pushed me through daily and made my moments writing more meaningful- because your eyes brimmed with pride whenever you told someone that I was an author.

Bruce, you kept me company til the wee hours of the morning while listening to one song on repeat after I'd drank too much caffeine. Oh, and you reminded me to get up to walk around.

Ana, Laura, and Sara, you rode this ride with me and never once tired of my giving you droll updates on my book. You cheered me on every chapter, every decision, every milestone. I'm eternally grateful for you three and your sharing of your talents to help me.

Joe, thanks for alpha'ing. Not only did you help me see the bigger picture, but you tore the bandaid off for people reading the sex scenes.

Britt, I will think of you every time I read this book. Both for your kickass attitude and all of the editing you did for me. I listened to at least 70% of it!

Thank you to my betas: Aoife, Renna, Rini, Amber, Gavin. Your feedback was essential, both to giggle with you and to improve the story.

Mom and Papa, thanks for all those hours we spend watching westerns together. I've put my own generation's spin on them to hand to the next generation.

To Courtney, Abbie, Gabs, and Abby, you are the ultimate cheerleaders!

To my street team, you took a chance on my book when you had no idea what you were getting into. A thousand thank yous for believing in this novel.

Finally, thank you reader for taking the time to read and finish this book! It's a different type of read, and I'm so delighted that you took a chance on it. Hopefully it left you with visions of dragons flying and handsome men bathing.

About the Author

Maggie grew up with a strong love of reading. As an avid beta reader, others have inspired and encouraged her in her dream of writing. She is co-founder of the Indie Romantasy Reads Book of the Month Club. She lives in Chicago with her husband, daughter, and Duck Tolling Retriever who lovingly support her in her endeavors.

You can follow her reading and writing antics on Instagram (@maggiehoopis.author) and her website (maggiehoopis.com)